Slow *Fire*

Slow *Fire*

Ken Mercer

Minotaur Books · New York

This is a work of fiction. All of the characters, organizations, and events portrayed in this novel are either products of the author's imagination or are used fictitiously.

Grateful acknowledgement is made for the permission to reprint the following material:

Excerpt from "Thou Shalt Not Kill" from *The Selected Poems of Kenneth Rexroth*. Copyright © 1956 by Kenneth Rexroth. Reprinted by permission of New Directions Publishing Corporation.

Excerpt from the lyrics to "I Feel Like I'm Fixin' To Die Rag." Words and music by Joe McDonald © 1965, renewed 1993 Alkatraz Corner Music Co. Used by permission.

www.minotaurbooks.com

Library of Congress Cataloging-in-Publication Data

Mercer, Ken, 1962–
    Slow fire / Ken Mercer.—1st ed.
        p. cm.
    ISBN 978-0-312-55835-2
    1. Crime—Fiction.   I. Title.
    PS3613.E7S57 2010
    813'.6—dc22

                                2009039816

10   9   8   7   6   5   4   3   2

You roasted him on a slow fire.
His fat dripped and spurted in the flame.

—Kenneth Rexroth, "Thou Shalt Not Kill"

Los Angeles, California
April 2006

How the hell had they found him?

When he opened the small metal door to his post office box, he saw the letter lying there all by itself, the edges of the envelope curling up inside the tight confines of the space. He took it back home, not bothering to open it.

He was living in the trailer then, out on the ragged edge of the county. An old Airstream, not much bigger than a minivan, its aluminum shell gone dull and oxidized in the salt air.

He was alone except for the dog. Laurie living in the house in Van Nuys, Sean already gone. More than two years now since he'd worked.

The inside of the trailer was as orderly as a sailboat. He didn't own much; what he did was kept stowed away in its designated place. In the long fog-filled evenings he would cook elaborate dinners for himself. After he finished eating, he would carefully wipe off the fake wood-grained surface of the dinette table before flipping down the cushions that converted it into his bed.

Lying there, listening to the waves through the glass louvers of the jalousie window, he rationalized things; telling himself this was his monastic period, romanticizing it as a kind of spiritual quest. But when his thoughts gnawed at him and kept him from sleep, he'd worry that there was no way back, that he had somehow managed to let himself drift too far off course.

When he finally slit open the envelope, he thought it was a joke. Perez, or one of the others over at Rampart, goofing on him.

The letter was printed on cream-colored letterhead, some kind of curious crest at the top, a drawing of a pickax superimposed over a pine tree. He'd never heard of the town, Haydenville, had to walk the four long miles to the library to look it up on the Internet.

The town was a long haul from anywhere, all the way up in the far northern reaches of the state. Seventy-five miles down from the Oregon border. A protracted and treacherous drive inland from the coast.

He followed up, found out the job offer was, indeed, for real.

In the end, there really wasn't much to think about.

Haydenville, California
May 2006

ONE

Her skin was the first thing he noticed.

Already deeply tanned on only the fifteenth day of May, it was flecked here and there with droplets of water from the river.

She wore a pair of green board shorts, stripes down the sides featuring some kind of exotic Hawaiian foliage. Above the chrome snap of the waistband, her stomach was undulated with small hills of muscle. The angle of her body caused the fullness of her breasts to spill from beneath the nylon triangles of her bikini top.

She lay on a bed of cobbles that thrust out into the rush of the river. The morning sun flashed off the water in discs of light, wrapping about her head like a halo.

Will Magowan stood over her, studying her youthful face. Just beneath her hairline was a circular purplish bruise. She stared up at him, as if asking for some kind of assurance, her eyes not blinking. A milky white film covered the pupils and irises, robbing them of color.

The air vibrated with the drone of blowflies, their metallic green bodies swarming over her nose and mouth. The insects had already managed to fill her nostrils with tiny white eggs.

He began to feel as if he were looking down at her from a great height, like a stilt walker. All of a sudden, there was the sensation of having too much saliva in his mouth. When he swallowed, the sheer volume of it surprised him.

Somewhere within his abdomen, his stomach shifted, making him conscious now of its weight. He forced himself to take a deep breath, to try to calm it.

Then, before it was too late, he spun away from her, hunching over into the willows just as the spasms began.

He could hear them laughing.

". . . supposed to be some big kahuna, just moved up from L.A." It was the one called Thomas, the police officer who seemed young enough to still be in high school.

"Don't exactly look like it right now," said the older one, the Forest Service ranger.

Will's back was to them. He was still folded over at the waist, staring at the remains of his breakfast strewn on the sandy ground. A Balance Bar and black coffee. He thought the energy bar looked pretty much the same way it had when he'd eaten it, only deconstructed now, no longer in its original rectangular form.

He remembered how he used to brag about how his stomach was bombproof. He'd eat anything with impunity, would even risk the *cabeza* and *lengua* from the illicit taco trucks parked in the shadow of the 710 Freeway.

But all of that was before Eucalyptus Knolls, with its vinyl-covered mattresses and echoing hallways that reeked of Pine-Sol. Before seventeen straight days of detox. No methadone, no clonidine. Nothing but a molded plastic vomit pan.

"Shit," Thomas said. "It's like the dude's never seen a dead body before or something."

Will ripped a sheet from his pocket notebook and used it to wipe his mouth. A second skin of sweat clung to him, the temperature already in the high eighties, so early in the morning.

They were staring at him.

Thomas and the ranger, waiting for him to say something. The ranger puffed at a slender cigar with a white plastic tip, his Smokey the Bear hat casting a semicircular shadow down across his face.

Will realized that they were waiting for him to tell them what to do, and he experienced a momentary pang of panic. What was he supposed to say? He'd never been in charge of anything like this before. He'd been around enough crime scenes, seen his share of DOAs, but he'd worked Narcotics ever since getting out of uniform.

He looked around, searching for the usual crush of activity— evidence techs, photographers, patrolmen—but this appeared to be the whole show. He reached into his back pocket and pulled out a leather badge holder. He flipped it open to expose a brass shield and slid it down into the waistband of his jeans.

CHIEF, the badge read. First day on the job. At this rate, he thought, probably his last.

An orange whitewater kayak was sitting on the stones next to the woman's body. Scattered around the kayak were various articles of paddling equipment: a neoprene spray skirt; a personal flotation device; a sparkle-painted red helmet with a spiderweb crack in the front. He had the nagging sense that something was missing but at the moment couldn't put his finger on what it might be.

Red earth rose up steeply from the aquamarine river, nothing but the empty road above them on one side, dense Northern California forest on the other.

They were staring at him.

The young officer, Thomas, wore his full dress uniform despite the heat, his black boots shined so they reflected the corona of the sun. His braided leather garrison belt sagged with the weight of what appeared to be every accessory that could possibly be ordered from the Streicher's catalog.

Will tried to figure out how he might proceed here. He flipped through his memories of homicide detectives past as they arrived on scene, mustard stains on their ties, the reek of Cutty thick on the breath.

When Will began to speak, he tried to channel those men, to somehow transplant their tone of bone-tired boredom.

"All right," he finally said. "So what've we got?"

TWO

The pane of glass in Will's office window was old and rippled, giving his view a distorted, dreamlike quality.

Outside, Haydenville sweltered in the bright late morning heat. Squat turn-of-the-century brick buildings lined a grassy square that held a painted wooden bandstand at its center. Marching away down oak-studded streets were carefully maintained houses flaunting widow's walks, mansard roofs, and iron weathervanes that spun on the rare gust of wind.

After a few short blocks, the town simply ended, as if surrendering itself back to the thick forest that surrounded it.

"You're not hungry?"

A wicker basket holding a collection of muffins was sitting on Will's otherwise empty desktop. They had been placed there by Haydenville's mayor, Bonnie Newman. She'd been sitting in Will's office, waiting for him, when he'd come in from the river.

"I think I'll wait," Will said. "I appreciate it, though."

She took one of the muffins and tore off a chunk of it. Her hair was gray, although Will guessed that she was only about ten years older than he was, in her early fifties. She wore glasses with golden metal frames.

"I was just about to leave," she said. "I thought you'd get in a little earlier on your first day at work."

"Sorry. Something came up."

Will looked around his new office. The Haydenville Police Department was comprised of four wooden-floored rooms, more than sufficient, considering the entire department consisted of Will, Thomas, and a receptionist.

"Something bothering you, Will?"

He told her about the body.

"My God, what happened?" she asked.

"She was kayaking. It looked like she hit her head on a rock and drowned. Hard to say for sure."

"Why's that?"

"Arriving officers moved everything around before I got out there."

Hopelessly fucked things up. That was a more accurate way of putting it. Thomas and the ranger had moronically pulled the woman from her boat, taken off her spray skirt and PFD, and removed her helmet.

"Where'd they find her?" she asked. "The body."

"About twelve miles outside town, past that steel bridge. She was still in her boat, floating in an eddy. I'm going to push the coroner to order a postmortem."

She stopped chewing on the piece of muffin and frowned. "What for? It's a river accident."

"I think it's an accident," he said. "But I don't know it."

"Do you really want to waste your time?" She set what was left of the muffin down on the corner of his desk. "We've got more pressing matters to deal with, and you know it. We didn't bring you all the way up here to waste your time on boating accidents."

"Her paddle was missing," he said.

"So? It's probably at the bottom of the river."

Will shook his head. "They float."

"Excuse me?"

"Paddles. They don't sink, they float."

"Then it's floating somewhere out in the Pacific by now."

"Let me ask you something, Bonnie. What if she were your daughter? How would you feel then?"

"That's not fair. But if it *was* my daughter, I don't know that having the coroner slice her open would really brighten my mood."

He picked up a paper clip and fiddled with it, bending it open. "I thought I was here to run the department, such as it is. To run my own show. Isn't that what you told me?"

"Yes."

"Not to have someone—"

"Looking over your shoulder?"

Will said nothing. Outside the window, a lumber truck rumbled past, sections of redwood trunks the size of missiles strapped to the bed.

"Look, Will, I stuck my neck out big-time to hire you. There're people on the city council hoping you'll fall on your face, just to get at me."

He bent the paper clip, trying to get the metal to go back to its original shape. "It's *my* face."

She nodded. "You're in charge," she said. "I know I told you that. And I'll honor it."

"Thank you—"

"But we were also clear that this town has a serious problem. That's why we brought you here, because of your experience."

He forced himself to smile at her. "So would you stop worrying?" he said. "I told you, I can handle it."

THREE

A brass plaque was attached to the front porch of the house, bearing the name of a long deceased milliner who had commissioned the home's construction in 1896.

The house was square and compact, clad in wide clapboards that were lumpy with successive coats of paint, the most recent of which was a pale shade of green. It was owned by the city and was being provided to Will as part of his compensation package.

He sat at his dining room table, the double-hung windows opened wide to let in the evening breeze, the air still so warm and parched that it felt like the discharge from a blow-dryer. A cordless telephone stood upright on the polished surface of the table, beside an open bottle of Anchor Steam that sweated beads of moisture.

Will lifted the bottle and took a sip. He knew that, technically speaking, he wasn't supposed to be doing it. The counselors at Eucalyptus Knolls had drilled it into the clients that it was too easy to simply trade one addiction for another. They warned that even caffeine could prove troublesome, many ex-addicts becoming coffee fiends, the friendly baristas at Starbucks their new dealers.

But one beer, he reasoned, couldn't hurt.

Will reached for the phone and hit a number already programmed into speed dial. He listened to the faraway ringing.

"Hi, this is Laurie." The sound of her voice was digitized, fake sounding. "I can't come to the phone right now, so please leave a message. *Namaste.*"

Will clicked the phone's OFF button without leaving a message, then began to worry that his number might show up on her caller ID.

Namaste. That was a new one. Laurie getting sucked deeper and deeper into her obsession with yoga.

After what happened to Sean, the doctors had put Laurie on a variety of antidepressants. But after four months when she rarely got out of bed, they wanted to try electroconvulsive therapy. Then a friend literally dragged her off to a yoga class, which led to a meditation retreat, which to Will's utter amazement actually started to turn things around for her.

The buzzing sound of crickets was loud through the window screens. It was just before nine, the sun disappearing behind the ridge of mountains off to the west. The lights inside the house were still off, the room illuminated only by the glow from a muted television playing a Giants-Dodgers game.

Will had already finished unpacking, knowing he would never be able to relax until the job was done. His glassware was neatly arranged on the kitchen's open shelving. Framed oil paintings hung on the wall, along with a solitary photograph. It pictured a golden retriever, the animal looking into the camera, his mouth cracked open as if smiling.

Through the open door of the bathroom, Will could see the dog now stretched out on the cool tiles of the floor, his head pressed against the base of the toilet.

Will took another sip of beer, then picked up the phone and hit REDIAL.

When he got the beep at the end of her message, Will began to speak. "It's me." He paused, conscious of the fact that whatever he said next would acquire a kind of permanence. "I really need to talk to you. I moved, and there's no cell service up here, but here's my home number."

Will left the number, then clicked off the phone.

Only one moving box was left for him to go through, sitting there on the tabletop, its flaps still sealed with a strip of shiny brown packing tape.

He snapped open the blade of his pocketknife and used it to slice open the box. He reached inside and pulled out a translucent plastic container filled with envelopes bearing the logo of a fast photo place on Cahuenga. He placed the container on the seat of the chair next to him, not looking at it.

He reached back inside the box and took out a sheaf of papers held together with a binder clip. The papers had the well-thumbed look of a popular magazine at a dental office. The first page bore the letterhead of a Century City law firm.

He looked up when a sound startled him in the otherwise silent house. He realized it was coming from the bathroom. Through the doorway he could see the dog standing at the toilet, lapping at the water.

"*Buddy*," Will yelled. "Cut it out."

The dog pulled his head from the bowl and gave him a puzzled look, but obeyed, turning in a small circle before settling back down on the floor.

Will began to read the document in his hand, for the umpteenth time, as if it were a liturgical text. Below a listing of the firm's partners was a date:

March 8, 2006

He stared down at the subject line, the letters breaking apart and becoming abstract:

LAURIE A. MAGOWAN v. WILLIAM S. MAGOWAN
ACTION FOR DISSOLUTION OF MARRIAGE

Will flipped through pages of dog-eared court documents until he reached the last one. Above a line marked PETITIONER, he saw his wife's signature. A pink Post-it note was stuck to the page, beside the empty line marked RESPONDENT.

In Laurie's handwriting, it read:

> *Will,*
> *I need you to sign this and send back ASAP.*
>
> *Love,*
> *Laurie*

FOUR

The next morning, he went into work early.

He organized his office, arranging the items on his desk and lining up his books on top of the credenza, his California Code books and a worn copy of Tony Alvarez's *Undercover Operations Survival in Narcotics Investigations.*

He had just sat down in his swivel chair when he saw Lila, the department's receptionist-cum-dispatcher, standing in the doorway. She was young, her body slight and birdlike. She was still wearing her headset. Her hands clawed anxiously at the dangling cord as if it were a noose, her face flushed with blood.

When she opened her mouth to speak, the words tumbled out in a breathless stream.

"Something real bad's happening over at the Dig Inn," she said.

The Dig Inn was Haydenville's only bar. An old neon sign hung from its brick exterior, an enormous miner clutching a pickax.

Will and Thomas stood out front in the dusty heat.

The open doorway was a dark rectangle, the noon sunlight making it impossible for them to see anything inside. Old-time swinging saloon doors hung at waist level across the opening.

A sound floated out from the darkness. A dull thudding, like someone pounding at a slab of meat with a huge tenderizing mallet. The sound repeated itself over and over again with the regularity of a metronome.

Will's duty weapon rested inside a leather paddle holster that was clipped to his belt. As an undercover officer, he hadn't had the luxury of being able to carry in most situations, was forced to rely on his wits to survive. He drew the gun, racking back the slide to feed a round into the chamber.

Thomas was frozen in place, transfixed by the odd sound coming from inside the bar. His upper lip was filmed with perspiration, as if he'd suddenly grown a mustache.

"Look at me," Will said. "You gonna be okay here?"

Thomas parted his lips with a forced smile. "Long as you don't puke."

The inside of the Dig Inn was a large rectangular room, the bar running along the far wall, a mounted five-pointed rack from a deer hanging above bottles of liquor. A sad collection of chipped Formica tables and some chairs were off to the left.

An old man sat alone at one of the tables, in the shadows against the wall. At the far end of the bar, a small group, mostly male, huddled together, their heads turned away from what was taking place on the floor.

A man lay face up on the worn linoleum, in a lake of blood that glowed with the greenish light from an electric clock that advertised Sierra Nevada Pale Ale.

A shirtless man crouched above him, his naked torso so thin that it appeared skeletal. He held the bleeding man's head with both hands, rhythmically slamming it, over and over, against the linoleum squares.

It was obvious to Will that the man on his back was already dead. His skull was collapsed like a deflated basketball; the sharp tang of excrement that hung in the air suggested that he had evacuated his bowels for the last time.

But none of this seemed to have registered with the skeletal man. He continued on with his grim task, pounding the head against the floor to the beat of some atavistic rhythm only he could hear.

Will drew his gun from the holster and held it at his side. "Police," he said. "Don't move."

The skeletal man swiveled his head around to face Will. His face was coated with perspiration and freckles of blood, the pale skin so tightly drawn across his cheekbones that he had the appearance of an anorectic. He muttered in a way that sounded somehow mournful, the words only vaguely human, as though the vocal center of his brain had short-circuited.

"Slow down," Will said.

On the floor to the left of the man was a chromed stanchion, of the sort that a velvet rope might be clipped to outside an exclusive nightclub. The man reached out to it, the skin on his arms covered with angry red scabs that were like boils. Using the stanchion as a cane, he rose to his feet.

Will thumbed off the gun's safety. "I need you to stop moving," he said.

The man looked in Will's general direction, but his eyes did not focus, watering so profusely that it looked as if he were crying. The man picked the stanchion up with an ease that was surprising, given his emaciated frame. He gripped it like a baseball bat, swinging it slowly back and forth, the heavy base cutting lazy arcs through the air.

Will pointed his gun at the man's chest. "Drop it," he said.

The skeletal man smiled at Will, exposing teeth rotted down to blackened stubs. He stepped toward them, the stanchion cocked back over his shoulder, loaded up to swing.

Beside him, Will could sense Thomas begin to shuffle backward.

"Hey, man," Thomas said. "We're not gonna tell you again."

Will held up his hand, silencing Thomas. It was precisely the wrong thing to say to a suspect in this situation. After all, what if they *did* need to tell him again? They'd have lost their credibility.

"Look," Will said to the man. "I don't know what just happened, but I'm sure you've got a good explanation for it. Nobody else needs to get hurt here."

The man cocked his head to the side and stared back at Will, his eyes blank.

Will's palms felt slick against the checkered grip of the pistol, his sweat mixing with gun oil. "What's your name?" he asked.

The man ignored him, continuing with his running monologue of muttering. It was unintelligible, like a record being played in reverse.

"I can't understand you," Will said.

The man stopped babbling and grinned at Will. He slowly raised the gleaming stanchion high above his head, like some medieval crusader.

Then he charged them.

Will's shot bloomed high up in the chest, just to the right of the sternum. The man staggered backward from the impact but managed to remain on his feet. His respiration acquired an odd sucking sound, his nostrils flaring as he labored to breathe.

Will realized that his bullet had punctured the man's lung. From the far end of the bar, he could hear a woman sobbing.

The skeletal man took one hand from the stanchion and brought it to his naked chest, as if forming the sign of the cross. His palm came away slick with wetness. He brought it to his lips and licked at it. The taste of his blood seemed to act as an elixir, reviving him. Spittle flew from his lips as they began to move, churning, forming angry words that Will could not understand.

Will's peripheral vision was gone, his entire world collapsed down so that he now peered through a long tunnel.

It was through this tunnel that Will watched as the man drew back the stanchion, lowered his head, and ran at him.

There's a name for this.

Will tried to recall what they called the condition where something caused a suspect's nervous system to become so flooded with adrenaline that he became almost superhuman. He could remember seeing the words for it written on a chalkboard at the old academy out in Elysian Park but couldn't seem to remember the words themselves.

Thomas fired. He was holding his gun only inches from Will's ear when it went off.

The explosion was so loud inside his head that it transcended the realm of sound, becoming only pain, as if someone had plunged an ice pick into his eardrum.

The shot grazed the charging man's right cheekbone and sheared off his ear.

What the hell are you aiming for, Thomas? You weren't supposed to take a head shot if you had the choice.

Blood poured from the man's wounds. But still he kept coming, his smell of body odor and Old Spice overpowering.

Will struggled to center the phosphorescent dot of his front sight on the man's advancing chest.

Green neon reflected off the chromed base of the stanchion as it began to whip toward him through the air.

Excited delirium.

Will finally remembered the term, now that he'd stopped trying to, now that he was simply squeezing the trigger over and over as fast as he could.

FIVE

"Why the hell did he do that?"

Thomas kept repeating the same question, over and over, pacing back and forth in front of Will. "Why didn't he stop when you told him?"

Will was down on one knee, cinching a Flex-Cuf down around the man's bony wrists. The man wasn't moving, but at this point Will wasn't about to take anything for granted.

He pressed his shaking hand against the man's carotid but couldn't find a pulse. Seven red blooms were grouped on the left side of the man's chest where he'd shot him. Will wasn't sure where Thomas's bullets had gone, other than the head shot, but was relieved to see that none of the bystanders had been hit.

"You recognize this guy?" Will asked.

Thomas nodded. "Name's Wes Keller. I went to high school with him."

Will's right ear felt dead, deaf except for a disturbing metallic ringing. "Any record?"

"Negative," Thomas answered without looking down. "Normally he's a solid citizen."

"Any history of violence?"

Thomas shook his head. "Not that I'm aware."

From the bar, Will could hear the sound of hushed murmurs.

"We need to talk to them," Will said. "Find out what happened before we showed up."

"Why didn't he stop when you told him?" Thomas asked again. "Why the *fuck* did he do that?"

Will began to go through the dead man's pockets. He pulled out a wallet, a round tin of Skoal, a Bic lighter. The wallet was distended, bulging with something stuffed inside.

Will took a ballpoint pen from his shirt pocket and dug around inside the folds of leather.

A small cellophane envelope that was heat-sealed along the top fell to the floor. It was filled with clear crystals that were like pieces of rock salt.

Will picked up the packet, studying it in the dimness of the bar.

Here's the answer to your question, Thomas.

The crystals seemed to glow with a bluish inner light.

I've got your answer right here.

Up close, the old guy sitting at the table wasn't as elderly as Will first thought. He now estimated him to be somewhere in his mid-sixties. It was hard to tell.

The man was still sitting alone at his table in the shadows. He wore eyeglasses with frames of heavy black plastic, like something from the 1950s. A long white beard sprouted from his face before spilling down his chest.

"You doing okay here?" Will asked him.

"This one's a bitch." The man looked down at the crossword puzzle in a folded copy of the *New York Times*. "They get tougher as the week goes on. This is only Tuesday. I don't even want to *imagine* Sunday."

Will was concerned the man might be mentally ill. "Did you see what just happened?"

The man shook his head. "I was pretty caught up in the puzzle, just minding my own." His voice was a baritone rumble.

"A person has their head smashed in, you don't have anything to say?"

The man answered while writing letters into the squares of the puzzle. Saying it softly, so Will couldn't quite hear. It sounded like he had said, "Boo-fucking-hoo."

Will looked at him. "Say that again?"

"Some morons wanna fuck themselves up, that's why they call this a free country."

Will heard the man's words in mono. He still couldn't hear anything through his right ear.

"Sir, I need for you to watch the language."

The man looked up at him and smiled. "You kidding me? We're in a fucking *bar*."

Will's eyes had become more accustomed to the darkness. He could now see that what he had first taken to be the colorful sleeves of the man's shirt weren't sleeves at all. They were tattoos. From shoulder to fingertip, the man was covered with a mosaic of imagery.

Will found himself being drawn into the swirl of colors, recognizing the oddly familiar objects arranged on the man's flesh, a greenish lamprey with jaundiced eyes and a horned man standing erect on the legs of a goat, a human skull sprouting the wings of an enormous bird and a deep red mushroom covered with warts, and an intricately rendered butchering diagram of a cow. On the back of the man's left hand was a black wasp, so lifelike that it looked as if it might fly away at any moment.

"So you're the new sheriff in town." The man smiled, his teeth yellow and pointed. "Hope you last longer than the last guy."

Will took a breath. "I have the authority to arrest you for

obstructing an investigation," he said. "One more time: Tell me what you *did* see."

"All right." The man nodded his large head. "What I saw was you go all Dirty Harry, blow the shit out of an unarmed guy."

Will used his chin to point at the stanchion tipped over on the floor. "You wouldn't consider that a weapon?"

The man grinned at Will. "Only if I wasn't on the guest list."

Will pinched the bridge of his nose. "Look, this has been a real long day. I'm not gonna stand here with you playing Whose Dick Is Bigger—"

"Dicks???" The man laughed, his eyes alive with electricity. "Now you want to talk about *dicks?*"

"Enough." Will flipped his pocket notebook open. "I need your name. Now."

The man rose to his feet. He was bigger than Will had expected, his upper torso broad. Will now found himself forced to look up at the man's bearded face.

"Frank Carver," the man said. "Need me to spell it for you?"

Will hesitated. He had dealt with famous people before, working in L.A., so it wasn't that. It was the context that surprised him, like running into the president in a crack house. It left him standing there, feeling stupid, trying to think of what to say next.

But that was as long as it took.

The man's engineer boots clomped away across the worn floor. He pushed through the batwing doors, leaving them swinging in opposite directions, flapping back and forth in his wake.

SIX

That evening, a cool breeze picked up from out of the west.

For a fleeting instant Will thought he could detect the metallic scent of the sea, then dismissed the idea as an impossibility given the considerable distance involved.

He let Buddy out of the fenced backyard, and the dog moved along the edge of the sidewalk, off leash. They turned right at the corner, the homes becoming larger and more elegant, Victorians and Greek Revivals looming behind trimmed hedges.

One of the largest gold claims in California history had been discovered outside Haydenville in the summer of 1849, and the town's housing stock was a beneficiary of the resulting economic boom. The surrounding forest was still littered with the abandoned mine sites.

Will and the dog reached an intersection, the street abruptly coming to a dead end at the edge of the national forest.

He stood at the border of the woods, thinking about taking the dog into them. He tried to see into the shadowed darkness, silhouettes of massive trunks and long branches reaching out in every direction, growing into one another. The tall trees seemed to drain all of the light from the air, so that it was like trying to peer into a mineshaft.

If the dog took off after a squirrel, Will might not be able to find him.

Something in the periphery of his vision captured Will's attention, and he found himself staring at a black-and-white photograph of a German shepherd. Above the photograph were block letters that spelled out the words LOST DOG, the xeroxed flyer stapled to the splintered surface of a telephone pole.

He flinched when something brushed against the backs of his legs.

Will spun around. He looked down and saw the dog there, a stick now held in his mouth.

He pried the stick away from the dog and sent it flying end over end up the street, away from the woods. It went off course, landing in a front yard.

In contrast to the neighboring lawns, the grass there was dried up, the yard an arid patchwork of dirt and yellow weeds. The house's front porch was crowded with detritus that included a filthy velvet couch, a cracked porcelain toilet, and the metal frame from an old hospital bed.

Through the screen door, Will could see tall piles of magazines and stacks of cardboard boxes, transforming the living room into a labyrinth.

A young woman dressed in a matted velour sweat suit came to the door. Her face was that of a crone, her thinning hair charged with static electricity that made it hang in the air around her skull like pieces of dull thread.

Will raised his hand in greeting, but the woman turned away and slammed shut the wooden front door.

Buddy waited for Will at the next corner, beside a telephone pole. As Will approached, he could see it was covered with paper notices. He stopped to look at one of them, thinking it might be an announcement for a picnic or barbecue, somewhere for him to meet people.

But it was another missing dog poster, this one for a dachsund whose legs looked so short it seemed as if its stomach would scrape the ground.

Will looked at the next notice, for a missing pug, and saw just below it one offering a reward for the return of a rottweiler.

The notices overlapped one another as they stretched around the circumference of the pole. Will took a step back and looked up, the notices stretching far above his head. Whoever had put them up there would have needed a ladder.

There were dozens of them, for cocker spaniels and boxers and Labrador retrievers and beagles and malamutes and collies, their eyes staring out at him from the pole.

Will made a mental note to ask Thomas if he knew anything about this.

SEVEN

"I've got a Special Agent Nolan from the DEA on line two," Lila's voice announced over the intercom.

Will took his hiking boots down from the top of his desk and looked across at Thomas, who was sitting in the guest chair. "Put him in here."

A nasal voice came over the speakerphone. "*Will the Thrill.*"

"Kirk," Will said. "I've got you on speaker with Thomas Costello, one of my officers."

"One of your *officers*," Nolan said. "To be honest, I never thought they'd even let you wear a badge again. When I saw your name on the lab request, I almost crapped my pants."

"That's why they make *Depends*," Will said.

"Same old Will," Nolan said. "How about it? You still the same guy, or did you clean up your act?"

Will's hand tightened into a fist. "It's a clean act. All the reviewers say so."

"The good people of Bumfuck know about your problems, Will?"

Thomas gave Will a puzzled look.

"They prefer to call it Haydenville. And yeah, I told the mayor, but she thought it best to keep it under wraps from the people working for me. Thomas here, for example."

Thomas stared at him from the other side of the desk, a hurt look on his face.

"There I go, popping off my big mouth again," Nolan said. "Hey, Thomas?"

Thomas scooted forward to the edge of his chair. "Yes, sir?"

"Forget I ever said anything, would you?"

Will waved Thomas back from the phone. "What do you want, Kirk?"

"You submitted a sample to the state lab, they sent it on to us."

"Why would they do that?"

"Because it's the cleanest sample we've ever tested," Nolan said. "Ninety-nine percent pure methamphetamine. How'd you happen to come by it?"

"More like it came to us. Found it in the pocket of some tweaker who tried to kill us."

"Not surprised. Shit would send Gandhi on a rampage."

"This town has a meth problem," Will said. "That's why they brought me up here."

"It's not Hicksville, or whatever you call it, I'm worried about. This shit finds its way to a major city, can you imagine the kind of hell that will break loose? Makes me glad I live in the burbs."

Will moved closer to the speakerphone. "We'll find where it's coming from and shut it down."

"Laboratory results indicate the crystal was Nazi method. You're probably looking at a clan lab, and with that kind of purity we're not talking Beavis and Butthead cooking in the back of a Winnebago."

Thomas opened his mouth, as if to ask a question. Will shook his head, quieting him.

"Trust me, Kirk. I can handle it."

"I don't mean any disrespect here, but frankly this is too impor-tant for me to just *trust* you."

Will sat back in his office chair. "Why is it that whenever some-one starts out a sentence by saying they don't mean any disrespect, they always do?" he said. "We've got it under control, we're tracking the source as we speak."

Thomas shot him a confused look but didn't say anything, cross-ing his arms across his chest.

"It's your funeral," Nolan said over the speakerphone. "But one word of advice."

"What's that?"

"Don't fuck up."

EIGHT

The pages of the book fluttered in the stream of chilled air blowing from the air-conditioning system.

Will sat alone at a dark wooden table inside the Haydenville Public Library and read from a hardbound copy of Frank Carver's novel, *The Silent Men*.

He'd never read it before, even though it had been an international bestseller back in the seventies. He always suspected—and now that he was reading it felt that his suspicion had been correct—that the book's sales were based on the notoriety of the man who had written it rather than on the quality of the book itself.

As Will remembered it, sometime in the early seventies Frank Carver and his wife had attended a party in the Berkeley hills.

After a long evening of drinking and drugs, Frank announced to the guests that he had something he wanted to show them. When a crowd of revelers had gathered around him, Frank said that he was going to perform a historical reenactment of the legend of William Tell.

He then took an apple and placed it on top of the head of his wife. According to eyewitnesses, Frank staggered as he paced off a distance across the lawn. He picked up an arrow and blew theatrically on the feathers before nocking it in the bow.

He drew back the bowstring and aimed the metallic point of the arrow at the apple perched on his wife's head.

The crowd stood there and watched, too afraid of Frank to intervene on her behalf. Frank released the arrow, which went low of its mark, burying its shaft into his wife's left eye.

She was loaded into the back of a Volkswagen Microbus and rushed to a local hospital, where she was pronounced dead upon arrival.

Frank Carver was arrested while attempting to board a flight to Tangier. He was found guilty of voluntary manslaughter and sentenced to eleven-to-life at the state penitentiary at San Quentin.

It was while incarcerated there that he became a voracious reader; he told journalists that his favorite authors were Genet and Dostoyevsky. Frank successfully petitioned the warden for a typewriter and set to work on a novel of his own. He also began corresponding with some of the decade's leading writers, including Norman Mailer, Gore Vidal, and William Styron.

Frank became a cause célèbre in the literary community. Famous authors wrote letters on his behalf and came to testify at a specially convened parole hearing.

The parole board was duly impressed, and Frank was released from prison in the summer of 1977. *The Silent Men* was published later that year, a picaresque tale of a career criminal's bloody journey through America during the Summer of Love. Frank had appeared simultaneously on the covers of both *Time* and *Newsweek*.

In 1979, Frank purchased property in Haydenville and moved there to begin work on a follow-up.

It had still not been published.

Will placed the book facedown on the library counter.

"You want to check that out?" asked the teenaged boy behind the desk.

"No thanks," Will said. "I don't have a card."

The kid pointed at the book. "You like it?"

"It's pretty melodramatic."

The boy had a blank look on his face. "What's that mean?"

"Melodrama?" Will tried to think of how he might explain it. "Basically, it's when the characters solve their problems with guns."

The boy shrugged. "So what's wrong with that?"

"It's not the way the world works."

The boy picked up the book and looked at the black-and-white author's photograph of Frank Carver on the back cover. "He's in here all the time."

"Who is?"

"Frank Carver. He gives readings sometimes. Ernie's real tight with him."

"Who's Ernie?"

"The librarian."

"Is he here?"

"*She*," the boy said. "Ernestine. She's off until Tuesday."

Will thought it might be useful to talk to her, see what he might be able to learn about Frank Carver. He'd already run Frank through the California Department of Justice and NCIC databases and was surprised to see that, aside from the manslaughter conviction, there was nothing else on his record.

Will opened his wallet, took out one of his brand-new business cards, and slid it across the desk. "Do me a favor? Let her know I'll be coming back."

NINE

"You feel any calmer today?" Will asked.

Thomas sat across the table from him on the outdoor deck of a restaurant that everyone in town simply referred to as the Café. Wisteria snaked along the wooden arbor above their heads, shading them from the heat of the morning sun.

"I don't know." Thomas pushed a pile of crumbs from his order of toast back and forth on the table with the edge of a knife, not looking up at Will. "Why didn't you tell me?"

After the conference call with Nolan, Thomas had gone to his desk and packed up his Thermos and lunchbox, then stormed out of the office, even though it was only three in the afternoon.

"I didn't think it was relevant," Will said. "It's past history."

"Not when we have to work together, it isn't. Not when my life might be on the line."

"Your life *was* on the line, remember?"

Will could still hear the high-pitched ringing in his right ear. It set him on edge, the constant buzzing of a gnat. He wondered if he should try to find a doctor to take a look at it.

"If I'm gonna work for you, I need to know what I'm dealing with," Thomas said. "That dude from the DEA seems to think you're a complete fuckup."

"What do you think, Thomas?" Will asked.

"I don't really know what to think. I need you to come clean with me."

"Come clean with *you*? You work for me."

Thomas looked up and met Will's gaze. "I look like a slave?"

Will wondered how he should proceed. He had never managed an employee before, was unsure of the correct approach. He wanted to just tell Thomas to go to hell but realized that he needed to keep him around.

"All right," Will said. "What is it you feel you need to know?"

"That dude on the phone, how do you know him?"

"We were on a task force together."

"He kept saying you had a problem."

Will took a sip of his coffee. "I had a drug problem. But I've been clean for more than two years."

"What kind of drugs are we talking?"

"Heroin, mostly," Will said. "Sometimes I'd mix it with fentanyl."

"You snorted it?"

Will shook his head.

"Shit," Thomas said. "I thought you were supposed to be a narc."

"I was. A detective in the LAPD Narcotics Division."

"But you were shooting heroin."

"I was undercover, working cases against major distributors. You get close to them, they expect to see you use. They *need* to see you use, or they peg you as a cop."

Thomas nodded his head. "And your case is blown."

"At that point, you don't really care."

"How come?"

"Because you're already dead."

Will took a sip from his glass of ice water. The morning was warm, the temperature already somewhere up in the eighties. "The way you're trained is to make excuses for not using. You tell the bad guys that you're on parole, and you're gonna get your piss tested tomorrow. Or you say you've got some medical problem. But when you work the kind of cases I was, when you work *deep*, where you're under for sometimes months, the excuses wear out."

"So what do you do?"

"You have a choice. You can either bail on the case and throw away everything invested in it, or you use in front of them."

"And that's what you did."

Will nodded. "It was a choice, and I made it."

"And then you were a junkie."

"No," Will said. "I only used in front of the perps, and chipped on the side to keep my tolerance up. So I wouldn't get too high when I did have to shoot up. I had it under control."

"So what went wrong?"

"Something bad happened." Will said. "Then I didn't have it under control anymore."

"What was this thing, that was so bad?"

Will saw Sean's face, his blue eyes looking up at him from his crib

(i wasn't there—)

Will blinked the image away, looking off into the distance, at the snow that still capped the mountain peaks despite the summer heat. "It was personal, OK?"

"No, not OK." Thomas shook his head. "I want to know."

Will slammed his coffee cup down on the saucer. "Yeah? Well, you can go fuck yourself."

Thomas stopped fiddling with his pile of crumbs, his cheeks turning the color of an old-fashioned hot water bottle. It was quiet now, except for the sound of the crows pecking at the lawn of the town's square.

"Look," Will said, the expression on the boy's face filling him with a sense of remorse. "It's just not something I'm willing to talk about, all right?"

Thomas nodded his head while looking down at the table. He looked as if he might begin to cry. "Why'd he call you that name, Will the Thrill?"

"It's just something cops do sometimes, give each other nicknames."

"But why that one?"

"I don't know, probably because I was willing to take chances."

"Like what?" Thomas asked.

Working without a net. That's how he had come to think about it. He'd push the brass to let him work deeper and deeper, sometimes not checking in for days at a time. They never even knew if he was still alive until he surfaced again, like a man in a diving bell emerging from the depths of the sea.

"I was the lead on the Faustino Rodriguez bust," Will said.

"That was you?" Thomas looked up at Will now in a way that was somehow different. "I remember seeing that on the news."

Damn right. It still stood as the biggest heroin bust in the history of the LAPD. Will had kept a file folder with newspaper clippings, though he had no idea where it was now.

Thomas ripped open a packet of sugar and poured some of it into his mouth. "What's the Nazi method?"

"Shit, Thomas, didn't they give you any training up here?"

Thomas looked down at the tabletop, but didn't say anything.

"There are basically two ways to manufacture meth," Will said. The Nazi method uses anhydrous ammonia and lithium. It's called that because it was the process Hitler used to manufacture the methamphetamine to fire up his troops."

A young woman pushed a stroller along the sidewalk in front of the Café. Her hair was matted and shiny with grease, the pale flesh of her face covered with red sores.

Will recognized the sores as symptoms of formication, a delusion common to meth addicts that causes them to scratch compulsively at the imaginary insects they feel crawling beneath their skin.

"What's happening to this town, Thomas? How long has this meth problem been going on?"

"Not long. But once it started, it spread real fast. Kind of like *Invasion of the Body Snatchers.*"

"Why is everyone who lives here just sitting back and letting it happen? Why don't they do something?"

"I don't know," Thomas said. "They probably don't want to get involved."

"What about you?"

"I grew up here. I hate what's going on. But what am I supposed to do?"

"We bust users, then try to flip them. Follow it back up the line to the source," Will said. "Narcotics Investigation 101."

Thomas nodded. "Hey, Will, can I ask you something?"

"Last question of the day."

Thomas brushed the crumbs from the front of his shirt, then looked up at Will. "You think I could maybe have a nickname?"

TEN

The Johnson & Burdette Funeral Home sat just off the town's square in a converted Second Empire home, its mansard roof topped with cast-iron spikes that pointed upward at the bright and empty sky.

Will pushed through the heavy oak front door and found himself standing inside a room decorated to give it the appearance of a bucolic family home.

"May I help you?" A small older man in a dark suit spoke in a whisper. To his left was a showroom, gleaming caskets resting on biers.

"I'm here for the autopsy," Will said.

The man brought his finger quickly to his lips and made a shushing sound. "Could you please keep it down?" He glanced into an adjoining room. "There's a family in there."

Will lowered his voice. "Sorry."

The man pointed a finger toward a door at the far end of the foyer. "Down in the basement."

Klamath County was too small to have a morgue facility of its own, so it had worked out a series of arrangements with private mortuaries to perform autopsies using their premises. An independent patholo-gist under contract with the county had driven out to perform the postmortem on the dead kayaker.

Coming from the brightness of the upstairs rooms, Will's eyes took a long time to adjust to the dark stairwell. He gripped a metal handrail attached to a wall made from roughly hewn stones that were damp with condensation. The wood of the treads felt soft beneath his feet, as if they might give way at any moment, send him plunging down into the blackness.

Will's stomach growled. He'd made it a point to skip breakfast because he'd never attended an autopsy before and wasn't sure what to expect.

The basement was dark except for a circle of light cast by a stain-less steel surgical lamp hovering over an old porcelain embalming table.

One of the dead kayaker's co-workers from a local whitewater rafting business had come forward to report her missing and been able to identify her body. The kayaker's name was Caitlyn Johnson. She'd been living in Haydenville for the summer while attending California State University in Humboldt.

She now lay faceup on the white table, her body naked. Her legs were splayed wide, and as Will walked toward her he could see the exposed folds of her vagina and the clean-shaven mound of her mons verneris.

"Beautiful girl, isn't she?" The pathologist wore a Plexiglas face shield and a disposable white Tyvek jumpsuit over his street clothes, as if she were somehow toxic.

"Dr. Crosley?" Will extended his hand to shake. "We spoke on the phone. Thanks for getting out here so quickly."

The pathologist held up a hand encased in a long black rubber glove that was slick with fluids. "I don't think you really want to do that."

He turned away from Will and reached his gloved hands inside a deep Y-shaped incision that ran upward from her pubic bone, curved under each of her breasts, and finally ended at the tip of each shoulder. He emerged clutching her heart, then dropped it into the metal basket of a scale hanging from the room's ceiling.

"This town's really gone to hell since the last time I was here," he said.

"How do you mean?" Will asked.

"Isn't it obvious?" Crosley scribbled the weight of the organ on a whiteboard that was smeared with blood that looked as dark as coffee.

"I just moved up here from L.A." Will said. "It seems pretty nice to me."

"Yeah? Well, you should have seen it before."

Metal shelves held plastic bottles of Tiss-U-Tone and Cavamine. Will flashed on Sean's face, what they had done to him, the waxen skin and bad makeup, as if his son had been switched with a grotesque doll.

Dr. Crosley waved his gloved hand in the general direction of the woman's vagina. "There was no evidence of recent sexual activity, or presence of semen. Her hymen was intact."

"She was a virgin?"

Crosley seemed amused by the question. "As in *vestal*? I really wouldn't know."

Will was confused. "You said——"

"You've never done this before, have you?" Crosley said. "A significant percentage of sexually active postpubertal females have intact hymens."

Will looked down at the woman's form, the chipped white porcelain of the table taking on a pinkish hue from the fluids that ran down into a drain hole between her feet. Her face had been pulled off, the flesh now in a heap at her throat. A yarmulke-shaped piece of skull was missing from the top of her head.

"She didn't drown," Crosley said.

Will looked at him. "How do you know?"

Crosley smiled. "Because there was no *water* in her lungs."

"So how did she die?"

The pathologist grabbed something off a wooden board and thrust it toward Will in his gloved hands, as if cradling a small animal.

Will saw that it was a brain. It was smaller than he would have expected, wrinkled and gray. He opened his mouth to ask a question, but Crosley cut him off.

"Her brain swelled up after an impact caused it to collide with the inside of her skull." Crosley pointed to an area on the brain that was purplish and slick with blood. "You can see the cerebellar hematoma. Once the swelling started, without intervention she would have died in a matter of hours."

"She was kayaking in a river. If she hit her head, how could she not have drowned?"

"The simple answer is that she stopped breathing before she respirated water. But looking at the condition of her skin, I'd say she never was in the water at all."

Will wondered how that could be possible, to lose consciousness in a kayak, in a fast-moving river, but not fall in.

"This struck me as somewhat odd." Crosley pointed at a series of circular bruises that ran across her upper chest, like a necklace. "See how they're almost identical in size and shape to the wound on her forehead?"

He lifted Caitlyn's body, exposing her back. "Now look at this."

Will could see more of the circular bruises wrapping across her shoulder blades. "So you agree with me, then?" Will asked. "That it could be homicide?"

The pathologist set her body back down on the table, what was left of her head banging against the hard surface. "Who said *that*?"

"You just said it was odd."

"I didn't realize that 'odd' was a synonym for homicide," Crosley said. "Your report and the physical evidence are consistent with accidental death."

"Then how do you explain the bruises?"

"My guess is that she crashed into a rock. The current pinned her against it, smashing her body against it repeatedly, resulting in the multiple contusions."

Will had done some kayaking back when he was in college. He couldn't picture her being held against the rock so that it smashed the front part of the body, then somehow turned her around so that it smashed her back.

"I've got this gut feeling, this wasn't an accident," Will said.

Crosley blew some air out through his mouth. "Good for you."

"If you rule this an accident, my mayor will shut the investigation down."

"Why do you care?"

He opened his mouth to answer the question but wasn't sure what to say. He remembered her lying there, dead on the ground. Not like seeing a dead junkie, or some corner dealer who'd been gunned down in a drive-by.

"Can you do me a favor here? Could you at least rule it undetermined, while I check things out?"

The pathologist flipped up his Plexiglas face shield and looked at Will with eyes that now seemed smaller.

"Mr. Magowan, I'm getting the sense that you don't understand how this is supposed to work. You called me up and begged me to hustle out here, because you said this case had to be resolved immediately. Isn't that right?"

"Yes, and I appreciate it."

Crosley picked up a long, hooked needle and began to thread it with what looked like twine. "Well, let's resolve it, then. Pending the lab work, my finding is that the proximate cause of death was a cerebral edema, sustained while striking a blunt object while the sub-ject was engaged in whitewater kayaking. In other words, the manner of death was accidental."

Then he jabbed the needle into her abdomen and began to stitch her closed.

ELEVEN

When he arrived home from work that evening, Will could hear the ringing of the telephone coming from inside the house.

He fumbled with the dead bolt, then realized that he was using the key for his office. By the time he managed to get the door open, the ringing had stopped.

Inside the living room, he heard Laurie's voice floating from the answering machine.

Will grabbed the cordless from the cradle and hit the TALK button. "Laurie? Sorry, I just walked in."

"Where are you?" she asked. "What do you mean you moved?"

Her voice sounded fuzzy. Then he realized what he was doing wrong and switched the phone to his good ear. "I wanted to tell you sooner. Things have been happening kind of fast."

"It doesn't matter," she said.

He pulled out one of the chairs from the dining table and sat down. "I'm in a town called Haydenville. It's up north."

"Why?" she asked. "Is there someone up there you know?"

"I got a job."

"Really?" She sounded surprised. "Doing what?"

"You're gonna think I'm putting you on, but really, I'm not. I'm the chief of police."

Will could feel Buddy watching him. The dog lay on his side on the living room floor, eyes wide open.

"I don't know what to say. Are you sure you're ready to go back? To handle all the pressure?"

"It's just a small town."

"I still don't understand," she said. "Why *there*?"

"I need to work, Laurie. It's not exactly like people were standing in line to hire me."

"But you're a good cop."

"If you're willing to overlook the heroin addiction."

She let out her breath. "Do you ever cut yourself any slack?"

"What for?" he said. "I'm the one who screwed up."

"After what happened to Sean, was it really a surprise?"

"People go through worse."

"Yeah? Like what?"

He didn't answer.

"The people you worked for, they put you in a position where you had to use drugs," she said. "Then they have the nerve to fire you when you get hooked?"

"Too bad you couldn't testify at my hearing."

In the wake of the consent decree, and with the new police chief appointing the Blue Ribbon Rampart Review Panel, the department had been looking for ways to make object lessons, to publicly demonstrate how the new LAPD would no longer brook misconduct from its officers. He had been an easy target.

They took away his gun and badge, and put out a press release.

"I was really hoping to hear about you," Will said.

"I'm good," she said. "I started subbing for some of the teachers at the yoga studio."

"You're really going for it. I heard the message on your machine."

"You mean the *namaste*? It's what we say after the blessing for all sentient beings."

"What about the nonsentient beings?"

"Fuck 'em," she said.

"Wow, that's pretty harsh."

"They don't have any feelings," she said. "That's the point."

Will laughed; he had almost forgotten her sense of humor. He sat up in the wooden chair, sensing that this was his opportunity. "You know those papers?"

"The divorce agreement? Don't tell me you still haven't signed them."

"What I'm thinking, we're going too fast. We should give things another chance."

"We've been through this a million times, Will. You've got to stop running away from what *is*."

"But it's different now," he said. "I've got this job. I've got a great house, I'm clean. I'm thinking it could be like old times."

"No," she said. "It will never be like that again."

He became aware of a pain deep in the bones of his hand, and he realized that he was gripping the phone too tightly. "It's not like I'm asking you to renew our wedding vows, Laurie. Just come up for a weekend. I'll sleep on the couch."

"Look, Will, I love you, OK? But I just can't be with you anymore."

He hadn't had the chance to turn on the lights when he came in, the room now illuminated only by the silver light of the moon coming through the skylight.

"Not even for a *weekend*? You'll love it here. It's like this postcard-perfect little town."

"Let me think about it."

"Sure," he said. "Why don't you think about coming up for the Fourth of July?"

There was an awkward silence before she answered. "Why'd you pick that day?"

"Because they have this great old-time parade. Shriners in little cars, the whole deal."

He waited for her to say something, listening to the static of their connection, like running water.

"Do you even *know* what day that is?" she asked.

Will saw it now, but too late. "It was his birthday."

He saw smoke rising from the tips of slender blue candles, a bright and conical hat perched on his son's head, the taut elastic band digging into the soft flesh of his cheek

(i wasn't there—)

"Say his name," she said quietly.

"What for?" His voice now sounded weak to him, like a boy going through puberty.

"It's Sean's birthday. Sean. Can't you even say his *name?*"

Will opened his mouth to speak but couldn't find the right words, floundering once again in the river that had somehow come to run between them.

He heard an electronic click and realized she had hung up on him. His thumb moved to the REDIAL button, but he didn't press it.

Will sat there in the dark, then pushed the chair back from the table, the sound loud inside the empty house. He crossed the room and lay down on the wooden floor, beside the dog.

TWELVE

The plastic probe was cold and sharp inside his ear canal. The doctor hunched over at the waist, peering into the instrument, his breath moist on the side of Will's neck.

"Tell me again?" the doctor asked. "How it happened?"

"A gun went off next to my ear."

"If you don't mind my asking, why were you holding it next to your ear?"

"It wasn't mine. It belonged to another officer."

Will looked at the pattern of cabbage roses on the wallpaper. The doctor's offices were on the first floor of a Victorian home just off the square, the examining room occupying what must originally have been a bedroom.

The doctor removed the probe from Will's ear, stepped on the pedal of a garbage can, and ejected the plastic tip inside. "The news isn't so good, I'm afraid." He leaned back against a counter and crossed his arms. "I see a lot of inflammation. You complain of tinnitus, but what bothers me is the hearing loss. It's significant."

"What should we do?"

"*We* shouldn't do anything. You need to get yourself to a good ENT man right away. The closest one I know is in Redding."

Redding was two hours each way, best case.

"This isn't a good time for me," Will said. "Things are pretty crazy at work."

Will and Thomas had started working their way through the list of those who had been arrested on drug-related charges. Using last known addresses, they had been conducting field interviews, seeing if they might learn something useful about Haydenville's meth scene.

So far, it had been a series of dead ends: four instances of moved with no forwarding address; two currently encarcerateds; innumerable blank stares accompanied by protestations of clean living.

"Is it a good time for you to go deaf?" the doctor asked.

Will took this to be a rhetorical question and therefore didn't answer it.

"You need to see somebody now, while the hearing loss may still be reversible," the doctor said. "Tell me, how are you feeling otherwise?"

"How do you mean?"

"You look exhausted. How are you sleeping?"

"On and off," Will said.

"Something bothering you?"

Will breathed in the pungent aroma of rubbing alcohol. "Like I said, there's a lot going on."

"My advice? You better start taking care of yourself."

"I know. I just need for things to calm down a little."

The doctor stood up. "Is there anything else?"

"There is one thing." Will hesitated. "My knee. I've got this old injury, and lately it's been killing me."

The doctor reached for the cuffs of Will's jeans. "Which one? Let's have a look—"

Will got up from the table. "I've gotta run right now. But I could really use something, for the pain."

"Take four ibuprofen, every eight hours."

"I tried that," Will said. "It's not cutting it."

The doctor took a pad from the pocket of his lab coat. "I'll write you a prescription for some Vicodin."

THIRTEEN

The morning sun blasted through the glass doors of the library, making him feel as though he were inside a greenhouse. Will shifted on the wooden bench that was set just inside the entrance and watched the minute hand of a clock hanging on the wall tick forward.

"You want a coffee?" It was the same young clerk from the other night.

"I don't know," Will said. "You think she'll be much longer?" He'd been there for almost fifteen minutes now, waiting for the librarian to emerge from behind the closed door of her office.

The teenager shrugged. "She's on the phone with somebody."

Will thought about whether he should just leave, come back some other time.

He had left Thomas at the office to finish going through the records of everyone the department had arrested for narcotics violations over the past two years. They'd also started contacting farm products dealers, getting lists of recent purchasers of anhydrous ammonia and inquiring if there had been any thefts.

For the past several nights they had alternated pulling night duty, patrolling outside the Dig Inn and along Main Street, hoping to arrest users.

So far, it had amounted to less than nothing.

The door to the librarian's office opened, and a middle-aged African American woman came toward him.

Will stood up and held out his hand. "Ernestine, I'm—"

"Ernie." She looked at his hand but didn't take it. "That's what people around here call me. And I know who you are."

Will stood there feeling awkward as the woman started gathering books out of a metal cart. "I was hoping you might be able to provide some information about Frank Carver."

She started to walk away, holding on to the stack of books. "I've got to reshelve these. Why don't we walk and talk."

Will followed her into the maze of tall shelves. "What can you tell me about him?"

She turned to face him. "I can tell you that he's a great man."

Will took the stack from her as she fitted one of the books into a vacant spot on the shelf. "What is it, that makes him so great?"

"You see all these books?"

Will nodded, not sure why she was asking.

"They're all here because of Frank. There was no library in this town before he came up with the money to renovate this building, to pay for all the rest of it." She took more of the books from his stack. "He did it on his own, understand? He came to us. Nobody had to go and ask him to help."

"Why do you think he did it?" Will asked.

"He saw for himself how books could change a person's life. Books gave Frank a second chance. How many people get that?"

She stared at him, waiting for him to respond. When he didn't she said, "He's a single parent. He raised his two boys, all by himself. That makes him a hero in my book."

"Frank killed their mother."

She gave him a withering look. "That was his first wife. The twins are from a second marriage."

"What happened to her?"

"Who knows?" she said. "Just up and disappeared not long after those children were born."

Will tried to help by trying to put away some of the books.

Ernestine watched him, a frown on her face. "You know the Dewey?"

"No."

"Then you best leave it to me." She took several books from the top of his stack and began sliding them into place on a shelf.

"I understand you know him fairly well," he said. "What can you tell me about him that hasn't been in the press?"

"Everything else's just a bunch of rumors," she said. "There's always been all kinds of nonsense floating around about Frank Carver."

"Like what?"

"I don't traffic in rumors," she said.

She took the last book from Will and started to walk away down the narrow aisle.

He reached out and touched her shoulder. "Please. You never know what could turn out to be important."

She wheeled around. For a second he was afraid he had gone too far by touching her, but her features seemed to soften when she looked at his face.

"Since you asked so nice, there is one thing I do know for a *fact*," she said. "But I'm sure you already know it."

"What's that?"

"Frank was an Angel."

"An angel," he repeated, lost.

"Are you a real cop, or what?" She strained to keep her voice low in the hush of the library. "An *Angel*. Frank used to be with the Hell's Angels."

FOURTEEN

On Saturday, his day off, Will dragged a yellow kayak across the stones of the river's bank until its pointed bow came to rest at the edge of the current.

From the interview with the owner of the rafting company where Caitlyn Johnson had been employed, Will had learned that she set out for a solo paddle after work, at approximately 6:30 P.M., putting in at this spot. Any of the rapids between here and the eddy where they had found her floating could be the site where she died.

He wanted to re-create her final voyage, to see with his own eyes the rocks that had supposedly killed her. Even with everything else that was going on, he found he couldn't get her out of his mind. He'd wake up in the middle of the night and see her face; not as he'd found her, lying dead on the ground, but undefiled and beautiful, filled with life. When he saw her, she was always smiling.

The boat was a rental, dented but serviceable. Will had done a little paddling back when he was in law school, some of his only happy memories from the years he had spent at Duke—before finally deciding to drop out.

He slid his legs inside, surprised by how snug the fit was. He was forced to cant his feet forward at an uncomfortable angle to fit them inside the narrow bow, then struggled to stretch the neoprene spray skirt onto the boat's coaming, sealing himself inside.

He pushed himself off the bank, angling upstream before making an eddy turn that launched him into the main current of the river.

He found himself floating downriver on a section of water that was broad and flat. The sun was high up in the open sky, the temperature close to the century mark. A pair of red-tailed hawks glided together on a thermal.

He figured that this would be as good a place as any to test out his Eskimo roll.

He drew in a deep breath and then flipped the boat over so that he was inverted, his body suspended in the clear water by the kayak, which floated along up above him.

It was quiet now, the sound of the world shut off. The sunlight raked down through the greenish water, so that he felt as if he were encased inside an emerald. Will reached up with both hands so that the blades of the paddle rested on the surface of the water. Then he slowly swept one of the blades out, away from the edge of the kayak. When it was at the proper angle, Will executed his hip snap, and he felt the boat begin to come up.

The layers of green water became lighter as he rose, his face almost breaking the surface of the water.

Then his momentum abruptly stopped, and he began to plunge downward, the cold water rushing up into his nostrils.

He hung upside-down in the room of green water, trying to figure out what he'd done wrong. His head began to fill with recriminations, aware now that this had been a bad idea, pure hubris, attempting the river alone after a seventeen-year layoff.

He felt himself accelerating, the stones of the bottom speeding by above his head. The water began to grow cloudy, filling with bubbles of turbulence, the sound of it becoming a low rumble.

Rapids. He tried not to think about how much time he had before he would run into them. He tucked his face up, against the deck of the kayak, trying to protect it from oncoming rocks. He was desperate to breathe now, had to fight the screaming instinct to inhale.

He thought about popping the skirt and doing a wet exit, but swimming the rapid was a dangerous proposition.

He set up to roll again. He thought he had it figured out now, what he'd been doing wrong with his roll. His *head*, he'd been lifting it too early as the boat was coming up, so that it was acting like a giant counterweight.

This time, he forced himself to keep his chin tight against his shoulder as he snapped his hip, and he popped up, back into the warm and bright air.

He blinked the river's water from his eyes, alarmed to see that he was about to enter the rapids, and that he wasn't ready. The bow plunged downward into a hole, the water loud and white. There was no time to react. Instinctively, he lay forward on the front deck of the boat, preparing to capsize.

The rapid took hold of the kayak, shaking it, spinning the bow back and forth like the needle of a compass.

But the boat didn't capsize. On its own, without his even using the paddle, the kayak came through the rapid, floating once again on an untroubled section of calm water.

He could now see how it was possible.

The rapids here were so easy that even if she had been lying unconscious on the front deck of her boat she could have moved downriver to her final resting place without tipping over.

Will looked up at the red earth and granite of the bank on the far side of the river and saw dark smoke drifting up through the trees. It rose from the metal chimney pipe of a ramshackle cottage, like something that had been trucked there from Appalachia.

Will wondered why anyone would be using a fireplace in this kind of heat. Then, catching the smell, he realized that they were burning garbage. When he had the time, he thought it might be worth paying a visit, both to ask them to refrain from burning and to see if they might have seen Caitlyn on the evening of her death.

He wasn't sure how he might get there. To his knowledge, there were no roads on that side of the river.

FIFTEEN

The Haydenville Police Department's only vehicle was a white Ford Explorer with a light bar mounted to the roof and 140,000 miles on the odometer. Will sat in the passenger seat as Thomas drove. The truck's air-conditioning labored to cool the interior.

An aluminum clipboard rested on top of Will's thighs, and he read from the printout of a rap sheet:

NAME: Bell, Henry, NMI
DOB: 5/2/70
SEX: M
RAC: W

They were working their way through the last of the known offenders list they had compiled. Henry Bell had been arrested for possession of one gram of methamphetamine the previous year. The Klamath County district attorney had declined to prosecute, citing the relatively small amount involved.

"Remember how you wanted a nickname?" Will asked.

"Yeah." Thomas kept his eyes looking forward, out at the road.

"I've been giving some thought to the matter." A rack holding two shotguns was placed between them, just behind the front seats. One of the guns had an orange muzzle, to indicate that it fired non-lethal ammunition. "What I came up with is this: Mr. T."

"Mr. T?"

"You know, like the guy on that old TV show?"

" 'I'm gonna git you, sucka'," Thomas said in a ridiculously poor impersonation of the Mohawked actor from *The A-Team.*

Will laughed. "Glad you like it."

" 'I pity the fool'," Thomas growled, still in character.

"Enough of that, or I'll take it back."

But the boy wouldn't stop. He was laughing now, thoroughly enjoying himself, as he tried out another line from the show. " 'Don't make me *mad* . . .' "

Will tried to ignore him, looking back down at the paperwork in his lap, wondering if the whole thing had been a mistake.

The last known address for Henry Bell was down a pothole-riddled gravel road on the southern fringe of the national forest.

A frayed blue tarp clung to the roof of an old two-story house. Peeling patches of paint like torn scabs hung from the clapboards, exposing the old-growth redwood beneath. Thick vines snaked up the balusters of the wraparound porch, making it appear the house was being reclaimed by the earth.

They walked through the heat of the front yard, nothing but dry weeds and clods of dirt.

Next to a raised garden filled with dead tomato plants stood an abandoned nativity scene caked with dried mud, the sun-faded figures leaning at odd angles, as though they were drunk.

Thomas banged on the front door.

No sound came from the other side. In the yard, the Explorer's cooling engine made a ticking noise.

Thomas pounded on the door, more forcefully this time, using the heel of his fist.

Will could hear footsteps now, someone heavy, leather heels on a wooden floor.

The door opened inward a few inches on a brass security chain. Thomas extended his badge holder through the opening. Will made a mental note to speak to him about that, since it wasn't proper procedure.

"Police," Thomas said.

No answer from inside. Only the smell of body odor and moldering garbage.

"Open up," Thomas said. His hand was still extended through the crack.

Will reached out to pull back the younger man's arm.

Too late. Like the spring mechanism of a rodent trap, the door snapped shut with a crunching noise.

Thomas screamed.

Will took a step back, then threw his shoulder squarely at the door. It didn't move, something powerful and unyielding pushing back from the other side.

"Police." Will thought it might help to say it again, just to be sure there was no misunderstanding. "Open the door. *Now.*"

There was no response from whoever was inside the house.

Will looked at Thomas. His face was bloodless, dripping with sweat.

"Look at me," Will said, keeping his voice low. The boy's head turned toward him, but his eyes were unfocused. "On three, we hit it together, okay?"

Thomas nodded.

Will held up his hand and began to stick his fingers up into the air, counting. When he reached three, they pushed, the rubber soles of Will's hiking boots sliding away on the painted wooden boards of the porch floor. The front surface of the door began to splinter, flakes of paint fluttering down.

The door started to open. An inch that with great effort became two.

"Push," Will said.

But whatever was on the other side now pushed back even harder. The door jerked back to its original position, causing Thomas to let out a scream of pain.

Will surveyed the wraparound porch, trying to figure out what to do. "Hang on, Thomas," he said. "I'm gonna get you out of there."

Will ran along the porch to the side of the house, until he came to a window.

Will looked through it. It was dark inside the house. He could just make out the silhouette of a male figure, pressed against the inside of the front door. Will couldn't see any evidence that the man was armed, but in truth he couldn't be sure.

Will wanted to break out the glass and charge through the window, getting the drop on the man. But the window was divided into individual panes by a grid of thick wooden muntins. Will pushed against them with the palm of his hand, but they were sturdy.

"*Will?*" Thomas called from the other side of the porch. "Where are you?"

"I'm here. Hold on."

Will looked around the yard, his eyes coming to rest on a stone birdbath. He figured it had enough mass to crash through the window.

He took hold of the edges of the saucer, grunting with the effort of trying to lift it, but it was too heavy. He thought about whether he should try to drag it through the dirt.

"*Will?*" Thomas's voice was shrill, as if he'd been castrated. "Something's *happening*, Will."

"Hold on." Will looked around the yard for something else he might use.

"Will, my hand—it's BURNING."

Fuck it.

Will bent down and pulled the tops of his socks up over the cuffs of his jeans. He buttoned his shirt collar against his neck. Then he jacked a round into the chamber of the pistol, slid it back inside his holster cocked and locked, and snapped the thumb break on.

He started about ten yards back from the lip of the porch. He ran toward it and launched himself into the air like a hurdler.

He brought his arms up, wrapping them around his face to form a protective veil in the long moment before the window exploded around him in a fury of splintered wood and jagged shards of glass.

He came down off balance, stumbling forward before he could bring himself to a stop.

The man at the door swiveled his bald head toward him, a look of surprise on his face.

Will reached down to draw the pistol, but it wouldn't come free of the holster. He tugged harder, then remembered that he had left the thumb break snapped, afraid that the gun would come loose when he crashed through the glass.

His index finger found the snap. He popped it loose and drew the gun, thumbing off the safety as he came into a Weaver stance.

"FREEZE."

The man continued to push against the door, Thomas's arm protruding from it. Will now saw that the bald man was holding something in his right hand. Shiny and metallic.

"DROP IT."

The phosphorescent dot of the gun's front sight trembled, centered on the man's chest.

Don't make me have to shoot you. Will watched the man, waiting for him to comply. *Please don't make me have to shoot you.*

Will took some of the slack out of the trigger.

"DROP IT," he repeated.

Will watched as the man's hand came open and something heavy clattered down onto the floor.

* * *

The inside of Henry Bell's house was a cross between a labyrinth and a pigsty.

There was barely room to move between the various piles: mountains of soiled underwear and other clothing; dirty dishware covered with velveteen layers of mold; precarious cairns of pornographic magazines.

Will had retrieved the first aid kit from the truck and was applying burn cream to a pattern of angry weals on the back of Thomas's hand. The man had been using a lighter on Thomas, the heavy brass Zippo what he'd dropped to the ground.

Will had already examined Thomas's arm and wrist. He didn't think anything was broken, but the boy would need X-rays to be sure.

Will struggled to make his voice sound steady. "You okay, T?"

Thomas nodded. "Dude's a lot stronger than he looks."

Will looked at the man, lying facedown now on the living room floor, his wrists and ankles chained together. He suspected that the man's strength was not all natural.

They began to search the room. The plastic case of the television set had been removed, pieces of electronic guts spread out across the dust-covered top of a cabinet.

"This dude an inventor or something?" Thomas asked.

Will shook his head. "It's something tweakers do. They take things apart, like a compulsion. Then have no clue how to put them back together."

Framed photographs hung on the wall. Various pictures of Henry Bell posing with a woman and a small blond girl who seemed to like dressing in pink.

Thomas pointed at Will. "You're bleeding."

Will touched his face. His hand came away wet with blood. He ran his fingers through his hair and found a long but shallow cut on the crown of his head. He didn't think it was anything serious; scalp wounds were notorious for bleeding.

The downstairs bedroom was painted pink, the twin bed made up with a Winnie-the-Pooh comforter. A wooden shelf over the head-board held a carefully arranged menagerie of plush animals, the room a small oasis of order amid the slovenliness of the house.

As they worked, Will periodically checked on the man. He was aware of several civil suits that had been brought against police depart-ments after agitated suspects had asphyxiated while being restrained in a prone position.

In the kitchen, a syringe stood soaking inside a jelly glass of water. The syringe was a disposable, although judging by the flecks of dried blood along the shaft of the needle, it wasn't being used as one.

Will found Henry Bell's stash buried at the bottom of a box of Frosted Flakes, five small heat-sealed cellophane envelopes.

He held one of them up to the light filtering through the dirty kitchen window, saw crystals that were like pieces of rock salt glow-ing with a bluish inner light.

SIXTEEN

The department's interview room was small and square, the painted gray walls blank except for a two-way mirror. Henry Bell sat facing Will across a small table, his ankles shackled to a bolt drilled into the floor, hands cuffed behind his back.

"Henry?" Will said in a comforting voice, just two friends shooting the shit. "You sure you don't want to say where the dope came from?"

"How many times do I have to tell you? I can't remember."

They had been at it for over an hour now, Will getting nothing from the interrogation except a tension headache. He decided to change it up a little.

"I saw pictures of a little girl back at your house, and a woman," he said. "That your family?"

Henry nodded. His face had probably been handsome at one time, but now had a haunted look, his mouth framed by an unkept goatee, the leathery skin patterned with scabs.

"Where are they, Henry?"

"Gone. Moved in with her folks."

"Because of the meth?"

Henry nodded again.

When he was with the LAPD, Will had received training in the Reid Technique. It was mostly designed to obtain a confession of guilt, which wasn't an issue here. But he'd found some of the methods useful in eliciting information.

He now framed what was known as an alternative question. Rather than asking an open-ended question that Henry Bell could simply evade or deny, he offered two choices, both of them incriminating, but one meant to seem less so.

"Did you cook the meth yourself, or did you just buy it from someone?"

"Just bought it."

"That's good, Henry. I didn't think you were the type to get messed up with manufacturing. So tell me, who'd you get it from?"

"I want a lawyer."

This was a new development. Usually, if they're smart enough to ask for an attorney, they say it at the beginning.

Will nodded. "Like the other officer told you when he read you the Miranda, you're legally entitled to that. Do you have one to call?"

"What about the public defender?"

Will could see that he was heading for a dead end. Once Henry got lawyered up, there'd be no more interviews. *Time for Plan B.*

"I can call for you," he said. "But, Henry?"

Henry Bell looked at him. The air-conditioning was cranking full blast, but rivulets of sweat coursed down his angular face.

"Before we get someone else involved," Will said, "I'd like to offer you a chance."

"What chance?"

"I need to explain something to you. If that ice is as pure as I think it is, it gets special treatment under the sentencing guidelines. Were you aware of that?"

"What do you mean?"

"If it's more than eighty percent pure, the actual amount gets multiplied by ten. So your five grams gets treated like it's fifty. That's a mandatory five-year jolt in state prison."

"You said 'chance.'" Henry frowned. "How's that a *chance?*"

"If you cooperate with us, help with our investigation, I could get you into a diversion program. You'd go to a treatment center and get cleaned up—"

"I'm no *rat*."

Will leaned forward in the chair. This part was always a little delicate. "Who said anything about being a rat, Henry? All I said was you could go away, spend your days making license plates in Folsom and let your daughter grow up without a father."

Henry Bell looked at him now, paying attention.

"Or you could get a second chance. Be a good father, a good husband again. And, also, help us get this meth off the street before it ruins anybody else's life. Under the circumstances, I don't see how anyone could see you doing that as being a rat."

He was afraid he might have laid it on a little too thick. But then he watched Henry uncross his arms, always a good indicator.

Will slid his chair closer to Henry Bell. Up close, the stench of the man's body odor was overpowering. "Henry, you told me that you bought the meth, right? So tell me something. Is it being made by somebody here in town, or is it coming from outside?"

"I'm not an idiot," Henry said. "I ain't saying squat, till I see something in writing."

"That's not a problem," Will said. It wasn't exactly a lie, but it made it sound a lot easier than it was. "But before I can do that, I need you to give me something, Henry. To see if you've got something that can actually help us."

"It's made here."

"In Haydenville?"

Henry nodded. "In the woods."

"Where?"

"I don't know. I heard there's some big lab out in the national forest."

"How big?"

"I don't know."

"What would you guess?"

Henry grinned, dark holes where he was missing teeth, reddened gums receded down to black roots. "What I heard, it can crank out seventy-pound batches."

Seventy? Will did the math in his head, figured it was enough to keep tens of thousands of serious addicts tweaking for a week. "C'mon, Henry. You must have some idea where it is, right?"

Henry shook his head. "No, he's real secretive about it. Always talking about how no one will ever be able to find it in a million years."

"Henry, you just said 'he.' Who're we talking about here?"

"I don't know his name."

Henry's eyes slid to the left when he said it. Will recognized the tell. After spending all those years undercover, forced to lie to survive, he had become exquisitely sensitive to the act in others.

"I've been straight with you, haven't I?" Will said. "Just tell me his name, that's all I'm asking."

Will watched the expression in Henry Bell's eyes change, deception now replaced by fear.

"You don't know this guy," Henry said. "You have any idea what he'd do to me?"

"*Who?*"

"If I give you his name, I need to go in the Witness Protection Program."

Will shook his head. "You've been watching too much TV, Henry. You won't have to worry. Give us his name, he'll go away for a long time."

Henry crossed his arms again. Hugging himself now, frightened. "Prison won't stop him from getting to me."

Will took a plastic evidence bag off the table and started to take something out of it. "I want you to look at something, Henry."

Henry looked at the framed photograph, his eyes filling with tears as he studied a younger version of himself standing on a sun-filled beach with his wife and daughter.

"What would they want you to do, Henry?"

Henry continued to stare at the photograph as if trying to climb inside it, tears running down his ruined face. "All right," he said. "But I want something in writing first."

SEVENTEEN

Using the photocopied list he kept beneath his desk blotter, he found the home telephone number for the Klamath County district attorney.

His name was Stuart Isgro, and when he came on the line Will laid out the details of the situation for him. When he got to the part about offering Henry Bell the diversion program, Isgro interrupted him.

"You don't have the authority to make deals."

"I know, that's why I'm calling you." Over the phone line, Will could hear a television playing in the background.

"Do you realize it's nine thirty on a Friday night?"

Will took a sip from his mug of black coffee. "I'm not asking you for a detailed plea agreement," he said. "I just need a memo I can show him, something over your signature."

"I'm at *home*," Isgro said. "With my family."

Will stared at his reflection in the blackened rectangle of his office window. "Bell says this lab can make seventy pounds of pure crystal in a single batch. The DEA classifies any place that can make more than ten pounds of meth in a single run as a superlab. We need to shut it down now, before any more of this shit gets out there."

"I hear you," Isgro said. "I'll give it some thought and get back in touch."

Will fought to keep the anger out of his voice. "You don't under-stand. I need to do this right *now*. Before he has a chance to change his mind."

"Let me ask you something," Isgro said. "How do you know this guy isn't just yanking your chain?"

"I got a solid baseline on him at the beginning of the interview. I can tell when he's lying."

Isgro's laugh was loud through the receiver. "That's quite a talent. Remind me to take you along next time I go car shopping."

A gust of hot air came through the open window, carrying with it the smell of smoke from a distant forest fire.

"I'll draft the memo for you," Will said.

"You an attorney now, too?"

Will took a breath, the sound of buzzing loud in his damaged ear. "I'm just trying to make it easier for you."

"You're missing the point," Isgro said. "I'm not inclined to just let this guy walk."

"It really shouldn't be that big a deal to you."

"Why do you say that?"

"Because you already did, the last time he was arrested. Only that time you didn't get anything in exchange."

Through the phone, Will could hear the sound of the other man's breathing.

"Fax it to my house," Isgro said. "If I like what I see, I'll sign it."

By the time Will walked back into the interview room, it was almost midnight.

He was holding the signed fax from Stuart Isgro, along with a can of Dr Pepper that he'd just purchased from the vending machine for

Henry Bell. He made sure that the door to the room was locked behind him before he turned to face the prisoner.

Will's first thought was that Bell had somehow managed to get out of the chair.

Then he realized that the chair wasn't there, either.

He scanned the room and spotted the legs of the chair sticking out from under the table. As he came around the tabletop, he saw that the chair was tipped over.

Will dropped the can of Dr Pepper. It fell to the floor and broke open in a geyser, soaking the legs of his jeans. He crouched and looked beneath the table. Henry Bell lay facedown on the floor, the chair on top of him.

Trap.

Will reached for his gun before remembering that he had no weapon with him, following SOP by leaving it outside the room.

Using the toe of his boot, Will nudged Bell's arm.

No response.

Will bent down to check the cuffs, saw that they were still locked. He pulled the chair away, tossing it aside. Will grabbed Henry Bell's shoulder and rolled him over. A stream of blood flowed from his mouth and pooled on the gray vinyl floor.

The door banged open and Thomas rushed into the room. "I saw you through the glass," he said. "What's wrong?"

Will opened Henry Bell's mouth and peered down inside it. The few teeth he still had left looked like tiny islands floating in a sea of blood.

"He chewed off his tongue," Will said. "I think he swallowed it."

Will pulled Bell up into a sitting position and wrapped his arms around the other man's chest, clasping them into a ball just below his sternum. He counted silently to three before jerking his clasped hands inward. A soft gust of air came from Bell's mouth, but nothing else.

Will tried again, jerking harder this time, and a slender object was expelled from Henry Bell's mouth in a spray of blood. The piece of tongue skated across the floor, coming to rest against the painted wood of the baseboard.

Will opened Bell's mouth and saw that his airway was now clear. He put his good ear close to Bell's nose and mouth, but couldn't hear any sign of breathing.

Will looked up at Thomas. "Get me the CPR shield."

"The what?"

Will gestured with his hands. "You know, the *thing*. So I don't have to swap fluids with him."

Thomas nodded, then turned and ran from the room.

Will unlocked the cuffs and laid Henry Bell on his back, tipping back his head to open the airway, preparing him to receive CPR. He placed his hand against Bell's neck, checking for a carotid pulse, but felt nothing. Not much time left to try to save him.

Will felt something on his leg. When he looked down he saw that the puddle of Dr Pepper had spread across the floor and was soaking through the leg of his jeans. The stickiness of it made him feel uncomfortable.

For as far back as he could remember, even when he was a kid, he'd always hated feeling unclean. Laurie had teased him about his constant hand washing, calling him "Lady Macbeth."

What the fuck was taking Thomas so long?

Will picked up one of Henry Bell's hands and squeezed it. "Hang in there, Henry," he said. "Don't you die on me."

Thomas appeared in the doorway, out of breath. "I couldn't find it," he said.

Will looked down at Henry Bell's scab-covered face, the leathery skin beginning to turn blue from cyanosis.

Will started to rise up from the floor. Then, quickly, before giving himself another chance to think about it, he reached out and pinched Henry Bell's nostrils shut and clamped his lips down on top of the other man's.

He felt Bell's unhealthy teeth shift from the pressure, the prickling hairs of his goatee moving against his lips. The taste of Bell's blood was metallic, like an old penny.

Will blew into the other man's mouth, shifting his eyes to watch the chest rise. He gave him a second rescue breath, then placed two fingers against Bell's carotid artery and felt for a pulse.

When he was certain there was no heartbeat, he placed the heel of his left hand on Henry Bell's sternum and laid his right hand on top of it. He locked his elbows and pushed down hard thirty times before giving him two more of the rescue breaths.

Will lost himself to the rhythm of it, counting silently to himself as he thrust downward against the chest, then inhaling the room's chilled air before blowing it into Henry Bell's mouth.

He remembered bending over Sean's crib that last morning, already dressed for work, the sky outside the windows not yet light. Reaching down to run his fingers through the boy's blond hair, inhaling the smell of his grape-scented shampoo. His son's blue eyes coming open, looking up at him with something that he would think of forever as expectation.

(i wasn't there——)

Will pushed the thought out of his mind and blew into Henry Bell's mouth, then sat up to begin another cycle of chest compressions.

"Will—"

Thomas was saying something to him.

"*Will—*"

He looked up at Thomas, still standing there in the doorway.

"Will, I don't think it's working."

He looked down at Henry Bell's face, as gray and lifeless as the floor tiles beneath it. Will glanced at his watch, surprised to find that more than five minutes had somehow gone by.

He heard his knees crack as he sat back on his heels. He spat, his saliva pink as it splashed against the floor. His stomach turned over, and he was afraid that he might be sick.

Thomas came fully inside the room, standing over Will, gazing down at Henry Bell's inert form. The air-conditioning kicked on, the rushing sound of air moving through the ductwork.

"Why would he . . ." Thomas stared at Henry Bell's dismembered tongue lying on the floor. It looked as if it had been sawed off with a steak knife. "What would make him do that?"

"You mean *who*."

Thomas looked at Will, not understanding.

Will spoke quietly, as though he were talking to himself. "Who the hell could he be that afraid of?"

EIGHTEEN

The forest, along with the mountains and rivers, spread out along the wall.

Will stood in front of the topographic maps, United States Geological Survey, 7.5 Minute Quadrangle Series, lined up edge to edge.

He had spent a good part of the morning tacking them up along the entire length of the department's conference room wall, from the floor all the way up to the crown molding of the high ceiling.

He'd intended to put up the entirety of the national forest but had run out of room. More of the maps still lay on the carpet.

Thomas sat at the long oak table. Next to him was the forest ranger from the morning at the river. The two of them were eating triangles of pizza from an open cardboard box that had just been delivered.

Will looked down at the notes he had typed up on his computer.

He'd never led a meeting before and was feeling pressure to have it go well. It was important to gain the full cooperation of the Forest Service for the work that lay ahead.

"Gentlemen," he began, hearing how foolish he sounded as soon as his words hit the air.

At least he wasn't slurring. He'd taken three of the Vicodins earlier, chased down by his morning coffee.

The pills were a poor substitute for the real thing; there was no rush, none of the flooding warmth. But he found that if he took enough of them, he could experience some of the old familiar sensations: the cotton mouth; the sense of feeling at ease within his body; a lightening of the weight of thought and memory.

Will motioned toward the map and pressed on. "From what we've learned to date, we believe that hidden somewhere out there in the national forest or surrounding wilderness area, there's a clan lab."

The ranger smiled at him. "You talking about guys with pillowcases on their heads?"

Thomas laughed, and the ranger turned to him and grinned.

The ranger's name was Mike Lopez. He'd finished eating the pizza and now had a slender unlit cigar with a white plastic tip perched between his lips.

"Clan, as in *clandestine*," Will said. "Meth isn't that hard to make. You can find recipes for it on the Internet. Most of it's cooked in small labs. Low-quality stuff made from Drano and camera batteries."

He felt a drop of sweat course down along his side. The air-conditioning had broken down, and the awning windows were tipped open as far as they would go. But the room felt airless, thick with the smell from the pizza.

"From the quality of the meth we've tested, and from what we've heard from our sources, the lab we're looking for is what's called a superlab—"

The ranger started humming something out loud. He held his arms straight out in front of him, pantomiming that he was flying. Thomas laughed again.

Will looked at them for a moment before realizing that the ranger was doing the theme song from *Superman*.

I'm losing them. He was unsure of what, exactly, he should do about it, afraid that if he came down like a hard-ass he would end up pissing Lopez off.

"A superlab like this one, we're dealing with suspects who are highly organized. From the lab reports, we know that this lab is using the Nazi method, which means they need access to a supply of anhydrous ammonia."

He had gotten a call from Nolan earlier in the week. The DEA agent had told him that the lab had matched the crystal from Henry Bell's house with the sample from the Dig Inn. Will had assured Nolan that they were "hot on the trail" but was careful to omit any mention of Bell's suicide.

"Thomas here has been contacting farm product dealers," Will said. "One over in Fortuna thinks they're missing one hundred and fifty gallons of anhydrous ammonia, which is a lot. There was no evidence of theft, so the manager thought it was just a leak in their tank."

The ranger struck a wooden match and brought the flaming tip to his cigar.

"Please don't do that," Will said. "There's no smoking in here."

The ranger dipped the smoldering end of the cigar down into his soda can, where it made a hissing sound.

"Anhydrous ammonia is *extremely* dangerous," Will said. "We had an officer in L.A. who stuck his head over an open container of it, not knowing what it was. It literally melted his face."

"And my wife tells me *I'm* ugly," the ranger said.

Thomas laughed again, and Will turned to glare at him. "He's had six plastic surgeries so far. His kids still won't go out with him in public."

When Thomas looked down at the table, Will continued. "Anhydrous ammonia is a gas at room temperature, so you need something to contain it. Most of the time, the bad guys'll use the propane tank from a barbecue grill. You can tell if you come across one of them, because the ani corrodes the nozzle, so that it turns blue."

Will took a step closer to the maps. They were mostly solid green to indicate the forest land. But there were also patches of white that represented areas of elevation above the treeline, and veinlike blue lines that were the creeks and rivers tumbling down from the alpine peaks. Symbols of crossed pickaxes marked the locations of old mine sites.

Will tapped the back of his hand against the dry paper. "So, somewhere out here, there's a superlab. The question is, how do we search for it?"

Thomas and the ranger sat at the table. The pizza was gone, nothing left but a shadow of grease on the bottom of the box.

The ranger pointed his finger at the maps. "You're talking about one of the largest roadless wilderness areas in the entire country."

"So what do you do when someone goes missing out there?"

"We try and use the information we have about them to narrow down the search area."

"But what if you *couldn't*?" Will said. "What if you only knew that they were somewhere in the national forest?"

"Honestly?" The ranger locked his eyes on Will's. "I'd light a candle for them."

"What about using a helicopter?"

The ranger shook his head. "Forest canopy is too thick. You can't see squat."

"What about a chopper equipped with FLIR?" Will asked.

"To be real straight with you," the ranger said, "I don't know what that is."

"Forward-looking infrared. It shows areas of heat on the ground."

"Sounds great," the ranger said. "Too bad we don't happen to have one of those lying around."

Will looked out the open window, crows lined up along the high tension wires. "Then we need to set up surveillance," he said. "Look out for any suspicious vehicles driving in or out of the national forest. The lab needs to somehow get supplies in, move the finished product out."

Will felt his energy begin to pick up as he laid out the plan taking shape in his mind. "Also, we need to post flyers at every trailhead, telling hikers what to be looking out for, tell them to report anything suspicious immediately."

Lopez pushed his chair back from the table and shook his head. "No can do. All the cutbacks, we're down to just three full-time."

Will slumped back against the maps, not knowing what else to say. At least he'd given it a shot.

Thomas took a sip from his can of grape soda and then swiveled his chair around to face Lopez. "Hey, Mike?" he said. "This man knows what he's talking about here. We need your help. So will you just knock it off?"

The ranger sat in a rectangle of yellow sunlight, chewing on the plastic tip of his unlit cigar. He picked his hat up from the table, gazing down into the empty crown for a long moment.

Then he looked up at Will.

"I apologize for being such an asshole," he said. "Now tell me again, what it is you need."

NINETEEN

The ringing of the telephone woke him.

Will tried to answer it, but found it difficult to move, the sweaty bedsheets wrapped around his limbs like a straitjacket. He finally managed to wrestle the cordless off the nightstand and punched the TALK button.

"Hello?"

"I wake you up?" It was Thomas.

Will looked at the alarm clock, red digital numbers announcing that it was 6:04, the sunlight already fierce through the drawn window shades.

"What's up?"

"Remember when you asked me about the dogs?" Thomas said.

"Dogs?" He was calling at this hour to talk about *dogs*?

"You know, the ones that went missing?"

"The posters," Will said, remembering.

"I think there's something you better come see."

* * *

They walked along a narrow trail through the forest, Thomas in the lead, Will following a few strides behind. Even in the deep shade of the woods it was warm. A stain of sweat the shape of Texas spread across the back of Thomas's khaki uniform shirt.

The forest was mostly evergreen here, Pacific madrone and Douglas fir, the primeval green of the trees punctuated by flowering red bursts of columbine.

"Lopez called me," Thomas said. "From the Forest Service? He said a backpacker came into the station and reported it."

"Where?"

"About a mile in. Maybe a little more."

The trail now ran above the north fork of the river, the water liquid jade as it coursed around an obstacle course of boulders. Overhead, an osprey circled a nest made from hundreds of twigs, the bird's wingtips flared like fingers against the sky.

"I can't stop thinking about that dude," Thomas said.

"Which dude are we talking about here, T?"

"You know. Henry Bell. I keep seeing him, in my head."

Will didn't answer, concentrating on the trail, the ground under his boots cushioned by a carpet of fallen pine needles.

"You think we'll ever stop them?" Thomas asked.

Will had no clue who the boy was talking about. "You seem to have woken up on the cryptic side of the bed this morning."

"What do you mean?"

"Which *them* are you referring to?"

"The tweakers. You think if we bust enough of them, they'll stop using it?"

The trail had become narrower here, encroached upon by dry branches that were white as bone. Thomas pushed aside the foliage as he advanced, the branches whipping backward toward Will when he released them.

"Vollmer wrote that drug addiction isn't a police problem," Will said. "He thought it was a medical problem, and that it would never be solved by the police."

"Who's *Vollmer*?"

Will shook his head. "Didn't you learn anything at the police academy?"

Thomas shrugged his shoulders. "Never went."

"Then how'd you get hired?"

"Mr. Douglas, the last chief? I grew up next door."

Will ran his hand through his hair. "Jesus."

Thomas kept walking in front of him. "He always told me that the job was the best training."

Thomas pointed. "It should be down there."

The trail descended into a small oval-shaped clearing. Absent any trees, it baked in the full heat of the morning sun.

There were a couple of empty Budweiser cans littering the ground, crushed flat. In the center of the clearing someone had hammered an aluminum tent stake into the hard dirt.

One end of a leather leash was wrapped around it.

Attached to the other end was a dog, lying prone on its side. Will could see that it was a good-sized German shepherd, or at least what was left of one. Its head was mostly gone now. Scattered around it on the baked earth were several sharp and yellowed teeth.

"Shotgun?" Thomas asked.

Will knelt down to take a closer look, then shook his head. "There aren't any pellets."

Whatever it was, it had pulverized the dog's head, singeing the fur around its mouth. The dog's muzzle had been blown apart from the rest of the skull. A metal choke collar wrapped around the dog's neck, an identification tag hanging from it. Will turned it over and read the name engraved into the tarnished brass.

OTIS.

Will took a disposable pen from his shirt pocket and began to probe at the remains. He could see small pieces of shiny gray plastic attached to bits of fur. From the texture of the plastic he could tell that it was duct tape.

There was also something else, a ragged remnant of something that was red in color. It was easy to miss, blending in with the carnage. He poked at it with the tip of the pen. It was saturated with blood, but it didn't take him long to guess what it was.

"Look at this," he said to Thomas.

Thomas knelt beside him. "Paper," he said.

Will shook his head. "It looks like a piece of wrapper from an M-80," he said. "Somebody put it into his mouth and then duct-taped the muzzle shut."

Will rose to his feet and took a folded plastic evidence bag from the back pocket of his jeans. He collected pieces of the duct tape to send off to the FBI crime lab in Quantico. He thought it would be worth having the fragments analyzed and checked against their tape files, figuring that if he knew the brand of tape it might turn into some kind of lead.

He unbuttoned his short-sleeved shirt and stripped it off his back. The label was from a men's store on Melrose, the shirt an anniversary gift from Laurie.

He spread it out on the ground and swaddled the dog in it. It was difficult, because the shirt was too small for the task. He did the best he could, then hoisted the dog up on his shoulder in a fireman's carry, legs and fur sticking out from the fabric.

"What're you doing?" Thomas asked.

"Taking him with us."

"What for?"

"It's somebody's dog, Thomas." Will said. "I'm not just gonna leave him out here."

Thomas gestured with his hand toward the trail that climbed up out of the clearing. "It's a long way to be carrying a dog."

Will scanned the dirt floor of the clearing, trying to be sure that he wasn't forgetting anything important. Then he began to walk along the trail in the rising heat, holding on to the shirt-wrapped dog.

"Wait a sec," Thomas called out from behind him.

Will turned around and saw the boy scrambling to catch up, his open arms held out in front of him.

"Let me take him," he said.

TWENTY

The road leading to Frank Carver's house wound its way through the forest, covered by a thin layer of gravel and treacherous with deep ruts carved by the runoff from winter storms.

Will steered the department SUV through a hairpin turn. Even in the middle of the summer afternoon, the dense foliage seemed to suck the light from the air, throwing everything into shadowed relief.

The house came into view, like a ship that had somehow run aground deep in the forest. An enormous A-frame, it featured vast sheets of glass framed by strips of weathered cedar, the steeply peaked roof piled high with mounds of brown pine needles.

A short distance behind the house was some kind of tower that rose high above the earth on wooden stilts. At the top sat a small building, its windows reflecting the sun.

Will parked the truck and got out. Two men were playing a game of catch in the sun-starved dirt yard.

"I'm looking for Frank Carver," Will called to them.

They ignored him, the baseball speeding through the air in a flat trajectory before slapping into a leather glove.

They were both in their early twenties, powerfully built, with thin, dark beards trimmed like chin straps.

"*Excuse me,*" Will called, louder. "Is Frank Carver here?"

The men both turned toward him, and he could see now that they were identical twins.

"Inside," one of them said, before throwing the ball across the distance to his brother.

Frank Carver wore a faded yellow T-shirt with green letters that spelled out HAPPY FILLMORE NEW YEAR. The sleeves had been cut off, exposing tattoo-covered arms that seemed too muscular for someone his age. A longneck bottle of Budweiser dangled from the crook of two fingers.

"I'd like to ask you a few questions," Will said.

Frank turned his back without answering, Will taking it as an invitation to follow him into the house. The living room had a soaring cathedral ceiling of dark redwood planks and smelled of marijuana smoke and Ozium.

The side walls were taken up from floor to ceiling with built-in bookcases. The shelves sagged under the weight of books that seemed to be arranged without discernible method, a multiple-volume edition of *The Divine Comedy* shelved between a copy of *Steppenwolf* and a gilt-decorated *Une Saison en Enfer*.

"You've read all these?" Will asked.

The lenses of Frank's black horn-rimmed glasses seemed to magnify his eyes. "I collect rare books."

A wooden lectern held an opened volume, its pages covered with flowing calligraphic type and vibrant watercolor illustrations.

Frank watched as Will examined it. "That's William Morris's illuminated manuscript of Virgil's *Aeneid*."

Will looked down at an image of the sacking of Troy, the city engulfed in ocher flame. "It's beautiful."

"It's printed on vellum," Frank said. "Know what that is?"

"Paper?" Will said, not really getting the question.

"Paper made from *skin*." Frank's voice was a baritone rumble. "Ever read it?"

"The *Aeneid*?" Will said. "Who could forget the River Lethe?"

Frank opened his mouth, then stopped himself and smiled at Will, his yellowed incisors showing behind the coarse hairs of his white beard. "Good one," he said. "You're not just another dumb cop."

The River of Forget. Will could still recall the imagery, even though it had been decades since he had read it. The souls of the dead hovering over the waters of the Lethe like a swarm of bees, the river wiping clean their memories of earthly pain.

A barefoot young girl, not much older than twenty, entered the room and stood beside Frank. She wore a bikini swimsuit that was the color of flesh. A tattoo of a large marijuana leaf sprouted up from the suit's panties, reaching out across her tanned belly. She reached up and began to massage Frank's neck.

Will forced himself to look away, across the length of the house, out the rear windows. "What's that tower out there?"

"It's an old Forest Service fire lookout," Frank said. "I turned it into an office. Where I write."

"I would think the view would be a distraction."

Frank reached up and grabbed the girl's hand, pulling it away from his neck. "Why don't you leave us alone?" he said to her. "Go in the bedroom and smoke a joint."

Will looked at Frank. "You forgetting who I am?"

"It's medicinal. She's got a bad disk."

Frank watched the girl pad from the room, then pointed his bearded chin at a matched pair of avocado-colored couches. "Grab a seat."

Will sat facing him across a glass-topped coffee table that had wooden legs shaped like boomerangs. "I understand you used to be with the Hell's Angels."

Frank's head swiveled around on his neck. "I heard you used to be a narc."

Will was surprised that he'd found out. "Where'd you hear that?"

"Small town, it pays to know people." Frank's gaze was piercing, his eyelids never seeming to blink. "That's quite a career choice."

"How do you mean?"

"Spending your whole life lying to people."

"I never thought about it quite that way."

Behind the lenses of his glasses, the rims of Frank's eyes were as pink as those of a rabbit. "Wanna know who sold me my first bag of pot?" he asked.

"Not especially."

"Neal Cassady. And he ended up in *On the Road.*"

"Thanks for the tip," Will said. "But I'm pretty sure the statute of limitations has already run out."

Frank scratched at the copse of white beard piled on his chest. "You come all the way out here just for the fun of it?"

"Tell me about the Angels," Will said. "What chapter were you with?"

"Oakland." Frank smiled. "Why, you interested in signing up?"

"You guys cooked a lot of meth, right?"

"What do you mean?"

"Back then, the Angels controlled the manufacture and trafficking of methamphetamine. You guys had the recipe for it, kept it a closely guarded secret."

"Why're you asking me this?"

"As you're probably aware, this town has a serious meth problem."

Frank slammed the beer bottle down on the coffee table. "What the *fuck?*" Foam billowed up from inside the bottle and streamed down the dark glass of the neck. "You come here, into my house, and *what?* Accuse me of dealing speed?"

"No one's accusing you of anything."

"You sure could have fooled me. You're talking about something from forty fucking years ago."

"So let's talk about now," Will said. "What can you tell me about meth *now*?"

"You have any clue who you're talking to? I'm a famous author. Why don't you go and shake down Garrison Keillor?"

"I don't mean any disrespect," Will said. "But when was the last time you actually wrote anything?"

Frank Carver rose to his feet. Above the white tumble of facial hair, his face was dark with blood. It was not difficult now to imagine him as a younger man, wearing a jacket decorated with an image of a winged skull. "I think it's time for you to get the hell off my land."

Will sat there for a long moment, then got up from the couch and started toward the front door. He didn't see that he had any other choice, since he didn't have any legal justification to be there without an invitation.

TWENTY-ONE

When Will arrived back at the station, a green Forest Service truck was parked at the curb in front of City Hall.

Mike Lopez leaned against the bricks beside the doorway, his campaign hat pulled low on his brow to block the intense sunlight. "Sorry for being such a jackass, the other day," he said.

Will removed his sunglasses so the other man would be able to see his eyes. "Don't worry about it."

"We got the flyers up at the trailheads, like you wanted."

"I appreciate it," Will said. "Hopefully someone'll notice something."

"Reason I came by, we had a llama packer come into the station this morning—"

"Excuse my ignorance, but what's a llama packer?"

"They're outfitters, take groups out into the wilderness. They use llamas—you know, the animals—to carry the gear and supplies out into the woods. So folks don't have to hump everything in backpacks."

Will nodded. "You really do learn something new every day."

"This guy, he said they were taking a group of Boy Scouts out to Moriah Lake. You know where that is?"

Will shook his head.

"It's out the Sawtooth Trail, past an old abandoned mine site. He said one of the Scouts saw something lying there by the side of the trail. They thought it was pretty strange, finding it out there, so they brought it in."

"What was it?"

"That's what I wanted to show you."

Lopez moved around to the rear hatch of the green SUV and lifted up the tailgate. He leaned inside and slid out a long object, then handed it over to Will.

"It did seem like a weird thing to be out there in the middle of the woods," Lopez said. "And then I remembered that dead kayaker."

Will inspected the paddle. It was made of fiberglass, a long black shaft with wide yellow blades at each end. A decal was attached to one of the blades, the logo of a kayak manufacturer. On the other blade, Will saw that someone had scratched something into the surface of the fiberglass, what looked like some kind of symbol.

Will pondered it for a moment, wondering what it was. Then he rotated the paddle end over end, so that the symbol was now inverted.

He realized that he was looking at a pair of letters, and that they were initials, a way for the owner of the paddle to identify it as something that belonged to her.

TWENTY-TWO

Late the next morning, Will watched as an airplane painted a contrail against the flawless and blue dome of June sky.

The department SUV was parked just off the shoulder of the main road, across from where it intersected with a Forest Service road. All of the truck's windows were rolled down, but its interior was an oven. Will leaned forward in his seat, peeling his saturated shirt from the surface of the vinyl seat back.

He'd been sitting out here for almost four hours but had nothing to show for it. His handheld began to crackle from where it lay on the dashboard. He picked it up, recognizing Thomas's voice through the static.

"Will?" he said. "The mayor was just in here looking for you."

"You tell her I was busy?"

"I did, but she still said she wanted you to come to her office."

Will glanced at his watch. "I was about ready to hang it up anyway."

"Hey, Will?"

"Yeah?"

"Heads up," Thomas said. "She seemed pretty pissed."

*   *   *

The mayor's job was an honorary one, paying no salary. One of the few perquisites of the position was a corner office on the fourth floor of City Hall that possessed a commanding view of the square and surrounding buildings.

Bonnie Newman wore a shapeless cotton dress patterned with small blue cornflowers. A rock paperweight sat on her desktop, letters carved into it that read NOTHING IS ETCHED IN STONE.

She waited for Will to sit down before speaking. "I was just wondering," she said, "how you think things are going."

"So far, so good," he said. "There's a bunch of stuff I want to update you about."

"Really?" She picked up a gold-plated letter opener and used it to slit open an envelope. "Because I've been hearing some rather disturbing things."

"I don't understand," Will said. "Like what?"

"For one, an eyewitness has come forward, alleging that the man you shot at the Dig Inn was unarmed, that the shooting was improper."

"Improper?" Will's face grew warm. "I don't know who'd say that. The guy was totally out of control. He charged us with a metal stanchion."

She looked at him over the top of her glasses. "But he didn't have a gun, or even a knife?"

"No, but that doesn't—"

"Why didn't you just wound him?"

"You mean, like try to shoot him in the arm or leg?" Will shook his head. "That's not procedure. You have any idea how hard that is to do, on a moving target, the risk of hitting a bystander?"

"The witness claims that *you* were the one out of control. That it was a bloodbath, that you fired your gun over and over."

Will forced himself to take a breath. "Who exactly is this *witness*?"

"I'm not at liberty to say. But I can tell you that he's extremely reputable."

"Are we by any chance talking about Frank Carver?"

She looked away from him and picked up another envelope to open. "As I said, I'm not going to tell you that."

"Because that's quite a coincidence," Will said. "Considering I went out to his house the other day and leaned on him."

Her head jerked up. "You did *what?*"

"I questioned him. About our meth problem."

"Why in the world would you do that?"

"Did you know that Frank Carver used to be a Hell's Angel?"

She shook her head. "I know that he's close to a lot of the city council, he supports the Rotary, he's won the Pulitzer Prize—"

"He never won a Pulitzer."

She reached up and rubbed her forehead, as if she had a headache. "You're going to get us both fired if you keep this up."

"Can I ask you something? Why did you even hire me?"

"It wasn't as if we had a wealth of other options."

He wanted to tell her to go to hell, but instead changed the subject. "We found an informant that was prepared to give us the person behind the lab."

Her eyes widened. "What happened?"

"He became so afraid of retaliation that he committed suicide."

"Shouldn't he have been in some sort of protective custody?"

Will glanced out the window and watched a single white cloud float across a blue rectangle of sky, the air shimmering with heat.

The mayor shook her head. "How difficult can this possibly be? It's been a month. You need to show me some results."

Will kept looking out the window, not saying anything.

She crumpled an envelope into a ball and tossed it into the trash can. "This town, I swear it's going to hell in a handbasket. You walk down the street, these junkies practically bump into you. Merchants tell me they're up to their necks in shoplifters—"

"They're not coming to *me*."

One side of her lip curled up in a smile. "Well, that's a problem right there, isn't it?"

He tried to keep his voice even. "Look, I need some help from the people in this town. If they know what's going on, if they suspect something, they need to come forward."

She looked at him. "I wish you could hear how you sound. It's not their job. It's *yours*."

He nodded. "I know it is."

"Then why don't you start doing it?"

TWENTY-THREE

Sunday was Father's Day.

After breakfast, Will went out into the backyard and worked in his garden. The morning air was already filled with heat, the slight breeze carrying the charred smell of a forest fire burning somewhere off to the west. He knelt in the cool grass and carefully moved aside the blue petals of a forget-me-not, using a small hand trowel to place fertilizer into the flower beds.

A burst of static issued from the handheld radio that lay in the grass beside him, and then he heard the faraway sound of Thomas's voice.

Will used the sleeve of his T-shirt to wipe the sweat from his face and then thumbed the TRANSMIT button. "I'm here."

"I just pulled this guy over for not wearing his seat belt," Thomas said.

So why are you telling me this? For a minute, Will wondered if Thomas was seeking some kind of praise.

"I was parked out past the steel bridge," Thomas said. "At the intersection to that forest road. When I spotted him, he was coming out of the woods."

Will felt something wet brush against the back of his hand. He looked down and saw Buddy, a sodden tennis ball clamped in his jaws. Will worked the ball free and threw it across the lawn, bouncing it off the redwood boards of the fence.

"What's your gut?" Will asked.

"To be honest, he seems kind of hinky."

Hinky. It was as if Thomas had somehow become possessed by the Continental Op.

"Did you run his name?" Will asked.

"Not yet. I wanted to call you first."

Will rose to his feet.

"Hold him there," he said. "I'm on my way."

Will drove his personal vehicle, a five-year-old but well-maintained Volvo station wagon.

He spotted the department SUV parked on the side of the road in the shadows cast by a stand of Douglas fir. He pulled in behind the truck, his tires crunching on the gravel shoulder.

As soon as he got out of his car, he could see that Thomas had been right to call him.

When Will had been a rookie patrolman, he'd been assigned to a field training officer, a veteran named Leon "Ski" Szczepanski. Ski had drummed into him the value of observation, the importance of scanning a scene to look for anything that seemed out of place. Will had taken the lessons to heart. He'd come to treat everything in life like a game on a children's television show that he'd once watched with Sean, where you were supposed to guess which thing didn't belong with the others.

The car Thomas had pulled over was a chartreuse green Saab convertible that looked brand-new. The car was coated with a thick layer of red dirt from being driven on the Forest Service road, its rear fender splattered with mud.

The convertible top was down. The man seated behind the wheel was middle-aged and wore a yellow short-sleeved silk shirt. Perched on top of his head was a straw fedora.

Can you guess which thing doesn't belong?

Thomas waved Will over. "I had Lila run him through the computer," he said. "Name's Glen Sexton. He's got a prior for possession with intent to distribute, no wants or warrants."

Will walked up to the convertible. He kept his sunglasses on, even though he really didn't need them here in the shade. "Would you please step out of the vehicle?"

Glen Sexton was tall and lithe. He wore a pair of tight flat-front wool trousers and polished brown leather shoes. "What is this?" he asked. "I need to get back to the city."

"The city," Will knew, meant San Francisco.

"Can I ask you what you were doing back in the forest?" Will asked.

"I like nature."

"I don't mean any disrespect here," Will said. "But you don't seem dressed for it."

"I didn't realize you were the fashion police."

"Unfortunately for you, we're not," Will said. "Because Officer Costello, who's the *real* police, tells me you were driving without a seat belt."

"I was just about to put it on."

Will forced a smile. "That doesn't count."

"I'm sorry, all right? Now could you just give me a ticket, so I can be on my way?"

Will stared through his sunglasses at Glen Sexton. It'd been a long time since Will had last done a traffic stop, and to compensate he now found himself slipping into a kind of hard-ass cracker-sheriff persona.

"You *want* a ticket?" he asked. "Because most people in your situation, they do the exact opposite. They beg us *not* to give them one."

Will glanced over at Thomas and saw that he was smiling.

Glen Sexton blew air out through his pursed lips. "Can we please just get this over with?"

Will took a step closer to Sexton, getting in his personal space. "Glen, we've had reports that there's a methamphetamine lab operating in the forest. Would you happen to know anything about that?"

Sexton shook his head. "Absolutely not."

"No would have been a sufficient answer," Will said. "But you had to add 'absolutely.' Why'd you feel it necessary to do that?"

Sexton looked at Will in amazement. "What is this?" He said to Will. "Now you have a problem with my *grammar*?"

Will waited, making Sexton stand there in the heat before continuing. "Glen, I'd like your consent to search the vehicle."

"No way," Glen Sexton said.

Will had always been surprised at how many people would just agree to a vehicle search. Unfortunately, Glen Sexton didn't seem to be one of them.

"That's your right, Glen. As a United States citizen, that right is guaranteed to you by the Fourth Amendment."

Glen Sexton nodded his head at this, as though he made it a habit to read the Constitution.

Will continued. "But I'd like to tell you a little something about *my* rights, as a sworn law enforcement officer of the great state of California. I have the right to place you under arrest—"

Glen Sexton's mouth opened. "*What?*"

Will held up a hand to silence him. "Once I place you in custody, I'll need to impound your vehicle. For your protection, we'll need to inventory it. Go through every compartment from front to back."

Glen Sexton shook his head, looking down at the ground. "For my protection."

"That's right, Glen. To make sure that when you get it back, there's nothing missing."

"I don't fucking believe this."

Will made a big deal of scratching his chin. "Come to think of it, there is another alternative to consider. One that's a whole lot less bothersome, for both of us."

Sexton looked at him. "What's that?"

"You just consent to a quick search here, then you're on your way back to the city."

"What about the seat belt?"

"You cooperate with us here, I'd be inclined to look the other way."

Glen Sexton glanced over at his car, as if it could help him decide what he should do. "Fuck it."

He stepped aside. "Go ahead."

There were many places to hide drugs inside a motor vehicle, and Will had made it a point to learn most of them. He had once arrested a dealer after finding a kilo of heroin sealed inside a length of PVC pipe that was submerged inside the gas tank.

Will used this as an opportunity to teach Thomas the correct way to search a vehicle. After securing Glen Sexton in the backseat of the department SUV, they started with the car's interior.

After removing all of the Saab's floor mats, they used an angle mirror with a folding handle to look at the underside of the car's seats. They removed the radio and searched inside the dash. Will opened the air bag compartment and showed Thomas how contraband could be hidden inside.

They moved on to the trunk, removing the spare tire from its mount, then tapping on the trunk's walls to check for secret compartments. Will used a screwdriver to take the case off the CD changer, making sure nothing was hidden inside.

They searched the engine compartment, then finished with Thomas sliding underneath the car, following Will's shouted instructions on where to search.

When Thomas emerged from beneath the car, he had a grease stain on his forehead. "What next?"

Will shook his head. "Nothing. If there's dope in this car, I don't know where it is."

He was at a loss. His gut was screaming at him that Glen Sexton was dirty, but it had been proven wrong before.

He could arrest Sexton, impound the vehicle for further search, and drag him back to the station, but he didn't think it would do any good. At that point, Sexton would have the opportunity to call an attorney, potentially threaten a harassment suit. After his last run-in with the mayor, Will didn't think that would be a big plus for his career.

Will walked to the SUV and opened the door to let Glen Sexton out.

"Can I go now, Officer?"

Will looked down at the ground. A swarm of grasshoppers crawled across the dry pine needles. "Go ahead," he said. "I apologize for taking your time."

Will watched Glen Sexton walk to the convertible, remove his hat, and fold himself behind the wheel. When he turned the key in the ignition, the air-conditioning blasted on, Sexton's hair waving visibly in the artificial breeze.

Will walked quickly to the car, feeling like an idiot, realizing now what they had overlooked. What had been right in front of him the whole time.

Glen Sexton began to put the car in gear.

Will reached out and placed a hand on his shoulder.

Sexton looked up, an expression of surprise etched on his face.

"Just one more thing," Will said. "Would you mind raising the top for me?"

TWENTY-FOUR

The department's interview room was hot and cramped.

Glen Sexton wore an orange jumpsuit, his face shadowed by the beard he had grown during the time he had spent in custody. His attorney sat beside him, a slender blond woman with dark circles beneath her eyes.

Seated on Will's side of the table was Stuart Isgro, the Klamath County district attorney.

After Will had ordered Sexton to raise the convertible's electronically operated top, he had searched the compartment that it stowed inside of. Resting at the bottom was a plastic-wrapped package containing a pound of crystal methamphetamine. On the street, it would be worth at least thirty thousand dollars.

Preliminary lab results had showed it to be chemically identical to the samples recovered from both the Dig Inn and Henry Bell's kitchen.

Stuart Isgro was a tall man dressed in a three-piece suit. Clipped to his lapel was a pin in the shape of an American flag. He opened a file folder that sat on the table and removed its contents. The document was on ruled legal onionskin, a row of numbers running vertically down the left margin. On the first page, below the case number, underlined capital letters read CONFIDENTIAL SOURCE AGREEMENT.

"Before you sign," Isgro said, "I need to be sure you understand the scope of the agreement."

Isgro took a pair of tortoiseshell reading glasses from inside his suit coat and fitted them onto the bridge of his nose. "You agree to cooperate fully with any and all local, state, or federal law enforcement agencies. In exchange, we agree to press no further charges, except for one count of possession of methamphetamine. The maximum sentence the court will impose for this charge is twenty-four months, and a one-year term of supervised release."

Sexton's attorney looked across the table at Isgro. "We appreciate your need to cover all the bases," she said. "But I'd like to hear from your officer, re the specifics of what he's asking my client to do."

Isgro turned to Will and nodded.

"It's pretty straightforward," Will said. "He sets up a meeting with his source, to make a buy. When he goes to the meet, he's wearing a wire—"

"No way." Sexton pushed his chair back from the table. "He sees I'm wired, he'll kill me."

"He's right, Stuart," his attorney said. "Under the circumstances, that's unreasonable."

"I'm inclined to agree," Isgro said. He looked over at Will. "Can't you do it without the wire?"

Will shook his head. "The wire's for his own protection. It lets us listen in, so if anything goes wrong, if he's in danger, we can move in."

Sexton's attorney tapped a gold pen against a legal pad and considered what Will had said. "Okay," she said. "What else?"

Isgro continued to read from the document. "You agree that the information you provide to us while cooperating will not be used against you as a basis for additional charges."

He pushed the reading glasses up on his nose, his voice a bored monotone. "But if you violate the terms of this agreement, any and all statements made to law enforcement personnel while cooperating become admissible, and you waive your right to assert any claims under the U.S. Constitution, any statute, or Rule 410 of the Federal Rules of Evidence. Do you understand?"

"Not really," Glen Sexton said.

His attorney turned toward him. "Don't worry, it's the standard bullshit."

"It's a sweetheart deal," Isgro said. He slid the document across the table. "With the amount in question and his prior conviction, he'd be looking at a minimum of twenty years on the trafficking charge."

Sexton's attorney held out her pen to Sexton. "Just go ahead and sign."

After Sexton scrawled his signature across the last page, his attorney picked up the document but didn't give it back to Isgro. "I want my client released on bail," she said.

"No way," Will said. "Not until after the buy/bust."

Sexton's attorney looked at Will. "So when exactly is that going to be?"

"As soon as he sets it up. He can make the call right after this meeting."

"Fine," she said. "Anything else?"

"I want the name of his connection, right now," Will said.

Sexton slammed the pen down. "I already told you. His name's Sonny."

Will looked at him. "I need a last name."

"He never told me."

"Bullshit," Will said.

Sexton turned to his attorney. "What is this? I'm telling the truth here."

Sexton's attorney spoke to Isgro. "My client only wants to help," she said. "I'd appreciate it if you would instruct your officer to stop badgering him."

Isgro nodded. "That's enough, Will."

Unbelievable. Whose side was this guy on? It was already bad enough that Isgro had made him grovel to get the deal for Sexton, rubbing his face in the Henry Bell debacle.

"Look," Will said to Isgro. "We've gone through the files. There's nothing on anyone named Sonny in Haydenville or the surrounding areas."

"So?" Isgro said. "Who says he has to be from Haydenville?"

Will reached down onto the floor and came up with a black three-ring binder. It was a mug book that Will had put together, containing photographs of everyone who had been arrested by the Haydenville Police Department on drug-related charges in the last two years.

"It could be an alias," Will said. He slid the mug book over to Sexton. "See if you can pick out the man you know as Sonny."

Sexton quickly flipped through the pages of the book, one after the other, without pausing.

"Not here," he said when he had reached the end.

"Look again," Will said.

Sexton turned to his attorney, holding out his upturned palms. "He's not in there."

"Stuart," she said to Isgro, "your man here needs to start showing a little trust."

"Let's move this along," Isgro said to Will. "What else?"

Will sat back in the uncomfortable chair and blew out his breath. He instantly regretted it, knowing that it made him appear petulant.

He reached into his shirt pocket and removed a folded piece of paper.

"Take a look at this." Will slid the page across the Formica surface of the tabletop.

Glen Sexton unfolded the paper and glanced at it. He started to hand it back to Will but then seemed to change his mind. He brought it closer to his face, studying it, his eyes narrowing.

He tapped the paper with his fingertip and nodded his head. "Yeah," he said. "That's Sonny."

"You're positive?" Will asked.

"He's younger in the picture," Sexton said. "But, yeah, that's him."

Will held out his hand and took the piece of paper back from Glen Sexton.

Then he refolded the photocopy he had made of the author's photograph from the dust jacket of *The Silent Men*.

TWENTY-FIVE

"I don't like it," Will said to Thomas.

They were standing in the department conference room, the walls still covered with the topographic maps. Glen Sexton sat at the table, dressed in his street clothes. He had just called the man he knew as Sonny from his cell phone. The conference room was one of the only spots in the area that got a cell signal, due to its elevation and large windows.

"You couldn't have picked another place for the meet?" Will asked him.

"It's not like I get a choice," Sexton said. "He just tells me where to go."

The meeting had been set for seven that evening. But it was the location that bothered Will. Looking at the map, he could see that the spot was deep within the national forest, six miles in from the nearest paved road.

Will traced his finger along the closely grouped elevation lines on the map and could see that the meeting spot was in a bowl, a kind of natural amphitheater. It would be difficult for Will and Thomas to find a place that would have a visual of the meeting but still allow them to remain hidden from view.

Thomas pointed a finger at Glen Sexton. "Why can't he just call back, say he wants to meet somewhere else?"

"You out of your mind?" Sexton said. "He's already suspicious, me coming back for more so soon."

"He's right, T," Will said. "It'll be a dead giveaway."

"So what're we supposed to do?" Thomas asked.

Deal with it, Will thought. Find a way to make it work.

He pointed at a place on the map, probably three hundred yards away from the meeting spot. "We'll have to be somewhere back in here," he said. "Because of this rise, we won't have a visual. But we'll listen on the wire, move in as soon as the deal goes down."

On the table was a gray plastic Pelican box. Will rummaged around inside and pulled out a small microphone connected to a transmitter by a length of wire.

He looked over at Sexton. "Stand up and take off your shirt."

"What for?"

"This is your wire."

Sexton frowned. "The meeting's six hours away."

"I want you to get used to wearing it," Will said. "So you don't move any differently at the meet."

Will took a roll of surgical tape from the box and taped the transmitter in the hollow of Sexton's lumbar curve. He ran the wire around the other man's rib cage, attaching the microphone to his chest. He told Sexton to put his shirt back on, then took a step back to take a look. He felt confident that the rig would be undetectable unless Sexton was patted down.

"The key is to just talk normally," Will said. "Forget it's there."

Sexton began to put his shirt back on. "I wish I could. Are you really gonna make me wear this thing?"

Will ignored him and reached inside the equipment box. He

came out with a black plastic wristwatch. A Timex digital, a model popular with joggers.

He handed it to Glen Sexton. "Put this on."

Sexton held out his wrist to show Will the gold watch he was wearing. "Thanks, but I think I'll stick with my Rolex."

"The watch has a transponder in it." Will went back into the box and came out with a handheld receiver. "I can track your location on this screen."

Sexton looked at the watch and made a face. "Suppose he notices it?"

"Just put it on," Will said. "This way, if he puts you in a vehicle and drives off, we can stay with you."

Will looked over at Thomas. "Can you think of anything else?"

"Not really." Thomas shook his head and grinned. "This is gonna be cool."

TWENTY-SIX

Will lay flat on his stomach and looked down into the bowl where the meeting would take place. A dirt clearing, not more than thirty yards across, surrounded by a circular ridge of granite.

When he was satisfied that there was nothing more to see, he went back to the department's truck, hidden from view in a stand of cedars.

Thomas sat behind the wheel. "See anything?"

Will shut the SUV's door, careful not to make any noise. "Maybe we should forget the truck, set up at the top of the rocks."

"Fuck that." Glen Sexton sat in the backseat, his wrists cuffed in front of him. "He'll see you up there."

Will didn't say anything. Sexton was probably right. If nothing else, Will worried that if they were up there Sexton might glance up at them, giving away their presence.

Will looked at his watch: 6:02, still almost an hour to wait.

The temperature of the air had dropped, the wind turning around and coming from the south, buffeting the boughs of the trees. Anvil clouds the color of shale took shape in the darkening sky.

"Looks like we're gonna get a thunderstorm," Thomas said.

Will picked up the receiving unit for the tracking device Glen Sexton was wearing on his wrist and turned it on. There was a short delay while it picked up the signal, then a red dot pulsed to life on the LCD screen.

Thomas opened a hardcover library book wrapped in a clear plastic cover. Will looked over and saw that it was a copy of August Vollmer's *Police and Modern Society*.

"Catching up on your reading?" Will asked.

"I'm almost done with it," Thomas said. "Did you know they call him the father of modern policing?"

Will shrugged. "Who am I to argue?"

The woods all of a sudden became quiet, the birds falling silent. Then the ominous rumble of thunder sounded in the distance, followed a few seconds later by a flash of lightning.

Will looked down at his watch. "It's time," he said.

He got Sexton out of the truck. The other man stood there, holding his wrists out in front of him so that Will could unlock the handcuffs, shifting his weight from one foot to the other.

"You're gonna be fine," Will said.

"Easy for you to say."

Will paused, holding the handcuff key in the air, but not inserting it into the lock. "Hey, Glen?"

Sexton looked at him.

"If you're even thinking about running, get it out of your head right now," Will said.

"Where do you think I'm gonna go?"

"It doesn't matter," Will said. "Wherever it is, I'll track you down. That's a promise. I'll testify at your sentencing hearing that you're an escape risk. I'll make sure the judge sends you to the SHU at Pelican Bay. You know what that is?"

Sexton shook his head.

"You'll spend twenty-three hours a day in your cell. Your food comes through a slot in your door. You never see another human being. Trust me, you'll end up praying to get transferred to San Quentin."

"All right," Sexton said. "I get it."

Will removed the cuffs. They hadn't been tight, because Will had been worried about leaving marks, but Sexton rubbed at his wrists anyway.

Will handed the other man a green nylon gym bag. Inside was twenty thousand dollars in cash. The money belonged to Will. The Haydenville Police Department had no budget for drug buys, so he had withdrawn the money from his personal checking account, leaving him effectively broke.

"We need to test the wire," Will said. "As you walk away, say something."

"Like what?" Sexton asked.

Will started to get back inside the truck. "It doesn't matter."

He watched Sexton walk away toward the rise. Will turned up the volume on the receiving unit for the wire, until he could hear a voice.

"Bye-bye," Glen Sexton said.

TWENTY-SEVEN

Glen Sexton picked his way up the granite formation, ascending to the rim. When he reached the top, he paused momentarily, his slim body tiny against the western sky.

Then he dropped down into the bowl, disappearing from sight.

Thunder boomed, followed by a stroboscopic flash of light, the two events coming closer together now.

Will took a plastic vial of Vicodin from the front pocket of his jeans. He fumbled to open the childproof cap, his palm damp with sweat. He'd woken up with a terrible headache and had already taken three of the pills with his morning coffee, but they hadn't done the trick.

He shook out two of the tablets into his hand, then dry-swallowed them. He put the bottle down in the center console, not wanting to have the pills rattling in his pocket.

Thomas looked down at the vial, reading the label. "Is that a good idea? Because—"

Will cut him off. "What're you, my mother?"

Thomas opened his lips, about to say something else, then seemed to think better of it and sat staring out through the windshield. Will reached out and turned up the volume knob on the reception unit for the wire. There was the electronic hissing of static, but nothing else.

"Shouldn't we hear him?" Thomas asked.

Will looked down at the LCD of the tracking unit. "Not yet. He's still making his way down into the clearing."

It was as if the whole forest were listening along with them: the birds, the wind, even the leaves in the trees gone quiet. Then the silence was filled with another thunderclap, and a single heavy raindrop spattered against the windshield.

The rain began to pour down in a torrent, the sound of it like someone drumming on the metal roof. Will turned up the volume of the receiver to compensate, twisting the knob clockwise as far as it would go. He strained to hear any trace of Glen Sexton's voice. But there was only the static.

"How come we don't hear anything?" Thomas asked.

"I'm not sure," Will said. "The rain might have short-circuited the wire." He looked at the screen of the tracking device. The red dot had stopped moving: Sexton had reached the meeting site.

"What should we do?" Thomas said.

"Stop talking," Will said. "Let me think."

He had little doubt that something had gone wrong with the wire. But if they moved in now, before the deal was consummated, or at least under way, all would be lost.

"Let's give him two more minutes," Will said.

They both sat there, watching the rivulets of water stream down the windshield. The condensation from their breath began to fog the windows. Over the sound of the rain, Will could hear Thomas humming softly to himself, the melody vaguely familiar. He listened, recognizing it as the eighties hit "Everybody Have Fun Tonight" by the group Wang Chung.

"Hey, T?"

"Yeah?"

"You think you could hold off on the tunes?"

Even in the dim light, Will could see the boy's cheeks color.

"Sorry," Thomas said. "Guess I'm just nervous."

Will checked his watch. Just over a minute left now.

"Hey, Will?" Thomas said.

"What?"

"I need to take a leak."

Will let his breath out through his nostrils. "Can you hold it?"

"I don't know," Thomas said. "I'll try."

Will looked down at the LCD screen in his lap and saw that the pulsing red dot was now in motion. "He's on the move."

Will watched the screen. From the speed that the red dot was moving, he could tell that Glen Sexton was on foot.

"What should we do?" Thomas asked.

Will opened the truck's door and got out. "You wait here," he said to Thomas. "Monitor the wire, and listen for me on the radio."

When he reached the top of the rocks, Will dropped down on his stomach to keep himself hidden from sight, using his elbows to drag his body over the rocky soil.

He reached the edge and peered down, a clear view into the bowl. He scanned the clearing, forcing himself to go slowly, until he was sure.

It was deserted.

Thunder crashed, louder from up here. A bolt of lightning pierced the dark clouds, arcing down to strike the canopy of a lodgepole pine, startling birds into flight.

Will rose to his feet and worked his way down, into the bowl.

In the clearing, water ran across the earth in muddy streams. Will searched the ground for footprints, but whatever might have been there was already washed away. He looked at the LCD screen. The pulsing red dot was still moving, off in the woods to his left, moving diagonally away from him.

Will turned in that direction, running his eyes over the surface of the granite walls until he spotted an opening, just wide enough for a man to fit through. He walked up to it and saw the entrance to a trail.

He squeezed between the rocks and started running as fast as he dared given the treacherous footing. The trail was narrow, branches and leaves brushing against his shoulders. Rain coursed down his face, soaking his clothes. His body felt slow and leaden, and he wished now that he had not taken the Vicodin.

He tried to keep his thoughts from seizing on the consequences that would be in store for him if Glen Sexton was allowed to escape. There was the grief he'd have to endure from Stuart Isgro. But there was also the knowledge that the pulsing dot on the LCD screen was running away with the entirety of his life savings.

Will came to a fork in the trail. He stopped, gasping for breath, trying to decide which way to go. Then, feeling like an idiot, he remembered the tracking device.

The pulsing red dot on the screen was moving away to his right, so he took off in that direction. It was getting darker now, dusk beginning to press in, difficult to see very far ahead of him.

He heard the sound of water before he saw it, the trail dead-ending into a rushing stream. Will looked at the LCD screen and saw that Sexton was moving away from him on the far side of the water.

The rocks were slippery, thick with green moss. He forced himself to go slow as he made his way over the rushing water. When he reached the other side, the trail began to rise steeply, his breath coming in ragged gasps as he dragged himself up it.

At the top of the grade, he stopped to check the screen again. He cursed out loud, the pulsing red dot as far away now as when he had first started. It was a waking nightmare: He was going as fast as he could but gaining no ground.

He pushed himself to run faster, going all out now, any sense of caution gone. He felt a stitch in his side, a scalpel plunging into it with every breath. The sound of his breathing filled his head, mud splattering up against his legs.

Then he felt himself become airborne, and the ground flew up at him in the brief moment before his face slammed hard into the wet earth.

His head erupted with pain, his vision tinted red, flat on his stomach on the cold and wet ground. He turned to look backward and saw a thick vine snaking across the trail like a tripwire.

Will rubbed his hand over his lips, his palm coming away slick with dirt and blood.

He was no longer holding on to the tracking device. He pushed himself up onto his hands and knees and looked around, spotting the device in the deep shadows at the edge of the trail, lying at the base of a fir.

He went over and picked it up. A thin crack now snaked diagonally across the screen.

The red dot was still pulsing, but no longer moving. It just remained in place, slowly blinking on the screen. He gave the tracking unit a shake, afraid that it had been damaged by the fall.

Up ahead, the trail made a hairpin turn, disappearing from view. If the tracking device was still working, Glen Sexton was there, just a few yards up ahead.

Will drew his gun from the holster, pulled back the slide, and snicked off the safety. Then he began to walk up the trail.

The sun had disappeared behind a ridge to the west, as dark as night now. Thunder boomed somewhere off in the forest.

He came around the turn, the gun held out in front of him, the trail beginning to rise up once again.

Lightning flashed. In the brief moment of illumination, he saw that there was something on the trail, just ahead of him.

Will dove for cover, pressing himself against the rough trunk of a cedar.

He took a deep breath, then used one eye to peer around the tree, out at the trail. Without the lightning it was difficult to see, but he could make out the dark form, crouching low to the ground.

Will brought the pistol up, flinching when he heard the noise, almost pulling the trigger.

Growling.

The sight was almost surreal, the dog out here all by itself in the depths of the forest. A large and black mongrel, its teeth bared and yellow.

Will tried to move forward again, conscious that Glen Sexton was getting away. But the animal lowered its massive head and barked, blocking the trail.

Will glanced down at the LCD screen. He wondered again if it was broken, the red dot still not moving. Just pulsing in place, indicating a spot directly in front of him.

The dog crouched on its front legs, growling, saliva spraying into the air.

Will dropped down on one knee. The dog watched him, its growls becoming softer. He whistled to the dog and patted the ground in front of him.

The dog cocked its head, suspicious.

Will patted the ground again, and the dog trotted down the trail toward him, its tail swaying back and forth. Will held out his open hand to the animal. He let the dog sniff at it, ready to pull it back if he had to.

The dog was wearing a metal choke collar, something hanging from the front of it.

Will reached out and stroked the top of the dog's head, its fur matted and damp. The dog's tail wagged faster now. Will moved his hand around to the front of the dog's collar and took hold of the object that was hanging there.

As soon as his fingers touched it, Will felt the crushing certainty of what he was holding.

He pulled it around on the collar, until he was looking at it, staring down at the plastic wristwatch he had given Glen Sexton.

TWENTY-EIGHT

Late the next afternoon, Will pulled the department's SUV to a skidding stop in the dirt front yard of Frank Carver's house. It was still three hours away from sunset, but it was already dark in the woods, the lights inside the house burning brightly on the other side of the vast panes of glass.

Before Will could ring the bell, the heavy redwood front door swung open.

Frank Carver wore a faded Jimi Hendrix T-shirt that featured an illustration of a winged eyeball.

"What the hell is this?" he said.

Will plastered the search warrant against Frank's chest. "What's it look like?" he said. "Now step away from the door, or I'll put you in cuffs."

The twins were sprawled out on the carpeted floor of the living room playing a video game on a big-screen television. The house reeked of the smell of frying meat, greasy smoke hanging in the air.

The warrant covered the house, grounds, and outbuildings. Will and Thomas started with the living room, Frank and his sons watching from the sofa while they removed all of the many books from the shelves.

After they were finished with the main house, Will told Thomas to keep an eye on the others while he searched the garage and the old fire lookout tower that served as Frank's office. But he found no sign of Glen Sexton, or any other incriminating evidence that could be used to bring charges against Frank Carver.

When Will came back into the living room, Frank sprang to his feet, blocking his path. Once again, Will found himself surprised by the way the man moved, the primal power that seemed so dissonant with his age.

"Care to enlighten me now?" Frank asked. "The fuck's this all about?"

"Where is he?" Will asked.

Behind the lenses of his thick-framed black glasses, Frank Carver's pink-rimmed eyes did not blink. "Could you narrow that down a little for me?"

"Glen Sexton," Will said. "Where is he?"

"I've got no clue who you're talking about."

Thomas took a step forward. "This guy's so full of shit," he said. "Let's bust his ass."

Frank's head swiveled around on its broad neck to regard Thomas. "Who's that?" he asked Will. "Your son?"

Thomas took another step toward Frank and opened his mouth to speak. Will held up his hand to cut him off. "Let me handle this, T."

Behind his white beard, Frank Carver's lips spread out into a smile.

"Cut the crap," Will said. "Sexton already told us he was meeting you."

"Meeting *me*? What for?"

Will thought before answering, calculating the minimum amount of information he would need to reveal in order to move forward. "Glen Sexton is a person of interest in an ongoing investigation. He told us that he was going to be meeting with you. That's all I'm going to say."

Frank shook his head, smiling at Will. "What is this, a tribute to Kafka?"

"I was there when he called you to set up the meeting," Will said.

Frank tilted his head to one side. "You're telling me you actually heard this guy, talking to *me*?"

Not exactly. He had only heard Sexton's side of the conversation. The department did not possess a microphone tap for a cellular phone, even though it was an item that could be purchased for less than ten dollars at Radio Shack.

"He also ID'd you," Will said.

"What do you mean?"

"He picked your photograph out of a mug book."

"I don't understand." Frank said. "What was my picture doing in a *mug book*?"

"I put it there," Will said. "It was the author's photo from the back of your novel."

Frank Carver's laugh was deep, causing a web of wrinkles to spread outward from the corners of his eyes. "The city council must have been on acid when they hired you. That picture's been on the cover of *Newsweek*."

"So what?" Will could hear the lack of conviction in his own voice.

"This joker *played* you," Frank said, his eyes charged with energy. "What happens when you trust a rat."

Behind Frank, dusty framed photographs hung from the wall, depicting him posed beside famous people dressed in clothing that captured the changing parade of fashion.

There was Frank dressed in tennis whites while standing beside the net of a grass court with Jimmy Connors. Frank shaking hands with Spiro T. Agnew. Frank seated next to the comedian Flip Wilson in the circular booth of a nightclub.

"When I was in Quentin?" Frank spoke more loudly now, as if performing for an audience. "We found out this spic was working as a snitch for the guards. So we decided to teach him a lesson. This *rat*, he celled up on the fifth tier. Long story short, one morning at chow release I'm already up there, waiting at the end of the tier. When the guard throws the bar, this cheese-eater, he just comes sauntering out of his cell, not a care in the world."

The twins sat on the edge of the sofa, their eyes fixed on their father, as if listening to a favorite bedtime story.

"When he sees me coming toward him, he tries to boogie," Frank said. "I grabbed him by the back of his shirt and tossed him over the rail. Five stories onto a concrete floor. He didn't snitch anymore after that."

"What's your point?"

Frank stared down at him. "Rats deserve to die."

Will held the other man's gaze, fighting the urge to look away. "Tell me something," he said. "Where were you at seven last night?"

"That would fall under the category of none of your business."

"Not if I arrest you."

"I was at the library," Frank said. "Giving a reading."

Will smiled. "First rule of false alibis: Don't pick one that's easily disproved."

"Let me ask you something," Frank said. "I prove it, will you stay the fuck out of my life?"

"Sure. But you can't."

Frank walked to the dining room table and picked up a newspaper. He opened it to an inside page, then handed the paper over to Will.

The photograph was in black and white, Frank Carver reading from a book to a group of elementary school children who sat cross-legged at his feet. Will looked up at the date printed at the top of the page.

"It says it was yesterday, but how do I know what time?"

Frank Carver reached out and used his forefinger to point at something in the photograph. His fingernail was thick and yellow, in need of clipping.

Will saw what he was pointing to. It was small in the picture, but still visible. The clock that hung on the library wall, the hands reading 7:14 P.M.

"Don't look so glum," Frank said. "Ever read *Ulysses?* Stephen Dedalus says that mistakes, they're just portals for discovery."

TWENTY-NINE

The wall surrounding Thomas's cubicle was covered in a gray hopsack material. A flyer was tacked to it, block letters reading WANTED BY U.S. MARSHALS perched above the booking photo of Glen Sexton.

Will stood with his elbow propped on top of the partition. "You talk to SFPD?"

Thomas nodded. "They've got Sexton's apartment under surveillance twenty-four/seven."

"Good deal."

Will had a hunch that Sexton would eventually return to his Marina District condo, if only to retrieve some possessions.

Thomas's desktop was covered with copies of Sexton's credit card and bank statements. Will felt confident they would find him, that it was only a matter of time. It wasn't all that easy to stay hidden in the electronic age.

"He didn't escape on his own," Will said.

"What makes you so sure?"

"The dog, the way the whole thing went down. Trust me, he had help."

"From who?"

"If I was a betting man? Frank Carver."

Thomas looked up at him. "What about his alibi? Maybe it's time to move on, start looking at somebody else."

"Like *who*?"

Thomas didn't answer him, just chewed loudly on a piece of gum. On his desk was a garishly colored pack of bubble gum, something a child might buy.

Thomas noticed that Will was looking at it. "Want a piece?"

"Sure."

The piece of gum was shaped like a small cinder block, wrapped in waxy paper. The flavor was cloying.

"Maybe Sexton was bullshitting us," Thomas said. "Maybe he was meeting somebody besides Frank."

"Even if he was, the key is still getting Sexton back, so he can tell us who it was."

"How do you know he'll tell us the truth?"

"He broke the plea agreement, T. We've got the sword of Damocles hanging over his head."

"The *what*?"

Will thought of how best to explain it, then decided it would be easier to just change gears. "What I mean is, we've got a lot of leverage. He already copped to the possession charge, so it's automatic. Plus, we can hit him with possession with intent and willful failure to appear. Everything he told us can be used as evidence against him now."

"What about the DEA?" Thomas asked.

Will chewed his piece of gum. "What about them?"

"Maybe we should bring them in."

Will shook his head. "Not until we have something to bring them in *for*."

Earlier in the day, Will had endured an uncomfortable call with Kirk Nolan. The DEA agent had sounded apoplectic when Will told him about how they had moved ahead with the buy/bust operation without informing him.

The gum had already lost its flavor in Will's mouth. He continued to chew it, but it now felt more like a chore than a pleasure.

THIRTY

The campground was set on a rise above the river, a small general store in front, neon beer signs hanging in the window.

Will stood on top of a weathered log that lay on the ground at the edge of the dirt parking lot and scanned the campground. The early evening sun raked across an expanse of grass that had turned parched and yellow in the summer heat, interrupted by the dirt clearings of the campsites.

In his hand, Will was holding the kayak paddle that had been found deep in the woods. According to the owner of the rafting company, the campground had been the summertime residence of Caitlyn Johnson.

At the far end, beneath a stand of ancient oaks, Will spotted what he was looking for. A large campsite beside the trail that led down to the river, a clothesline strung between two trees. Hanging from the line were paddling tops, spray skirts, and a single yellow PFD.

A man dressed in flip-flops, cargo shorts, and a tie-dyed T-shirt stood over a wooden picnic table, adjusting the sputtering flame of a Coleman stove.

"I was hoping I could ask you a few questions about Caitlyn Johnson," Will said. He opened his badge holder and placed it on the picnic table.

The man frowned. "I was wondering if you'd ever show up." He was in his twenties, his sun-bleached hair the color of straw.

"What do you mean?" Will had to raise his voice, the sound of the river loud here.

"I wrote a letter, right after she died. But never heard anything back."

"You sent a letter?" Will felt confused. "To me?"

He shook his head. "The mayor. I told her someone needed to look into it. But it's been over a month. You didn't do shit."

Will felt himself shift to the defensive, the familiar feeling of guilt creeping to the edge of his consciousness. "We've been looking into it. But there's been a lot of other stuff going on."

"Like what? Rescuing cats from trees?" He opened a ziplock bag of dried pasta and dumped it into the now boiling pot of water on the camp stove.

Will took out his notebook. "I didn't catch your name."

"Mitch Powers."

"How well did you know her, Mitch?"

"We worked together for the past couple of seasons. We were friends."

"What can you tell me about her?"

"That she was a good person. She was studying so she could teach elementary school. When she was back home, she volunteered for ETC."

"I don't know what that is."

"Environmental Traveling Companions. They take disabled people out kayaking. She didn't deserve to die."

Will heard a mosquito buzzing around his ear. "Where did she live?" he asked.

"Over there." Mitch Powers pointed to the neighboring campsite.

"She lived in a tent?"

The other man shook his head. "She had a camper shell on her truck. Had a mattress inside."

"You live here by yourself now?"

"No. Everybody else is out on the river."

"Why aren't you?"

"My wrist's been hurting. I thought I'd give it a rest."

Will showed him the paddle. "You recognize this?"

The other man took the paddle and held it out in front of him with both hands, as if readying himself to paddle away. He brought the left blade close to his face, seeing the initials carved into the fiberglass.

"It's hers," he said.

"Is it the paddle she would have taken with her the night she died?"

"Yeah," he said without hesitation.

"What makes you so sure?"

"Because she only had one."

A plume of wood smoke rose from one of the campsites and drifted toward them, carrying with it the smell of roasting meat.

"She was supposed to go with us, that night," the other man said. "A bunch of us ran Burnt Ranch after work."

"What's that?"

"It's a class five run on the Trinity. We were heading out right after work. But Caitlyn had a group trip that showed up late. She was still on the water with them when we left."

A man and a young boy came up the trail from the river, both of them carrying fishing rods. Will studied the boy, matching him up with the images stored in his mind, how he imagined Sean would have looked as he grew older.

(i wasn't there—)

Will shoved the thought away, asking the other man the first question that popped into his head. "What made you write the letter?"

"Because it wasn't an accident."

"How do you know?"

"I've run Cherry Creek with her. It's class five-plus. She never even flipped. She was the best paddler I've ever seen."

"Accidents happen," Will said. "People slip in their bathtubs."

"But not in their kayaks. Accidents happen because people get careless. They're thinking about something else, not paying attention. Caitlyn wasn't like that."

"It was an easy stretch of water for her. Maybe she wasn't taking it seriously."

Mitch Powers jabbed a fork into the pot of pasta and stirred it. "This is a big waste of time, you aren't gonna do anything." He looked at Will. "There's no way she would have had an accident on that stretch of river. You couldn't hit a rock there if you tried."

Even in the shade of the campsite, the heat was still fierce.

Will reached behind him and pulled his damp shirt away from the small of his back. "I know," he said.

THIRTY-ONE

On Saturday, he found himself standing out in left field, dressed in a softball uniform and wearing a pair of cleats that were a size too small.

He had signed up for the team back in May, thinking that it would be a good way for him to meet people in the new town. He'd ended up missing the previous games because of work, but had gotten a call that he was desperately needed for today's tournament in Haydenville Park.

The sun was high up in a cloudless sky the color of a robin's egg, the hot air filled with the scent of sage and dry grasses. Down the foul lines of the diamond, people watched the game from folding deck chairs. Parked behind the backstop was a white beer truck, the Lions Club selling plastic cups of Budweiser.

It was a slow-pitch league. Will watched as the pitcher launched the fluorescent green ball in a high and lazy arc toward home plate. The batter swung early, hitting a weak pop-up. The shortstop caught the ball and then held a single finger up in the air to indicate that there was now one out.

Will looked out to the green mountains rising up to create a backdrop behind the brick buildings of the square, the highest peaks still dusted with snow. He found himself struck once again by the natural beauty of the place.

Nice place to live, if it wasn't for all the tweakers.

The second batter of the inning walked, tossing the bat away before trotting down to first.

The opposing team was sponsored by the Dig Inn, embroidered letters stretching across the front of their jerseys spelling out the team name, DRINKERS. They seemed to be living up to their name; in the deep shadows of their dugout, Will could see players tipping their heads back, draining cans of beer.

The next batter swung at the first pitch. Will watched as the ball rose off the barrel of the bat, the angle telling him that it was headed his way. He took a drop-step before realizing that the ball was going to fall in front of him, a dying quail.

Will took off at a sprint, his feet soundless on the carpet of green grass, his glove held flat against his side like a leather wing. At the last moment he dropped to his knees, letting his momentum carry him in a slide across the grass, the glove held out in front of him. His eyes never left the spinning ball, watching it all the way into his glove, snagging it in the webbing inches above the surface of the grass.

Then, out of the corner of his eye, Will caught a flurry of motion. The base runner had kept running on the play, figuring that Will wouldn't make the catch. He was now scrambling to get back to first.

Will rummaged inside his glove for the ball, then made a sidearm throw from his knees. He was afraid that it wouldn't make it, the ball losing altitude on its long trip across the diamond.

The first baseman stretched toward the ball as the base runner launched himself into a headfirst dive. The ball snapped into the glove a millisecond before the base runner arrived back at the base in an explosion of dust. The umpire pointed down toward the base runner before making a punching motion that indicated he was out.

Double play, inning over. Will trotted back toward the dugout, pin-wheeling his right arm in an attempt to shake off the twinge he felt in his shoulder.

Will led off the bottom of the inning. He let the first pitch go, the umpire calling it a strike. The Drinkers' middle infielders were Frank Carver's twins. In their uniforms they were mirror images, impossible to tell apart. Down the right field line, Will spotted Frank seated on a folding chair beside his young girlfriend. He wore a straw sombrero, the wide brim casting a circular shadow all the way down to his beard-draped chest.

Will drove the next pitch deep into right center field. It split the outfielders, and Will ran hard, turning it into a stand-up triple.

He stood on the bag, bent over at the waist, struggling to catch his breath. The third baseman came over and stood close beside him, exuding an aroma of hops and chewing tobacco into the warm air.

"Careful," the man said. "Payback's a bitch."

Will looked up and saw that it was the same player that he had just thrown out at first. He looked into the other man's eyes, trying to figure out if he was joking, but they were hidden behind wraparound sunglasses.

The next two batters walked to load the bases, so Will was forced to break for home on a slow ground ball hit to third.

He ran as fast as he could down the line, the catcher standing to the left of home plate, his mitt held up to take the throw from third base. Will stepped safely on the plate and then felt a sudden explosion of pain between his shoulder blades. He fell to his knees, collapsing on top of the plate as if he had been poleaxed.

He found that he could not breathe, his whole upper back crawling with spasms of pain. Laughter and scattered applause floated over to him from the sidelines. The umpire's face filled his field of vision, small eyes looking out at him from behind the cage of his face mask.

"You okay?" the umpire asked.

"I don't know." It was hard for Will to get the words out. He couldn't move his arms and wondered if he was paralyzed. "What happened?"

"The throw from third. It nailed you right in the back."

Will struggled to his feet, the pain in his back so severe that he had trouble taking a step.

The third baseman was staring at him, his weedy goatee framing a grin. He held up his palms toward Will in a gesture that said *shit happens.*

Then the man pursed his lips and blew a gob of spit out into the dirt.

THIRTY-TWO

When the game ended, Will gathered his gear from the dugout and headed for the parking lot. His back still ached, the pain wrapping across his upper back like a shawl.

An elderly man wearing a Lions Club T-shirt sat at a folding table, a roll of cardboard tickets set in front of him. "You look like you could use a beer," he said.

It was as if the man had read his thoughts. Will fished some dollar bills out of his pocket and handed them over.

The beer truck was the size of a moving van, the back of it gleaming and white, three chrome-plated taps sticking out from the side. Another man in a Lions Club shirt stood beside it. Will handed the ticket to him, and the man pulled the handle on one of the taps, golden liquid flowing out into a plastic cup.

Will found the vial of Vicodin inside his equipment bag and shook out four of the tablets into his palm. He washed them down with a swig of the beer. The wetness and carbonation scoured the dust of the playing field from his throat.

The sun had dropped lower in the sky, the hue of its rays shifting to orange. He brought the cup to his lips and gulped the beer, the sunlight coming through the translucent plastic, touching the liquid with fire.

He felt a tap on his shoulder and turned to see the third baseman from the other team.

The man was grinning, revealing dark gaps where teeth were missing. A plastic beer cup foamed in his hand. "Didn't I tell you payback was a bitch?"

"That's what you call payback?" Will fought to keep from raising his voice. "I throw you out fair and square, you drill me in the back when I'm not looking?"

The third baseman cracked his knuckles and made a big deal of flexing his biceps. The sleeves of his jersey were ragged where they had been cut off at the shoulders, his arms large and vascular. "You wanna do something about it?"

A half dozen of the man's teammates crowded in around him, staring at Will.

"I'm a police officer," Will said.

"I know who you are." In the mirrored lenses of the man's sunglasses, Will's reflection was distorted.

Walk away. Will tried to take a step, but a crowd of spectators from the game had drifted over, forming a semicircle, like in a schoolyard fight. The beer truck was at Will's back, so there was nowhere for him to go.

"C'mon," the man said, taking a step closer. "Show me what you're made of."

"What I'm made of?" Will said.

He thought about simply giving the man what he wanted, imagined driving his fist into this asshole's face, watching the cheap sunglasses fly off his head. But even through the warm embrace of the Vicodin and beer he could see the essential irrationality of this.

The weight of the crowd pressed in against him, giving off a barnyard smell.

"Kick his ass, Hank," a woman said, inciting a chorus of cheers.

"I'm a police officer," Will said.

"You already said that." The man was inches away from Will, his spittle misting against Will's cheek. "Don't you got nothing else to say?"

Will reached out and pushed against the man's chest, using the flat of his hand. "I need you to move back."

He hadn't pushed hard, but the man was drunk and unsteady on his feet. He stumbled backward, the beer spilling from the plastic cup, soaking the front of his shorts.

"Look," he said, staring down at his wet crotch. "Look what you did."

"I'll buy you another."

The man let go of the cup, letting it crash to the ground. Beer exploded upward in a mushroom cloud. "I don't want another one. I wanted *that* one."

The man balled his fists and brought them up high in front of his chest, adopting the stance of an old-time pugilist. He began moving them in small circles through the air.

His watch. Will saw that the man was wearing a digital watch on his right wrist, so the odds were good he was a southpaw.

Will ignored the circling right hand, focusing only on the left. It jutted forward, growing larger in size as it flashed toward his face.

Will slipped the punch, moving to his right.

The man's momentum continued to carry him forward. Will reached out and shoved the back of the other man's head, slamming his face into the side of the beer truck.

There was the wet snap of cartilage, the sound of a nose breaking. The man's knees buckled, and his face slid down along the side of the beer truck. He sank to the ground and lay there, unmoving.

The white surface of the truck was dimpled where the man's face had collided with it, joining with the thick trail of blood below it to form an inverted exclamation point.

Will spun around toward the crowd, the sound of his own heart loud in his ears. He saw them in fragments now, close-up flashes of feral eyes and bad teeth and writhing tattoos, angry sores and gaunt faces that were sheened with sweat.

Will steeled himself for them to set upon him. His gun was inside the equipment bag at his feet. His mind fast-forwarded to the consequences of drawing it in this situation, pictured the crowd surging forward and wrestling the weapon from his grasp before using it against him.

"STEP BACK," he screamed. His hands were clenched into fists, his head swiveling from side to side.

On some level, he realized that it was futile, that there were too many of them, but he was beyond rational thought now, operating at some atavistic level of consciousness, a cornered animal. His pain and anger and frustration mixed together with the drugs and alcohol in his bloodstream, a venomous cocktail welling up inside him.

He scanned the crowd, searching their eyes. What he saw there filled him with both revulsion and relief.

They were afraid of him.

Will took a step toward them, and they fell back. He waded into the crowd. It parted, a narrow corridor opening up before him as he walked away.

THIRTY-THREE

When Will walked into his office on Monday morning, he found Bonnie Newman seated behind his desk, using her long and manicured fingernails to peel the skin from a navel orange.

"Shut the door," she said.

He did it, then sat down in the hard plastic guest chair. "What's up?"

"There's no easy way to say this," the mayor said. "So I'll just say it. You're finished."

At some level, he understood what she was telling him, but he was stunned, his mind scrambling to catch up to the reality of the situation. "What do you mean, *finished*?"

"You're fired." She turned the orange in her hands, running her thumbnail beneath the skin, the peel coming away in long strips.

"Can you at least tell me why?"

She looked at him over the top of her glasses. "Do you really need me to?"

He nodded once, the buzzing in his bad ear loud. "I'd like to hear it."

She pulled a strip of the peel free and added it to a small mound on the top of his desk blotter. "When the chief of police is causing more problems than the people he's sworn to protect, something needs to change."

"You're talking about this weekend, the softball tournament?"

"The Lions are threatening to sue. They want us to pay to repair their truck."

"You can take it out of my salary."

She shook her head. "You're not getting any more salary."

He felt as if he were seeing her through surgical gauze, the details of the room indistinct. "He came after *me*. I was only defending myself."

"That's the second time you've used that excuse," she said. "The first time, someone died."

"He took a swing at me."

"According to *multiple* eyewitnesses, only after you struck him in the chest. He never laid a hand on you."

"Not for lack of trying."

She stopped peeling the orange. "What were you doing there in the first place? Hanging out and chugging beer."

"Is there some law against that? Me having a beer?"

She popped a section of the orange into her mouth. "What about the pills?"

"The *what*?"

"The Vicodin, Will. Taking it while you're at work."

How could she possibly know about that? He tried to remember if anyone had ever seen him taking them.

"I know all about it," she said. "My source is impeccable."

Her eyes slid away, to the desktop, and in that moment he had his answer. It felt as if a hand had slipped inside his chest, squeezing his heart.

Thomas. He saw the two of them, sitting inside the truck deep in the woods, at the stakeout. Will shaking the pills out of the vial.

There was a soft knock at the door.

The mayor looked up. "Yes?"

Lila, the dispatcher, peeked through the door. She looked embarrassed, avoiding eye contact with Will. "They called from upstairs, Your Honor," she said. "Your nine o'clock is waiting."

The mayor glanced at her wristwatch. "Tell them I'll be up in two minutes."

Lila shut the door behind her.

The mayor held out her hand toward him. "I need to take your badge," she said.

It was like L.A. all over again, only somehow worse. He'd thought that had been the bottom, but could see now that it was only a rest stop on his long descent.

Where was he supposed to go? His house belonged to the town. He'd given up the trailer in L.A. Gary Sexton had absconded with the entirety of his life's savings.

"Please," he said. "Just give me one more chance."

"You already had it." She swept the pile of orange peels into his wastebasket. "It's not just me, Will. It's the city council. I warned you not to mess with Frank Carver."

"I just need a little more time," he said. "We're getting so close."

"To *what?*"

"Taking down the meth supply. We've got a cooperating witness, someone who's buying directly from the source."

"*Really?*" She looked as if she didn't believe him. "Why don't you let me talk to him?"

"You can't."

"Why not?"

"He's not here," he said.

She shook her head. "I don't follow."

He felt hot and wondered if the air-conditioning had broken down again. "He escaped from custody."

She made a derisive clucking sound with her tongue. "Honestly, I don't know what I was thinking when I hired you."

"We're working with other law enforcement agencies," he said. "We're close to bringing him in. I just need more time."

"No."

"What about my contract?"

"You're being terminated for cause."

He couldn't stomach the thought of being stopped now, not at this point. There were so many loose ends, too many things left for him to do.

"You'll have to prove it," he said. "I'll get a lawyer and fight it."

She looked at him over the top of her glasses. "Do you really want that kind of humiliation?"

He was only trying to buy some time, knew that in the end he would lose. After all, how would he be able to prove his side of the story? He could think of no one who'd be willing to testify in his behalf. Before there had been Thomas, but that was no longer an option.

"I think it'll be worse for you," he said. "Do you really want word of this town's drug problem getting out? I can't see it being much of a boon for tourism."

She put the final section of the orange into her mouth. "Don't make this any harder than it has to be."

"Give me a month and I'll have the meth supply shut down. That's what you wanted, isn't it?"

"And what if you don't?"

"I'll leave. I won't make any trouble, I'll sign anything you want."

She looked off into an empty corner of the room, as if thinking it over. "I'll give you two weeks."

He nodded his head. "Fine."

"But, Will?" She turned her head back to look at him. "If anything should happen in the meantime? Any more of your public spectacles? You're history."

She stood up and wiped her palms against the front of her slacks. "Are we clear?"

THIRTY-FOUR

After the mayor had left the office, he got up and reclaimed his desk chair. He gazed down at the square, watching the cars move along Main Street, the bright sun flashing off their windshields. Everything seemed too far away, as though he were peering through the wrong end of a telescope.

He heard a gentle knock at his door and turned to see Lila perched at the threshold. She held a slip of paper in her hands, her fingers working at it like worry beads.

"Are you okay?" she asked.

It was all he could do to nod his head.

She held out the paper to him. "Your wife called."

"She called *here*?" He was confused—he'd never given Laurie the department's number.

Lila handed him the message slip. It was creased, damp with her perspiration.

He looked at it, recognizing the Los Angeles phone number.

"I'm sorry," she said. "I didn't think I should interrupt your meeting with the mayor."

"It's fine." He picked up the phone. "Would you please shut the door?"

Laurie answered on the third ring.

"Sorry to bother you at work," she said. "I tried leaving you a message at home."

"What's wrong?"

"Nothing, everything's great." She cleared her throat. "It's just that I've been thinking. What I think is, I *would* like to come up there. For the Fourth."

He was stunned. He looked at the hardware store calendar hanging on the wall, saw that she was talking about this coming weekend.

"Will? Are you there?"

"I'm here," he said.

"You don't sound very excited."

"I am," he said. "Really."

"Don't jerk me around." He could hear the pitch of her voice rise. "Did you change your mind?"

He spotted a tiny piece of orange peel stuck to the arm of his chair. He pried it loose with his fingernail and dropped it into the wastebasket.

"No," he said. "It's just—"

"Don't do this to me," she said. "I kept going back and forth about whether to come. It may not be a big deal to you, but it is to me."

"I know."

He heard only the hissing of the long distance connection, as if she were waiting for him to say something more.

"Forget it," she finally said. "This was stupid."

"No," he said. "*Please*."

"What is it, then? Are you okay?"

What, exactly, was he supposed to tell her?

"Why does everyone keep asking me that?" he said. "I'm fine."

"You don't sound like it."

"It's just things are a little crazy right now, at work. It'll all get straightened out by the time you get here."

"You're sure?"

"Look, I'm sorry if I sound a little preoccupied. I can't wait to see you."

"All right," she said. "I was going to drive up, turn it into a little road trip. Can you e-mail me directions to your house?"

"Sure. What time do you think you'll get here?"

"If the traffic cooperates, around dinnertime. On Thursday."

He jotted the date and time into his pocket notebook. "I'll take you to the most expensive restaurant in town," he said.

"You don't have to do that."

"Actually, I do," he said. "It's also the only one."

Over the hundreds and hundreds of miles of telephone wire, he heard the familiar sound of her laugh.

"Laurie?"

"Yeah?"

"It's really good to hear your voice."

THIRTY-FIVE

"I need to speak to you in the conference room," Will said.

Thomas sat at his desk, going through copies of Glen Sexton's credit card statements with a yellow highlighter. "Can you give me a few?"

Will shook his head. "It wasn't a request."

The morning sun was hot through the conference room windows. Will twisted the wand on the venetian blinds, throwing bars of shadow against the wall.

"What's the matter?" Thomas asked.

Will shut the door to the room. "What have you done, Thomas?"

"T."

Will shook his head. "What the *fuck* have you done?"

"I don't know," Thomas said. "I've been going through the phone records—"

"Cut the crap. What were you *thinking*?"

The younger man took a step backward, his eyes wide. "Calm down, Will."

"Don't tell me to calm down. After all I've done for you, this is how you pay me back?"

"What are you talking about?'

"You know perfectly well. The mayor."

"What about her?"

"She just tried to fire me," Will said.

"*What?*" Thomas seemed surprised by this news. "What for?"

"Maybe because you told her I was on drugs."

"No." Thomas shook his head. "That's not true."

"Stop lying."

"I'm not," Thomas said. "She came to *me*, told me she knew you were taking drugs again. She said she wasn't angry, she just wanted to know about it. So she could get you some help."

"And you believed her?"

Thomas looked confused. "I defended you, Will. I told her how you had things under control, that you were just taking some pills."

Will could see it now, what had probably happened. He pulled one of the chairs out from the table and sank down into it. "She didn't know anything, Thomas. She was only fishing. And you took the bait."

Thomas gazed down at the wooden floor. His eyes grew shiny. "I just wanted to help." Thomas wiped at his eyes. "I was worried about you, Will. I was worried all the time. Because of what you told me about L.A."

Will slapped his palm down on the surface of the table. "*Shit.*"

Thomas took a step closer to him. "I would never try to hurt you, Will."

Will looked at him. "For somebody who's not trying, you're doing a bang-up job."

"I'm sorry."

"Look, Thomas. From now on, don't tell anyone *anything* before speaking to me. You got it?"

Thomas nodded. "I'm sorry, Will."

"I didn't ask you to say you were sorry. I asked you if you understood."

"I promise." Thomas nodded his head and used the back of his hand to wipe his eyes. "Only you."

THIRTY-SIX

The afternoon was filled with golden light that did not penetrate the shadowed interior of the Dig Inn, the warm air inside the bar smelling of spilled beer and ancient dust.

Will perched on a vinyl-covered bar stool. He had changed out of his work clothes and now wore a T-shirt and a pair of shorts.

"What'll it be?" The skin of the bartender's face was creased and leathery, his thinning hair pulled back into a short ponytail.

"Jack Black, straight up," Will said. "And a bottle of Sierra on the side."

He had found that the alcohol was a way for him to take less of the Vicodin. Now that he had started drinking hard liquor again, he had been able to cut back to only six of the tablets a day.

A jar of boiled eggs sat on top of the bar. He realized that he hadn't eaten anything since breakfast, but the sight of the eggs was revolting, sightless eyeballs floating in a jar of formaldehyde. He downed half the shot glass of bourbon, letting the heat ignite on his palate before extinguishing it with some of the ale.

Will reached into the back pocket of his shorts and pulled out a folded document. Lila had handed it to him earlier in the afternoon, but he'd never gotten the chance to look at it. It was a fax from the FBI crime lab, results from the duct tape sample he'd taken from the mutilated dog in the clearing.

Since then, four more dead dogs had been found in the woods surrounding the town, all with their heads blown apart by M-80s. He felt a wave of guilt that he wasn't putting in more time trying to apprehend the person or persons responsible. With everything else going on, any investigation had pretty much been back-burnered.

Will drained the rest of the bourbon and held up his empty glass to signal the bartender that he was ready for a refill. The sounds of the bar melded into a pleasant hum, the coming and going of customers announced by the slapping of the batwing doors.

He skimmed through the FBI report. The techs had analyzed the adhesive on the tape sample and run it against their database. They had found a match, identifying the tape as *Duck* brand.

Will shoved the report back into his pocket. It was the most popular brand of duct tape; asking retailers to remember someone who'd recently bought a roll of it would be a waste of time, like trying to track purchasers of Ivory soap.

The jukebox switched to a new song, "Come Sail Away" by the band Styx. He heard himself humming along, even though it was a song he'd always despised.

The bartender set the fresh glass of bourbon directly on the scarred wooden surface of the bar.

"Which way's the bathroom?" Will asked him. He felt an urgent need to urinate, bordering on pain.

The bartender pointed a finger toward a doorway in the far corner of the room. Will stood up and walked toward it, careful to step over the faint rust-colored bloodstain that was still visible on the linoleum squares of the floor.

* * *

Will stared straight ahead at the green ceramic tiles, his bladder emptying.

Someone came into the men's room and stood at the urinal to his right, so that their shoulders were almost touching. The sound of the other man's stream was loud as it splashed against the porcelain surface of the urinal.

Something in Will's peripheral vision caught his attention. When he realized what it was, he tried to look away. But it was impossible, like turning away from a car accident.

The other man's penis was enormous, freakish in its length and girth, webbed with ropy veins.

The man cleared his throat. In a baritone voice he said, "We still playing Whose Dick Is Bigger?"

Will turned his head and found himself looking up into the face of Frank Carver. Behind the beard, his lips stretched into a smile that revealed a gold crown.

"Think you could handle it?" Frank said.

"What?" Frank was standing on the side of his bad ear, and Will wasn't sure that he'd heard him correctly.

"My dick," Frank said. "Think you could take it up your ass?"

Will started to back away, but he was still in the middle of urinating, the stream tethering him in place. His free hand clenched into a fist before he remembered the mayor's warning.

"Thanks," Will said. "But I actually prefer women."

"So do I," Frank said, "but you get sent away for as long as I did, you learn to adapt. 'Red in tooth and claw,' and all that crap."

Will tried to make himself urinate faster, wanting to get the hell out of there. "For some reason, I don't think Darwin was referring to sodomy."

A tumbler of amber liquid rested on the top of Frank's urinal. He picked it up and took a long drink, crunching ice between his teeth. "Tennyson," he said.

"What?"

" 'Nature, red in tooth and claw.' Everyone always thinks it's Darwin. But it was actually Tennyson. As in Alfred Lord."

"Sorry, but I don't think he was talking about sodomy, either."

Frank stared at him. The lenses of his heavy black-framed eyeglasses magnified his eyes, making them appear too large. "At Quentin? I had respect. After I went up in some punk, they walked with a *limp*."

"That must be strange, thinking of your dick as an instrument of torture."

Frank slammed the tumbler down on top of the urinal. "Fuck you, cop."

Frank took hold of his phallus and gave it a shake. He turned as he did it, a spurt of warm urine spattering against Will's bare knee.

Will felt his rage gaining control of him, the sense that he was no longer in his body, but was watching himself at a remove. He didn't care anymore if he lost his job. If he had to stand here and take this for even a second longer, he feared that something more important would be lost.

He stuck his finger into the other man's face. "You're going down. It's just a matter of time. I've got someone who's gonna burn you and your whole fucking organization."

There was an amused smile on Frank Carver's face. "You got to learn to control your temper, bud." He stuffed himself into his pants and zipped his fly. "I heard you got euchred."

"What's that supposed to mean?"

"That the mayor sliced off your sack. That you're one more fuckup away from being out on your ass."

Will had finally finished emptying his bladder. He zipped his shorts and stepped away from the urinal. "You seem to be pretty plugged in around here. What else can you tell me?"

"I know about your kid," Frank said.

Will felt as though he had just been kicked in the stomach.

Frank looked down at Will, the top of his head almost touching the ceiling of the bathroom. "Did you know that an article about it comes up when you Google your name?"

Will struggled to breathe, the chemical smell of urinal cakes overpowering inside the tiled room. He remembered the piece running in the *Los Angeles Times*, despite the LAPD media relations section's attempt to kill the story. The angle of Griffith Park and the child of a prominent detective too enticing for the editor to ignore.

Frank's eyes were electric with mirth, as if he were listening to a joke that only he could hear. " 'Each unhappy family is unhappy in its own way.' When you think about your son—about the way he died—do you blame yourself?"

(i wasn't there—)

Will's hand shot out, grabbing the front of Frank's shirt. The tumble of facial hair curled around his fingers like vines, dry and prickling. Will drew back his right fist. Frank didn't struggle, the grin on his face frozen in a rictus.

Then the bathroom door banged open against the tile wall. Will turned to see a man dressed in dirty work clothes frozen in the doorway, his eyes moving from Will to Frank.

Will let go of Frank's shirt and pushed through the door.

He worked his way through the now crowded bar, crashed through the batwing doors and out into the night, sucking down lungfuls of warm air.

He staggered along the sidewalk to his car and climbed inside.

He sat there breathing as though he had just completed running a marathon. It was hot and airless, but he did not bother to roll down the window. He sat there, alone inside the car, illuminated by the greenish light cast by the streetlamp.

He slammed the meat of his fist down on top of the dashboard. Then he did it again, harder this time, ignoring the pain that shot up his arm.

He struck the dashboard over and over until the vinyl surface split apart, revealing foam padding and tangles of wire that were like colorful snakes.

THIRTY-SEVEN

"Can I come in?"

Will looked up and saw Thomas framed in the doorway of his office. "You don't have to ask, T."

Thomas walked toward the desk, holding a yellow legal pad covered with scribbled notes. "I just got a call from SFPD," he said. "They spotted Glen Sexton entering his apartment."

Will sat up in his chair. "They got him?"

Thomas shook his head. "He got away. Building had a back exit they didn't know about."

Will slammed his hand down on the desktop. He winced from the pain, his wrist still sore from the beating he had administered to his dashboard. "Did Sexton make them?" he asked.

"They don't think so. They were down the block in an unmarked car."

"Did they get a good look at him?"

"Not really. They saw the lights in his apartment go on, but he was gone by the time they got up there."

"They go inside?" Will asked.

Thomas nodded. "They said the place looked like it'd been tossed. Stuff dumped all over."

"I do not fucking believe this."

Thomas looked at him. "They've got units posted on both the front and rear now."

"Talk about shutting the barn door after the horse's already run off."

"What?"

"It's just an old saying, T," Will said. "Don't worry about it."

THIRTY-EIGHT

Will walked into the house, the heat inside stifling. He went from room to room, sliding open the windows, leaving the back door ajar to let Buddy come inside.

In the kitchen, he opened a can of dog food. It was a brand called Iams, a name he'd always found strangely philosophical. He used a fork to empty it out into the dog's ceramic bowl.

"Buddy," he called out through the open back door. "Dinner."

He checked his watch. Two hours left until Laurie arrived.

Will changed into an old pair of shorts and a ripped T-shirt. He vacuumed the wood floors before moving on to the bathroom, scrubbing the tub and getting down on his knees to clean the toilet.

He changed the sheets on the mattress in the bedroom and then made up the foldout sofa in the living room.

When he had finished, sweat ran down his forehead and into his eyes.

Will went into the kitchen and opened a bottle of Anchor Steam. He looked down at the floor, surprised to see that Buddy's food was untouched.

He called the dog from the back door, but there was no response. He stepped out onto the patio and scanned the backyard. The dried pig's ear that Buddy liked to chew on lay abandoned on the grass, but he didn't see the dog.

Will started to call the dog's name again but stopped when he heard the metallic jangling of Buddy's collar. The dog trotted up to him and licked the back of his hand.

"Where were you, boy?" Will asked.

When the dog didn't answer, the two of them went into the kitchen together, and Buddy began to gobble the food from his bowl.

Will picked up the vial of Vicodin from the counter. It was new, a refill he'd just gotten from the drugstore. He hid it away on the top shelf of one of the kitchen cabinets. He'd made Laurie a promise after getting out of Eucalyptus Knolls, that he'd never use again.

He took the sweating bottle of beer with him into the shower and drank it while the tepid water washed over him. After, he stood naked in front of the closet for a long time, trying to decide what to wear, as if he were getting ready for a first date.

In the end, he decided on a pair of freshly laundered jeans and a Hawaiian shirt Laurie had given to him so long ago that it seemed like something from another life.

Tarnished lamps from an old mine shaft hung from the restaurant's ceiling, casting pools of dim yellow light on rough wooden walls decorated with pickaxes and dented tin miner's helmets.

"You look good, Laurie."

She sat across from him wearing a white summer dress with a scooped neck that exposed the freckled tops of her breasts. Her long blond hair was tousled from driving with the convertible top down.

"I wish I could return the compliment," she said. "But you look exhausted."

"It's work. It's a little crazy lately."

"But you're liking it?"

He nodded. "It's been interesting."

The waitress asked them if they wanted to start with drinks, and Will ordered a bottle of Clos Pegase chardonnay.

Laurie gave him a look. "Are you supposed to be drinking?"

He gave her a smile. "Only on special occasions."

When the bottle of wine arrived, they clinked their glasses together.

"So, have you been seeing anyone up here?" Laurie asked.

"You mean, like *dating*?"

She nodded.

"The last time I was inside a woman was when I visited the Statue of Liberty."

She laughed, brushing the hair back from her eyes. "You just come up with that?"

Will shook his head. "Woody Allen, *Crimes and Misdemeanors*. What about you?"

"There's this cute guy in one of my yoga classes," she said. "He keeps asking me out."

"What'd you say?"

"I turned him down."

"How come?"

"I don't know," she said. "I keep telling myself I should wait, until after the divorce is final."

Will took a long sip of the wine. When the waitress came back, Laurie ordered the filet mignon, cooked medium. Will didn't feel all that hungry anymore, but went with the roasted chicken.

Laurie looked around at the other diners. "I expected this town to be different."

"What do you mean?"

"You know, like *Mayberry RFD*. More friendly, people stopping by the table to say hello to their beloved sheriff." She used her head to indicate the tables behind him. "They're practically glaring at you."

Will looked and saw that she was right.

He decided to tell her everything. He started with his first day in Haydenville, trying to convey what he had felt looking down at the body of Caitlyn Johnson lying beside the river, then worked his way to the present. When he was done he felt depleted.

Laurie looked at him. "Why are you doing this to yourself?"

"Doing what?"

"Putting yourself through this. You're risking your life, for what?"

"Who else is going to do something?" Will gestured out at the other tables. "*Them?*"

"So why is it your problem?"

He tried to find the right words to explain it to her but found that he could not. "It's my job."

"Lots of people have jobs, Will. They go to work, they come home, they have a life."

He refilled their glasses from the wine bottle but didn't say anything.

"Can't you even see it?" she said. "You had a wife that loved you. You had a child who worshipped you. And you threw it all away. For your *job*."

They sat in silence until the food arrived. Laurie sliced into her steak but didn't try it.

"Something wrong?" he asked.

"It's undercooked."

Will looked at it. "You sure? It looks pretty good from here."

She turned the plate around so that he could have a better look. "It's bloody."

He managed to get the waitress's attention and sent the steak back. Laurie told him he should go ahead and start eating, but he waited.

"You ever miss L.A.?" she asked him after her plate returned from its trip to the kitchen.

"Sometimes. But I think I needed to get away." Will used his fork to push the mound of mashed potatoes around the plate. "When I was there, everything reminded me of him. I mean, I'd drive by the Tar Pits and I'd start to cry."

"Is something so wrong with that?" She was looking at him. "With crying?"

"Given the choice, I'll take laughter every time."

The corners of her mouth turned downward, as if he had somehow disappointed her. "You never cried," she said. "Not even at the funeral."

He remembered how, in the days after Sean had died, he had obsessively begun compiling a mental list of all the things he would no longer be able to do with his son. Among the items on this list were:

I won't be able to take him to the playground anymore.
I won't be able to read him stories anymore.
I won't be able to see him smile anymore.
I won't be able to hold him anymore.

He looked at her across the table and said, "People deal with things in different ways."

"You can't keep hiding from your feelings, Will. It just creates bigger problems down the road." Her eyes seemed larger now, the blackness of the pupils liquid. "I'm not saying you should wallow in them. I'm just saying you need to accept them."

He drained the wine that was left in his glass. "Do me a favor?" he said. "You think maybe you could spare me the yoga psychology?"

He regretted speaking the words as soon as he heard them leave his mouth, her head jerking backward, as if she'd been slapped.

He tried to think of what he should say. How to tell her that he hadn't meant it, how much he needed her, how his life felt when she wasn't in it. But then the waitress walked over to the table and handed them dessert menus. Laurie set hers facedown on the tablecloth, not bothering to look at it.

"You don't want any dessert?" he asked.

She shook her head and told him that she didn't want anything else, only to go to sleep.

THIRTY-NINE

Will drove along Main Street, lawn sprinklers casting lazy circles of water that sparkled in the early morning sunlight.

He'd gotten up at first light, dressed and made a pot of coffee. He left a note for Laurie on the counter, apologizing for his behavior last night at the restaurant.

He shifted around on the driver's seat of the station wagon, trying to get comfortable, his back muscles in spasm from his sleepless night on the worn-out springs of the sofa bed. He saw a green Forest Service truck coming the other way, and he raised his hand to wave. As they passed, he spotted Mike Lopez behind the wheel, the other man's eyes widening in recognition.

When he reached the next block, Will heard a car horn honking. He looked in the rearview and saw that the Forest Service truck was now behind him, Lopez gesturing for Will to pull over.

The gas station was up ahead. Will turned into the lot and parked. A rusted metal sign hung from the side of the building, a red horse with wings sprouting from its back. The Forest Service truck pulled in beside him, and Lopez walked up to his window.

"Just the man I wanted to see," Lopez said. "Saved me a trip down to the department."

"What's going on?"

Lopez took some xeroxed flyers from an aluminum clipboard and passed them to Will. "Take some of these. Let me know if you hear anything."

Block letters along the top of the flyers spelled out:

OVERDUE HIKER

Beneath there was a black-and-white photograph, obviously taken from a driver's license, of a bearded white man who looked to be in his early thirties.

Will reached down and turned off the engine. "Where was he headed?"

"According to the wilderness permit he filled out, out to Mosquito Lake. That's a sixteen-mile hike each way."

Will set the flyers on the seat beside him. "We'll be sure to keep an eye out, Mike."

Lopez nodded. "This guy, he's already five days overdue. He could have broken a leg, be lying out there somewhere."

"I understand. If we hear anything, I'll let you know."

Will restarted the engine, but Lopez didn't remove his hand from the door. "I'm getting a lot of heat from my supe."

"How come?" Will asked.

Lopez took out a slender brown cigar with a white plastic tip. He removed the cellophane wrapper, crumpled it into a ball, and stuffed it into a pants pocket. "This is the second hiker who's gone missing out there this month."

"Where'd you find the other one?"

Lopez fitted the plastic tip of the cigar into his mouth. "We haven't," he said.

FORTY

At lunchtime, they all gathered in the conference room.

It was Thomas's twenty-first birthday, and Will had asked Lila to order a pizza to celebrate the occasion.

The fluorescent lights were switched off, the room bright from the midday sun streaming through the tall windows. They sat around the big wooden table, Will and Thomas and Lila, sipping Mountain Dew out of foam coffee cups. Thomas was wearing his full dress uniform, the brass name bar pinned to his breast polished and gleaming.

"While we're waiting for the food, we've got something for you," Will said.

He reached beneath the table and came up with a clumsily gift-wrapped present, the paper patterned with colorful balloons floating in a cyan sky. He slid it across the table to Thomas.

Thomas ripped the paper from the present, revealing a six-pack of Anchor Steam.

"Congratulations," Will said to him. "Now you're legal."

Thomas smiled, holding up the beer. "Can we drink some now?"

"They're warm, T," Will said.

Thomas stood up and shook Will's hand, then bent over and gave Lila a chaste kiss on her cheek. "Thanks, guys."

"I just hope we're not leading you down the road to perdition," Will said.

The pizza was delivered by a teenaged boy with a bad case of acne. He pulled the cardboard pizza box from an orange vinyl carrier designed to keep it warm. Will counted out some bills from what little was left of his personal funds and handed them to the delivery boy.

"Enjoy," the kid said before he turned and left them.

Lila passed out paper plates and squares of paper towels, then opened the pizza box. Steam rose from it, along with the scent of tomato sauce and oregano. Will's stomach started to rumble, but he sat there sipping his soda, waiting for Lila and Thomas to take what they wanted first.

Lila picked up a wedge of the pizza but then stopped, not moving to set it down on her plate. She stood there, frozen in place, staring down into the pizza box, the color draining from her face.

Then her fingers let go, the slice of pizza falling to the wooden floor. Her mouth opened and she began to scream.

Will went to her and placed his hand gently on her shoulder. She jumped as if she had been struck by a cattle prod. She continued to scream, her arms hugged around her chest.

Will looked down into the box. The pizza was covered with a layer of sliced sausage, exactly what he had asked her to order. He moved his face closer, seeing now that one of the pieces of meat was different than the others. It was longer, lighter in color, creased with wrinkles.

At its tip was a yellowed thumbnail, a thin crescent of dirt trapped beneath the edge.

FORTY-ONE

Will crashed through the front door of City Hall, scrambling down the stone steps and out onto the sidewalk.

The sunlight blinded him. He lifted one hand to shield his eyes while he used the other to fumble his sunglasses from his shirt pocket. He pushed them onto his face and scanned the sidewalk for the pizza delivery boy.

A handful of people moved at a lethargic pace in the shimmering heat, but the pizza guy was not among them.

Hanging from the front of the hardware store was an old thermometer that advertised Dad's Root Beer, the red column of mercury hovering at a hundred degrees. Will had started to turn back inside when a flash of orange caught his eye, and he saw the boy emerge from the hardware store, the now empty vinyl warming bag held at his side.

Will began to run toward him. He'd worn his cowboy boots to work, and he now regretted the choice, the hard leather heels sending jolts of pain shooting up his shins.

"*HEY,*" he shouted.

The delivery boy turned and watched Will coming toward him. For a fleeting moment, their eyes locked.

Then the boy dropped the orange bag and took off in a sprint down the sidewalk.

Will chased after him, the Mountain Dew heavy inside his stomach, the sound of his footfalls reverberating off the sides of the brick buildings. He yelled at pedestrians to get out of his way, but they froze in place, watching him come, almost as if they were trying to create an obstacle course.

Where the hell is Thomas? Will looked around for him, but he was nowhere in sight.

The pizza boy reached the end of the block and turned left, cutting across the street in front of a honking pickup truck, then running away down Gold Street.

Will jumped out into the street to follow, looking up just in time to see the grill of a logging truck bearing down on him, the chrome ornament of a bulldog gleaming in the sun. He jumped back, then stood waiting on the sidewalk as it thundered past, its slipstream fluttering his clothes, his face peppered by bits of redwood bark.

The pizza boy was passing the drugstore. Will ran as fast as he could, the air hot and dry on his throat, but the kid was twenty-five years younger and ran like a track star.

At the corner, the boy hesitated for a moment, then turned right, onto Court Street. Will was a half block behind him now.

Will knew that Court Street would begin to head uphill, making for difficult running. He guessed that rather than dealing with the hill, the boy would opt for the flatter route and would hang his next right, onto River Street.

Will had been inside the drugstore before, knew that the building spanned the block, backing up onto River Street. He thought that if he could cut through the store fast enough, he might just be able to head the boy off.

*　*　*

Chromed bells suspended by a red ribbon hung from the door of the drugstore, jangling as Will shouldered it open.

Chilled air from the air-conditioning blasted him in the face. Shoppers, most of them elderly, turned toward him, clutching boxes of Kleenex and bottles of cough medicine. The store was long and narrow, with a counter at the far end. Behind it was an elevated platform lined with shelves holding bottles of prescription medication.

Will fought his way down the cramped aisle, trying to squeeze his way around the shoppers. His shoulder brushed against a shelf, and he heard the sound of glass smashing against the floor.

The druggist stepped to the front of the platform, looking down at Will. He wore a blue smock with his name embroidered onto the fabric in red thread. Will recognized him; the man had filled his prescriptions for Vicodin.

"What are you doing?" the pharmacist asked.

Will flipped open his badge holder and held it up. "Police. Where's your back door?"

"Why? What's wrong?"

"Just show me where it is."

The druggist led him into a dim storeroom filled with cartons of adult diapers, aluminum crutches and canes, and a leaning stack of bedpans.

The rear exit was a gray steel fire door with a metal push bar across it. Beside it was a grime-coated window, black security bars mounted on the outside.

Will looked out onto River Street. The sidewalk was empty, sunlight exploding off the windshields of cars parked along the curb. Will cursed to himself, afraid that he had guessed wrong, that the boy had chosen to head up Court Street after all.

The pharmacist cleared his throat. "Do you mind telling me what this is about?"

"*Quiet.*"

Will heard the boy before he saw him, the slap of his sneakers against the sidewalk. Will pressed his face against the glass and watched the boy running full-out toward the drugstore, his face flushed with exertion.

Will moved to the door and placed his palms against the push bar. He closed his eyes, concentrating on the sound of the approaching footsteps, trying to visualize the boy's progress.

When he thought the timing was right, Will threw himself against the door.

The door flew open. Will set his boot heels against the sidewalk and braced himself just as the door bucked hard against him, and he heard the grunt of pain as the boy slammed into the other side.

FORTY-TWO

The pizza boy clawed at the sidewalk, struggling to get back on his feet.

Will jumped on top of him, straddling the kid's chest. The boy was wiry and hard to pin down, flailing his arms and legs as he struggled beneath him.

"Get off me," he said.

Will managed to grab the kid's biceps and leaned down hard, pinning them against the sidewalk. "Why'd you do it?" he asked.

"Do *what?*"

"You put something on the pizza. *Why?*"

The kid continued to struggle. "I didn't do anything."

Will could feel the heat of the sidewalk coming through the thick fabric of his jeans, as if he were kneeling on top of a griddle. "If you didn't do anything, why'd you run?"

"You ran at *me*. It freaked me out."

The pharmacist stood framed in the doorway, watching, as if trying to choose sides.

"There was something on that pizza," Will said. "You've got three seconds to tell me who put it there."

"Not me, I swear. All I do is take the box off the counter and deliver it."

The kid's eyes were maybe two feet from his own, wide and white in his acne-covered face. The boy seemed scared, but it wasn't the fear of a criminal afraid of being caught.

The boy was scared of *him*.

Will started to ask the kid another question, but then stopped himself, recognizing that the boy was probably telling the truth.

Will had the urgent feeling that he was in the wrong place. He needed to get to the pizza restaurant. But what was he supposed to do with the kid? He didn't want to just let him go.

Where the hell is Thomas?

Will spotted a cast-iron pole standing across the street, in front of the library. At the top of it, a California state flag sagged in the dead air. Will pulled the kid up, marched him across the street, and sat him down with his back against the base of the flagpole. He had the kid place his hands behind him, wrapped around the pole, and zipped a plastic Flex-Cuf tight around the boy's wrists.

He tugged on the cuff, checking that it was secure.

Then he ran off toward the pizza place.

A plastic sign hung in the glass front door of the pizza restaurant. A single word, in red letters: CLOSED.

Will stared at it, standing out on the hot and bright sidewalk, struggling to catch his breath.

He noticed a small gap at the edge of the door. He pushed against the metal handle, the door making a scraping noise as it swung inward.

"*Hello?*"

No answer. Nothing moved except for an oscillating fan that

stood on top of the Formica counter, pushing around a warm breeze. The air held an unpleasant smell that Will couldn't quite identify.

The overhead lights were turned off, but the electronic cash register was still on, green electronic numerals frozen on the display. A backlit menu board mounted on the wall made a buzzing sound. He went behind the counter. A long wooden prep surface held plastic containers of grated cheese and various pizza toppings.

The sole of his boot slipped on the floor. He looked down and saw that he had stepped into a large puddle of spilled tomato sauce. He tugged a sheaf of paper napkins from the dispenser on the counter, then bent to wipe off his foot. When he looked at the napkin, he saw that it was saturated with blood.

Will stood there, staring down at the puddle of blood, trying to figure out where it had come from. He reached down to his hip, feeling for the checkered grips of the pistol, but the gun wasn't there. He realized he'd left it back at the office, inside his desk drawer.

A stainless steel door stood next to the pizza oven. Will pressed himself flat against the wall, then reached out and pulled on the handle.

He stuck his hand through the door and felt around until he found the light switch. He flipped it on to illuminate a storeroom, metal shelves lined with industrial-sized cans and plastic jars. He squatted to inspect the concrete floor, but there was nothing there.

As he was leaving the storeroom, Will heard the scraping sound of the front door opening, and he dropped to his knees behind the counter.

He listened to footsteps clicking toward him across the floor. He reached up, feeling along the top of the prep counter, searching for something that might serve as a weapon. His hand closed on a plastic handle. He pulled it down and saw that he was holding a spatula. He put it back and grabbed something else, something with a pleasant heft to it.

A butcher's cleaver.

Will jumped to his feet, the blade of the cleaver poised just in front of his shoulder.

A short man stood in front of the counter. He wore a pith helmet and a pair of blue walking shorts. A satchel hung from his shoulder, the profile of a bald eagle embroidered onto the flap.

"Who are you?" the postman asked.

"Police. I'm looking for somebody who works here."

"You mean Tony?"

"I guess." Will put the cleaver down. "Do you know where he is?"

The mailman looked at his watch. "It's lunchtime. Should be here."

"Except he's not."

The mailman reached inside the satchel and put a pile of envelopes and a copy of *Time* on the counter. From his side of the counter he couldn't see the blood on the floor. "I'm sure he didn't go far."

Will watched the mailman leave, then looked down and studied the puddle of blood, trying to figure out where it had come from. The soft hiss of gas came from inside the pizza oven. He went over to it and placed the palm of his hand against the steel door, immediately jerking it back from the searing heat.

Will grabbed the oven's handle and swung the door downward. A cloud of acrid smoke escaped, and he was now able to place the odd smell he had noticed earlier. Will reached out and took hold of the edge of the prep table to steady himself.

The man stuffed inside the pizza oven was wearing a soiled apron, a white paper hat still perched on top of his head. His throat had been sliced open by a sharp instrument.

The space inside the oven was narrow and cramped and the body had not been able to fit inside it in one piece.

FORTY-THREE

Thomas's lunchbox was sitting on top of his desk, but he wasn't anywhere in sight.

Will decided to just go ahead and process the pizza delivery kid into custody himself. Then he'd hustle back to the pizza place to deal with the scene there. When he left it, he'd shut the door and left the CLOSED sign in place, but he sure as hell didn't want anyone else going inside.

He inked and rolled the boy's prints on the booking card, since the department did not have a Live Scan terminal. He photographed him, let him call his mother, then locked him inside the cage.

He found Thomas inside the records room, hunched over an old steel desk that was covered with fingerprint cards.

"You mind telling me where the hell you were?" Will's anger was a physical thing, his heart hammering inside his chest.

"I wanted to get a print off the thumb."

"Why'd you feel the need to do that *now*? You left me chasing that kid all alone."

"I'm sorry." Thomas looked up at him, his face illuminated by the greenish light from the fluorescent gooseneck lamp on the desk. "I just thought you'd want to know whose thumb it was."

"I do, but you know we'll be lucky to hear anything back from the lab before Labor Day."

Thomas shook his head. "No, that's only for latents." He picked up a plastic evidence bag, showing Will the severed thumb. "I just rolled it, like it was still attached to a person."

Will could see where Thomas was headed with this. The state crime lab in Sacramento was backlogged with latent prints waiting to be processed by the small number of technicians qualified to process them. But a scan of the inked print could simply be fed into the lab's AFIS terminal.

"Did you e-mail it to them?" Will asked.

Thomas leaned back in the ancient steno chair. "I didn't have to."

"What are you talking about? Why not?"

"Because I got a match right here."

Will looked around the room, at the tall rows of steel filing cabinets. "*Here?*"

"I got a hit off one of the cards." Thomas picked up a booking card from the desk and held it out to Will along with the fingerprint card he had rolled from the severed thumb. "Looks like a perfect match."

Will looked at the cards, feeling what was left of his energy drain from his body. He studied them for a long time, comparing the two sets of prints, searching to find some point of difference.

But Thomas was right. The print on the booking card was an obvious and perfect match with the thumb.

"Are you all right, Will? You don't look so good."

Will stood there, not saying anything, just staring down at the booking card and its photos of Glen Sexton.

FORTY-FOUR

Will set the empty cardboard box on top of his desk and began to pack up his things.

He tore some sheets of paper from a yellow legal pad and used them to wrap his D.A.R.E. coffee mug, then placed it in a corner of the box. Outside the window, the bells from the church began to peal. When he looked at his watch, he was surprised to see that somehow it was already six o'clock.

And now comes Miller Time.

Will picked up his Shawn Green bobblehead doll, the plastic head of the Dodger gyrating from side to side, as if registering its disapproval. He shoved it down inside the box.

He wanted to clear out his office before calling the mayor to break the news about Glen Sexton's death, be ready to go as soon as she officially gave him the boot. He'd have to beg her to let him stay in the house a little longer, until he could find somewhere else to go.

He'd wracked his brain trying to find a way to put some other spin on the day's events, something he could use as leverage to bargain with her for more time. He couldn't come up with anything.

There was no doubt in his mind that Glen Sexton was now dead. He felt certain that the thumb wasn't some kind of ploy.

If Sexton had been trying to fake his death, he would have cut off some other finger. A pinkie, maybe. People didn't just chop off their own thumbs, since without one your hand was pretty much useless; you couldn't pick anything up. You might as well just whack off your whole hand.

He went to the bookcase and started to pack up his books, thinking that he'd need to take some time, reevaluate things.

Just a few hard knocks.

That's what he'd kept telling himself, these past couple of years, but now he had to consider a more distressing possibility. That perhaps the circumstances were not to be blamed, but only himself. He thought about the wrong turns he'd made, all of his poor choices, an ever expanding list.

He smelled smoke. Out the window he saw that the sky was filled with haze, a forest fire burning somewhere off toward the horizon, the sun a circle of orange flame. He looked down at the brick buildings lining the square and imagined how the town would simply go on without him, as if he'd never even been here.

In his mind's eye, he saw the face of Frank Carver, his spectacled eyes as bright as silver coins, his bearded chest convulsing with laughter.

"Will?"

He spun around to see Thomas standing there in his dress uniform, as if presenting himself for inspection by a commanding officer.

"You okay?" Thomas asked.

"Not a good question right now, T." Will picked up the carton and resumed packing.

"What're you doing?"

"What's it look like?" Will said. "My only shot was getting Sexton back. Soon as the mayor finds out he's dead, I'm finished."

Thomas stood and watched Will pack up his belongings. "Who says she has to find out?"

"What are you talking about?"

"The mayor," Thomas said. "What if we don't tell her?"

"She'll find out eventually."

"Okay, but it buys us some time." Thomas began to speak faster now. "We find the lab, bust the bad guys, and then who gives half a shit about Glen Sexton? At that point, we're frickin *heroes*."

Will looked at him. "We've got a dismembered corpse baking in a pizza oven, T. You really think we can keep that a secret?"

Thomas shook his head. "We don't have to. We tell her about *that*. Just not about Sexton."

Will stopped packing and stared at him. "Don't take this the wrong way. But I think you're completely out of your mind."

"I'm *serious*. What've we got to lose?"

"Me? Not much." Will said. "You, everything."

"Why?"

"It's called a cover-up, Thomas. If you take part in it, she'll fire your ass, too."

"I don't care," Thomas said.

"You should. You get fired over this, where're you gonna go? You willing to just flush your whole career?"

Thomas paced back and forth in front of the desk. "The way I figure it, I owe you. I mean, if I hadn't blabbed to her, you wouldn't even be in this situation."

Thomas stopped pacing and stood ramrod straight. His uniform was spotless, the shirt tucked tightly into his creased trousers, his leather garrison belt heavy with the weight of his duty gear. "What I'm saying? If you're not here, then I don't want to be, either."

FORTY-FIVE

"Something bothering you, Will?"

Laurie sat in the passenger seat of the station wagon. She wore a pair of yoga shorts, one long leg pulled up against her torso, her tanned knee sticking up in the air. Evergreens flashed by the open window behind her, a moving curtain of green velvet.

"No," he said. "Why?"

The car stereo was playing the song "Quiet Heart" from his old Go-Betweens CD. She bent forward and turned it down. "It's just that you seem a little preoccupied."

What was he supposed to say? He hadn't told her about yesterday's events, even though he'd gotten home well after midnight. After he and Thomas had gone back to the pizza place, he'd spent almost an hour on the phone with the state, begging them to lend him a scene tech. They told him they couldn't send anyone all the way out until after the holiday weekend.

So they had secured the pizza place as best they could, and he'd called the mortuary to have the body taken there until he could arrange for an autopsy.

He and Thomas ended up agreeing to keep the truth about Glen Sexton from the mayor. Thomas had phoned Lila at home, asking her not to say anything about the thumb. But, Will knew he had only a short window of time to try and wrap things up before Bonnie found out.

"Just work," he said.

Laurie's blond hair was pulled back into a ponytail, an orange bucket hat set on top of her head. The air inside the car was filled with the coconut scent of her suntan lotion.

"You're not at work now," she said. "You're here, with me."

"I know that," he said.

The north fork of the river flowed clear and cold, carrying snowmelt from high up on the mountain peaks.

The trail clung to the side of it, narrow and hard to follow in places. Will wore a pack filled with the picnic lunch that Laurie had prepared. At one point they were forced to climb over an up-rooted sycamore brought down by a winter storm, its massive roots exposed to the air.

After they'd hiked for over an hour, Will stopped and looked down at the river, studying a spot where the emerald water grew darker with increased depth, creating a swimming hole. They worked their way down to it, Will holding on to Laurie's hand as they descended the steep hillside.

Will went in first, walking across the pebble-covered bottom until it fell suddenly away and he was forced to tread water. He floated there, the current pushing against him, the cool water scouring away the dirt and dried sweat.

He watched Laurie as she stood on top of a boulder and pulled off her T-shirt and shorts. Underneath she wore a bikini patterned with small blue palm trees. The suit's bottom was tied with a bow at the crest of each hip.

She walked toward him, down into the rush of the water. Her body was sculpted from the yoga, different now from the softer, girlish figure he had first unclothed all those years ago. He felt himself growing hard beneath the cool surface of the water, straining against the rough nylon of his shorts.

She was staring at him. "*What?*"

"Nothing," he said.

He looked away, gazing down at his dangling legs and feet, tinted green by the clear water, as if he were viewing them through a piece of sea glass.

They swam together a few yards upstream, their hands slapping the water in front of them, water droplets exploding upward into the sunlight. Then they stopped and let the current carry them backward, to the spot where they had started.

They didn't speak, and Will became conscious once more of the wall that had somehow come to be built between them. He knew that he wanted to tear it down, but had no idea how he might begin to accomplish this task.

They laid their towels out on the sun-warmed surface of a flat rock that was perched above the rushing water.

Laurie unzipped the pack and took out their lunch: grilled chicken sandwiches on sourdough rolls, German potato salad, and plastic bottles of Calistoga.

While they ate, Laurie kept glancing up at the ridgeline.

"What're you looking at?" Will asked.

"Keeping an eye out. For mountain lions."

Will wiped his mouth with a paper napkin. "Do you know what to do? If you run into one?"

She nodded. "I read an article about it. You're not supposed to run away. Because then they see you as prey."

Will nodded. "That's right."

"And you try and make yourself look bigger, by climbing up on a rock or something, spreading your arms. They don't like to attack things that are bigger than they are."

"Do you know the odds?" he asked.

"What do you mean?"

"Of getting killed by a mountain lion?"

She shrugged her bare shoulders. "Pretty low, I guess. But I wouldn't want to try it."

A yellow jacket crawled along a piece of chicken that had dropped onto the surface of the rock, its mandibles working at the meat.

"I could think of worse ways to die," he said.

She stopped chewing. "Like *what*?"

"A plane crash," he said. "Plunging from the sky, but there's nothing you can do about it. It's out of your hands. You get attacked by a mountain lion, at least you can fight back."

He set the remains of his sandwich down on a napkin. "Plus, it's kind of an old-fashioned way to go, don't you think? Like something that would have happened to some homesteader along the Chisholm Trail. Call me a Luddite."

She looked at him, slowly shaking her head. "That's not exactly the word I had in mind."

They packed up the leftovers and then lay back on their towels. Sunlight raked down through the tall pines, the rays made visible by grains of pollen that floated in the still air.

It was quiet, the only sound that of the river running below. Will closed his eyes, the warmth of the sun making his body seem heavy. He heard Laurie move, then felt her head come to rest against his shoulder, the strands of her hair dancing against his skin.

Will came awake with a start, looking around for the source of the noise. In his dream, it had sounded like explosions, one coming after the other. Laurie was already awake, sitting up on her towel. She pointed her finger at something downriver, on the opposite bank.

He saw a group of teenagers dressed in bathing suits. They drank Mexican beer from clear glass bottles. A red plastic cooler sat on the cobbles at the edge of the water.

A shirtless boy crouched down and lifted a heavy stone from the bank and heaved it into the air, out into the rush of the river. The rock crashed into the current, water exploding upward in the shape of a crown.

The boy bowed to his friends with mock gallantry, then removed the cigarette from his mouth and flicked it, the tip still glowing, into the woods.

Will wondered if he should do something. Go over and check their IDs, lecture them about the hazards of forest fires. On the other hand, he didn't want to abandon Laurie.

He watched as another boy picked up a rock and threw it. This one carried farther out, into the center of the channel, its rounded shape catching the sunlight before plunging into the swirling water.

An image appeared in Will's mind for a fleeting instant. He closed his eyes and concentrated on it, seeing now the naked torso of Caitlyn Johnson, the necklace of dark bruises on her breasts and shoulders and back that were as round and perfectly shaped as stones from a river; and then he was up on his feet, shoving the damp towels and Calistoga bottles into the backpack, desperate to get back to the car.

"*Will?*" He heard Laurie's voice as though she were somewhere far away. "Where are you going?"

FORTY-SIX

Smoke drifted from the chimney pipe of the tumbledown cabin, just as it had on the day Will had spotted it from the kayak. It was dusk, but the windows were dark, some of the panes shattered.

He had dropped Laurie off at home before making the trip out here. There had been no direct route; he was forced to drive far to the west, cross the steel bridge, then double back along a gravel road.

The covered porch sagged away from the house, so that Will felt like he was walking uphill as he made his way to the front door. When he knocked, the door swung inward a few inches.

"Hello?" Will called out.

There was no answer from inside. Will knocked again, louder this time. The porch was littered with empty gallon bottles of jug wine.

When no one came to the door, Will used the toe of his boot to push against it, and it swung all the way open.

He stepped inside the cabin. It was dark, and he waited for his eyes to adjust, seeing only shapes.

Snick.

Will froze, recognizing the mechanical sound of a gun's hammer being cocked. He looked in the direction of the sound and found himself staring at the muzzles of a double-barreled shotgun.

He reached for his holster, but a voice in the shadows said, "Don't you *move*."

Will held his hands up in front of his shoulders. A match head flared to life in front of him and the room was illuminated by the yellow glow from a hurricane lamp.

"Give me one good reason I shouldn't pull this trigger," the voice said.

In the lamplight, Will could see that the speaker was old and frail looking, his head topped by a shock of unruly white hair. He held on to an aluminum-framed walker with one hand, the shotgun held low with the other.

"I'm a police officer," Will said.

"That don't give you the right to just waltz in here."

The floor was littered with paper plates covered with dried-up cat food that swarmed with buzzing flies. He could see the cats everywhere, their small eyes glowing from the dark corners of the room.

"The door swung opened when I knocked," Will said.

"You gonna lie to me now?" The old man snicked back the hammer on the other barrel. His eyes were clouded and milky.

Will took an exploratory step to his left, putting his weight down gradually on the floorboard, hoping that it wouldn't squeak. The old man's clouded eyes did not follow him, remaining fixed on the spot that he had just vacated.

"What's wrong?" the old man asked. "You ain't got nothing to say?"

Will took a step forward. He was close to the old man now, near enough to smell the scent of beer on his breath. Will reached out with his right hand and grabbed the long barrel of the gun. He twisted it to break the man's grip, then took it away from him.

The old man made a strangled sound deep down in his throat and raised his hands up to protect his face.

"Relax," Will said. "I just want to ask you a few questions."

"What kind of questions?"

Will eased both hammers of the shotgun back down. His eyes watered from the stench of cat urine and mildew. "Why don't we start with your name?"

"Harold," he said. "Harold Lane. I think I need to sit down."

Will gestured toward the living room's worn furnishings. "It's your house, Harold."

The man pushed his walker across the floor. A plastic tray was attached to the walker, an open can of beer set on top. When he moved, foam rose up through the hole in the can. He collapsed into a ripped recliner, motes of dust rising up into the air around his head.

"What the heck's so important, you come all the way out here?" he said.

"On the evening of May fourteenth, a young woman passed by here, out on the river. She was in a kayak."

"*Kayak?*" He stretched out the syllables, as if learning to speak a foreign language.

"It's like a canoe, but smaller." Will pantomimed a paddling motion with his hands, feeling stupid as he did it.

"Yeah." Harold Lane nodded his head. A piece of toilet tissue with a spot of blood was stuck to the side of his neck. "I seen them things."

Will handed him a color photograph of Caitlyn Johnson. "Did you see this woman?"

Harold scratched at the silvery stubble on his cheek, the eyes above them dull and milky. "Don't see too good no more. Got the *cat-racks*."

"You just said you can see the kayaks, out on the river."

"All depends," Harold said. "Comes and goes. Some days, I can't hardly see nothing at all."

Will's throat was getting scratchy, his allergies starting to kick in. "What about a woman who was in trouble, Harold? Did you maybe see that?"

"What kind of trouble?"

"Like someone was trying to hurt her."

Harold reached out to the tray of his walker and took a long drink from the beer can. "I'm sorry," he said. "I never invited you to sit down."

Will looked over at the stained sofa. It was covered with a thick layer of cat hair. He searched for a spot that looked the cleanest and then sat down.

"Did you see something, Harold?"

Harold Lane's clouded eyes stared at a spot somewhere above Will's head, not blinking.

"What are you thinking about?" Will said. "Just tell me."

"I was listening to one of my books," Harold said. "The state sends them to me on tape. On account of my eyes. I heard something outside, so I got up and turned down the book. That's when I heard all the shouting."

Will felt something brush against his shin. He looked down and saw a large gray cat that had the markings of a raccoon. The cat leapt up onto the cushion beside him and tried to step into his lap. Will attempted to gently move it away, but the cat pushed its head against his hand and began to purr.

Will looked over at Harold Lane. "Go on."

"I got my shotgun," Harold said, "and went out on the porch."

"What did you see?"

"They was killing fish."

"You mean they were fishing," Will said.

"No sir, I don't." Harold shook his head. "I mean they was dumping poison. Into the river. I seen them doing it before. They pull their truck right up to the bank down there and pour it out into the river. Out of a big barrel."

Will remembered a DEA report that he had in the file cabinet back at the office, detailing the environmental hazards of clandestine meth labs. In the appendix was a chart listing the various toxic chemicals they used. It ran to four pages of small type and included potassium cyanide, mercuric chloride, and benzene.

"The fish, they just come floating up on the bank," Harold said. "This one time? Cat ate one, started throwin' up all over the house."

"Harold, what does this have to do with the girl?"

"I just tole you."

"No, you didn't. What did the girl have to do with this?"

"She tried to stop them," Harold said. "Came along in that thing you said, the canoe. Saw them dumping the poison and started to yelling."

The gray cat walked in a tight circle across the top of Will's thighs, then curled up in his lap and shut its eyes. "Then what?"

"They was yelling all kinds of nasty things at her." Harold's face grew animated and he began to shout, reenacting what he had heard. "Like 'hey, *cunt*,' and 'you fuckin *dyke*,' and—"

"I get the picture, Harold."

"They was screaming at her, telling her to leave. But she didn't."

"So what happened?"

"They tried scaring her off."

"How?"

"I don't remember."

"What are you *talking* about? Tell me."

Harold looked down at his lap. "I'm a old man."

"You tell me right now, Harold. Or I swear, I'll arrest you."

Harold continued to stare down at his lap, as if something fascinating were taking place there. His body looked small and childlike, dwarfed by the big recliner.

"Did they throw something at her, Harold?" Will said. As a general rule, he tried to avoid asking a witness a leading question, but he didn't know how else to play it. "Were these men throwing rocks at her, is that how they tried to scare her?"

Harold looked up. "Not hitting her, just into the water," he said. "But she didn't get scared, she just kept on yelling at them. Then they hit her."

"Good, Harold." Will nodded at him. "Go on."

"She turned around and threw her paddle at them. But they just kept chuckin' them rocks. Kept hitting her. Over and over."

"How many men were there?"

"At first, I wasn't too sure." Harold took another swig from the can of beer. "I was afraid I was seeing double."

"What do you mean?" Will asked.

Harold set the now empty beer can on top of the tray, laying it down on its side.

He placed his hands on top of his thighs, bones and veins visible through the thin flesh. "Because the two of them? They both looked exactly the same."

FORTY-SEVEN

The Carver twins sat in the backseat of the department's SUV, their wrists cuffed in front of them.

As he drove, Will stole a glance at them in the rearview mirror. Except for their clothing, he would have been unable to tell them apart. Their faces were latticed by a pattern of shadows cast by the metal safety barrier mounted behind the front seat.

"Yo, *cop*. Wanna tell us what the fuck this is about?" Ike Carver spoke with the exaggerated mannerisms of a black rapper. He wore a New York Yankees cap, his thin chin strap beard running downward along his jawline.

"I need you to watch the language," Will said.

Ike Carver grabbed his crotch and said, "Watch *this,* mothafucka."

Thomas spun around in the passenger seat to face Ike. "Shut the hell up," he shouted.

Will reached over and touched Thomas on the knee to get his attention. "You'll just encourage him, T."

The windows were up, cool air from the air conditioner blowing from the vents. The truck labored to crest a hill, heat mirages rising up off the blacktop.

"I'll tell you what this is about," Will said to Ike. "You're under arrest in connection with the murder of Caitlyn Johnson."

"Never heard the bitch," Ike Carver said.

His twin brother, Trevor, had not said a single word since they'd been picked up. He pressed his face against the window glass, staring down at the river flowing through its narrow canyon.

The road began to descend, winding its way down into the town. Will could feel the heat of Ike's glare on the back of his skull, making the skin crawl on the back of his neck.

"Our pops finds out about this shit, he gonna fuck you up," Ike said.

Will glanced at him in the rearview mirror, their eyes locking. They had taken the twins into custody at their house, but Frank wasn't home.

"I hate to break it to you," Will said. "But I think you've got that the wrong way around."

Back at the station, Will left Thomas to process the twins while he went to check on Harold Lane.

The old man sat at the conference room table, eating from a bag of microwave popcorn and looking at a tattered copy of *Field and Stream*.

"Hang in there, Harold," Will said to him. "Not too much longer."

He wanted to see if Harold Lane could pick the twins out of a lineup. The department did not have a lineup room, so he was going to have the men stand against the wall of the interview room and have Harold observe through the room's two-way mirror.

Standard procedure was to fill out the ranks of the lineup with other prisoners from the jail. Since there were no other prisoners, Will was planning to call upstairs to City Hall and ask for some male volunteers. He checked his watch and saw that he would have to move quickly, since it was almost five o'clock, and everyone would be leaving.

When Will stepped into the hallway, Thomas was standing there waiting for him. He was holding one of the metal lockboxes they used to store the personal items of prisoners booked into custody. "I need to show you something," he said.

"Not now, T." Will tried to squeeze past him.

Thomas blocked his way. "It's about the twins," he said. "I had them empty their pockets—"

"I need you to get to the point, Thomas."

"After they were through, I could see a lump in the pocket. Of the one called Ike."

Thomas opened the lid to the lockbox and reached inside it. "So I just went and stuck my hand inside his pocket, and I found this."

Thomas held up a sandwich-sized ziplock bag.

Will took the bag, looking through the clear plastic at its contents. He felt his breathing stop, conscious now of his heartbeat.

There were two items inside the bag. One of them was a paper matchbook, the cover advertising Kool cigarettes.

The other was a red cardboard tube with a short fuse sticking out from its side, a powerful and illegal firecracker commonly known as an M-80.

FORTY-EIGHT

"Gimme a smoke, yo."

Ike Carver sat handcuffed inside the interview room, the greenish light of the fluorescent fixture making his pale skin look the color of absinthe.

Will sat down across the table from him. "I think you forgot the magic word."

"Fuck you."

Will shook his head. "Not the one I was looking for."

Harold Lane had ID'd both of the twins in the lineup, although not without some difficulty related to his poor eyesight. Will had already spent a frustrating hour attempting to interrogate the other twin, Trevor, but had gotten nowhere. He had refused to say a single word, just sat there at the table staring back at Will.

Now it was Ike's turn.

"Where were you on the night of May fourteenth?" Will asked him.

"Home."

"Can anyone verify that?"

Ike nodded. "Mos def."

"Do me a favor? Knock it off with the Tupac."

"What you mean?"

"I hate to break it to you, *homes,* but you're white. Now, who was with you that night?"

"My pops," Ike said. "We was all there. Kickin' back, watching the box."

"Yeah, what was on?"

"DVD," Ike said. "*Girls Gone Wild.* Some ho clockin' her weasel."

Will opened his mouth to ask what the hell he was talking about, then stopped when he figured it out for himself. "I don't think so. I think you and your brother were at the river, dumping chemical waste from your family's meth lab."

"Good luck proving that," Ike said.

"I already can. I've got an eyewitness who saw you and your brother. You're going away, Ike. The only question now is how long."

A green and black tribal tattoo showed above the neck of Ike's T-shirt, wrapping around his throat like a turtleneck sweater.

"I ain't spooked of doing time," he said. "My pops says it ain't no thing."

"Murder one is a capital crime. We're talking lethal injection."

Ike Carver's expression did not change. He moved his hands up and down in his lap, his hands moving in tandem because of the handcuffs, making the international symbol for masturbation.

Will waited for him to stop and said, "The eyewitness says Caitlyn Johnson caught you and your brother dumping the chemicals. You tried scaring her off. But she didn't get scared, so you and Trevor killed her."

Ike swiveled his head and spat on the floor. "I got two things to say. One, we never dumped nothing in the river. And two, we didn't throw rocks at no cunt."

Will looked at Ike. "Who said anything about throwing rocks?"

Ike held Will's gaze. "Suck my dick," he said.

Will smiled at him. "You know, when you talk like that you sound just like your old man."

Ike glared at Will, the pink skin of his scalp showing through the bristles of his buzz cut.

"Don't be stupid here, Ike," Will said. "The way I see it, you and your brother are just working for your father. It's his lab, the two of you were only following orders, right? Why carry the weight for him?"

"My pops is a writer," Ike said. "The fuck would he want with a *lab*?"

"Knock it off," Will said. "I already know the lab is out in the woods. Help yourself out. Show me where it is."

"Ain't no lab. So how am I supposed to take you there?"

Will took a breath through his nostrils. He could smell Ike's odor, like a goat.

"Why'd you kill the dogs?" Will asked him.

Ike made a snorting sound. "You mean them *strays*? Somebody's got to. Them little niggas out of control, crapping all over."

Ike lifted his hands and placed them on top of the table, the cuffs jangling. "My brother? He had this brand-new pair of Reebok. The first day, they got ruint. He tried cleaning them with a old toothbrush and rubbing alcohol, but they was *toast*."

Will fought the urge to launch himself across the table and wrap his hands around Ike's tattoo-covered throat. He forced himself to remain in his chair, to concentrate on how to elicit a confession.

Every criminal he'd ever interviewed had one thing in common: They all wanted to make excuses. Will thought that if he could offer Ike an excuse, some pretext that allowed him to rationalize his actions, he might be able to get him to admit murdering Caitlyn Johnson.

"Ike, from where I'm sitting, I think you've got a good reason for everything you've done."

Ike looked up at him, a slight smile on his face.

"The way I see it, you and your brother *had* to do these things. You were driven to it by a father who terrified you. Isn't that right, Ike? A father who abused you your whole life, who beat the crap out—"

"*LIAR*," Ike Carver shouted. "You a fucking *liar*. He ain't never beat on us." Spittle flew from his lips, the muscles of his forearms straining against the handcuffs. "We was bad, too. He shoulda beat our ass. But all he ever done was put us in isolation."

"What does that mean, Ike? What's 'isolation'?"

Ike froze, his lips pursed, staring down at his hands.

"C'mon, Ike," Will said. "You expect me to believe you, you gotta tell me. What's *isolation*?"

"It's just what he calls it." Ike nodded his head. "There's this old mine on our land."

"What about it?"

"He locks us down there."

"Down in the mine?"

Ike nodded.

"For how long?" Will asked.

Ike shrugged his shoulders. "Ain't like there's a calendar down there," he said.

FORTY-NINE

Will and Laurie had dinner outside on the patio at a wooden picnic table set beside the flower beds. After they finished eating, they lingered in the warm air, finishing off a bottle of sauvignon blanc.

The sun fell behind the range of mountains off to the west and a fast-moving shadow swept across the valley floor. The sky dimmed and turned the color of eggplant, the waxing moon low, shaped like a sickle.

A citronella candle in a galvanized metal pail flickered on the weathered tabletop, the whiteness of Laurie's teeth glowing in her tanned face. She reached across the rough surface of the table and placed her hand on top of his. Her skin felt smooth and warm, and he found himself trying to remember when he last had human contact.

"It's good to be here, Will." She left her hand there. "Thanks for inviting me."

They cleared the table and carried their plates inside. The two of them stood side by side at the kitchen sink, washing the dishes in the warm and soapy water.

Laurie looked over at the picture of Buddy that was hanging on the front of the refrigerator. "Where are all your pictures of Sean?" she asked.

"I haven't gotten the chance to unpack them yet."

She gave him a look that seemed meant to convey disapproval.

He tried to think of something to say, but was saved when the telephone mounted to the kitchen wall began to ring. Will dried his hands on a dish towel and picked up the receiver. He recognized the voice of Stuart Isgro, the Klamath County district attorney.

"Can we get together?" Isgro asked.

"What's up?" Will looked over at Laurie washing the dishes.

"I'll tell you when you get here," Isgro said.

The house was a large Gothic Revival, with arched windows and ornate bargeboards that ran beneath the eaves. A tall bush stood on each side of the front door.

Will went up the flagstone walkway, the door swinging open before he had the chance to ring the bell. Stuart Isgro wore a pink polo shirt and khaki shorts that were held up by a green belt made of canvas webbing.

"We need to keep it down," he said. "My family's already in bed."

He led Will down a dark hallway and into a study lined with fake wood paneling. A baseball game played on the television set mounted in the built-in bookcase, the Giants taking on the Dodgers down at Chavez Ravine.

Isgro dropped into a leather club chair and pointed at the couch. "Have a seat," he said. He picked up the remote for the television and turned the volume down, but not off, making the play-by-play announcer sound like he was whispering.

"I just got off the phone with Frank Carver's attorney," Isgro said, keeping his eyes on the game as he spoke. "It wasn't a very pleasant conversation."

"Why am I not surprised?"

Isgro picked up a tall glass that contained dark liquid and drank from it. "I've got some good news and some bad news."

Will sat on the couch, waiting for him to continue.

"Well?" Isgro looked at him. "Which do you want to hear first?"

"Just say it."

"The good news is that I got the attorney to agree to plead the twins guilty on the animal cruelty charge."

Will felt his fingernails dig into the upholstered arm of the couch.

"The bad news is we won't be pressing charges on the alleged homicide."

"*What?*" Will said. "And what do you mean, 'alleged'?"

Isgro turned to face him. "I need you to keep your voice down."

"We have a solid case—"

"You don't have a case," Isgro said. "You've got a wing and a god-damned prayer."

"What about the eyewitness?"

"Eyewitness?" Isgro placed his finger against his chin in a mock gesture of contemplation. "Oh, you must be referring to the drunk blind guy."

Will started to speak, but Isgro cut him off.

"Did you honestly believe I'd put him on the stand?" Isgro picked up a file folder from the coffee table and flipped it open, looking at the papers inside. "Do we really want to introduce such damning testimony as—and I quote—'when I first saw them, I thought I was seeing double'?"

"We can't do this." Will sat forward on the couch. "We *cannot* let those two skate."

Isgro watched with interest as the Giants turned a double play on the television. "Frank backed up their alibi. The twins were with him the whole evening of the incident."

"Give me a break," Will said. "He's their father. What else do you expect him to say?"

Isgro turned away from the television and looked at him. "Besides the old guy, do you have any proof that they weren't at home that night?'

"No, but—"

"Do you have any physical evidence I could use at trial?"

"Like what?" Will asked.

"A murder weapon always comes in handy."

Will stared at him. "She was killed by a *rock*. It's probably somewhere at the bottom of the river. How the fuck do you expect me to bring you *that*?"

Isgro didn't answer. On the television, the crowd cheered something that had taken place inside the stadium.

Will tried to keep his voice even. "Look, I know you'd prefer to have everything wrapped up with a bow, but you've got more than enough to indict."

"It's not the indictment that concerns me," Isgro said. "It's that pesky twelve ordinary citizens thing."

"I'm sure we'll be able to come up with more evidence as we prepare for trial."

"You're not listening to me," Isgro said. "We're not going to trial. We could end up spending years and hundreds of thousands of dollars only to lose. This way, we get the guaranteed conviction."

"On animal cruelty?" Will said. "What is that, a suspended sentence? Community service?"

"Keep it down," Isgro said. His shorts had crept up on his legs, revealing hairless thighs the color of cooked veal.

"Are you really that fucking lazy?" Will asked. "You can't go to trial, unless you're guaranteed not to lose?"

"I've got the taxpayers' money to think about," Isgro said.

"And your conviction rate."

Isgro stood up. "I think we're done."

"Do not do this." Will climbed up from the couch and stood close to Isgro. "I promise, I'll get you whatever you need for trial. I'm asking you to trust me."

"*Trust* you?" Isgro said. "You mean the way I trusted you with the defendant who escaped? Or like I trusted you with the guy who ate his tongue?"

Will's face was inches away from the other man's. On the wall behind Isgro's head he could see a framed diploma from Golden Gate University.

"Did I ever tell you I went to law school?" Will asked.

"You've got a J.D.?" Isgro seemed skeptical.

Will shook his head. "I dropped out."

Isgro grinned. "Too tough for you?"

"No," Will said. "I realized that I hated lawyers."

FIFTY

Late that night, an owl began to call from somewhere deep inside the forest, the sound loud and mournful inside the house. Will turned over on the thin and lumpy mattress of the sofa bed, the living room silver with moonlight.

The windows were wide open, but it was hot inside the room. He squeezed his eyes shut, willing himself to return to sleep, but the thoughts were coming without pause in his head. After some more time had passed, he realized that he was fooling himself, that there would be no more sleep for him that night.

He threw off the damp sheets, rose in the darkness, and dressed. In the kitchen he filled the coffee machine and switched it on. His back was killing him, making it painful for him to stand up straight. He reached a hand up to the top shelf of one of the kitchen cabinets, feeling around until he found the vial of Vicodin he'd hidden from Laurie.

He shook out four of the tablets into his palm. He swallowed them with the coffee, then left the house.

* * *

He turned off the road, his headlights illuminating the talus-covered trail that led down to the river. After a few hundred yards it turned to sand, and Will grew worried that the wheels of the station wagon would get stuck. He pulled off to the side, got out, and walked toward the sound of the rushing water.

The sky had started to brighten, reflecting off the sun-bleached rocks protruding upward from the water, the current turning white and agitated where it was forced to move around them.

He imagined her moving down the river in her small boat, the tall trees tinted crimson by the veil of blood streaming from her scalp, the world beginning to grow dim, as though an unseen hand were turning down a rheostat.

He thought about her parents, saw them sitting inside their darkened house, framed pictures of Caitlyn hanging on the walls. The two of them sitting together but not talking, just as he and Laurie had done after Sean died, staring endlessly into the fireplace or out the window.

There was a loud splash, and when he looked out into the riffles he saw a steelhead rise and break the surface of the water, becoming momentarily airborne, its iridescent body scattering the light.

Will walked along the bank, counting the stones as he went. He tried to guess how many of them there were along this stretch of the river. He looked down through the clear water and saw the smooth rocks that lay at the bottom, like prehistoric eggs, speckled and gray and dun colored.

Was it one of these stones that had struck Caitlyn Johnson high up on her forehead, causing the wound that had brought about her death?

Maybe he was staring down at it right now, watching the water course over it, scouring away any remaining trace of her blood.

Will looked up when he heard the sound of a car, the tires making a popping sound as they passed over the rocks of the trail.

He glanced at his watch and saw that it was just after six thirty, wondering who else would be coming down here at this hour. The vehicle's chrome grille emerged from behind the screen of willows, and Will recognized the truck even before he saw the light bar mounted on its roof.

Thomas dropped from the driver's side and walked around the hood. Will couldn't help but grin as he watched him approach. He looked like a boy dressed up in a costume, the gun and collapsible baton and radio and handcuffs that hung from his belt all jostling against his pants as he walked.

"What brings you out here, T?"

"Saw you from up on the road," Thomas said. "Doing some fishing?"

Will shook his head. "Just needed someplace I could think."

"Did it work?"

Will looked away, at the rush of the river. Then he filled Thomas in on his conversation with Stuart Isgro.

Thomas paced back and forth on the cobbles as he listened. "That's not right," he said. "That's just not *right*."

"Welcome to the real world, T."

Thomas stood there, his right hand resting on the butt of his gun. "Let me ask you something, Will. You have any doubt the twins are guilty?"

Will thought for a second. "No."

"You have any doubt Frank Carver is behind the lab?"

Will wondered where this was going. "No. But what's your point?"

The radio on Thomas's belt began to crackle. Thomas turned down the volume knob. "You know that meth we took off Glen Sexton?"

"What about it?"

"It's still in the evidence lockup," Thomas said. "We could just plant it somewhere in Frank's house. I mean, what's to stop us?"

Will couldn't believe he was hearing this. "The law, for one."

Thomas kicked at one of the stones with the toe of his polished black shoe, sending it skittering out into the river. "It's the *law* that's fucking us here."

"It's still our job to enforce it, Thomas," Will said. "We don't get to pick and choose."

FIFTY-ONE

Tuesday was the Fourth of July.

Will and Laurie rose early and walked to the square to stake out spots to watch the parade. The sidewalks were already crowded with families, children waving miniature American flags in the hot sun.

The air smelled of suntan lotion and frying oil from the doughnut stand that had been set up on the lawn of the square. Red, white, and blue bunting hung from the brick buildings, the jagged backdrop of the mountains rising behind them.

Inside the wooden bandstand, a public address announcer began speaking into a microphone. "Ladies and gentlemen," he said, "please welcome the Haydenville Volunteer Fire Department."

A Klaxon sounded, and an antique fire engine rolled around the corner, waxed red paint and gleaming chrome. The crowd began to cheer as the truck rolled past, the firemen tossing wrapped pieces of penny candy out to the children.

Will stood there in the bright light, seeing the parade pass by in a series of snapshots.

The sun reflecting off the brass bell of a French horn, the bare legs of a cheerleader turning cartwheels down the yellow line of the street and an overweight man in a fez driving a miniature car. A woman on horseback waving a California state flag, and a mallet being twirled in the air before striking the skin of a bass drum. A group of bagpipers wearing knee socks and green tartan kilts. A boy in a red plastic fire hat eating from a paper cone of cotton candy.

"This is so cool," Laurie said, clapping her hands together.

A spearmint-colored vintage convertible turned the corner. Bonnie Newman sat perched on the deck behind the rear seat, holding a red parasol. Her arm waved back and forth mechanically at the crowd, a smile frozen on her face, the sun hot on the sidewalk.

"Ladies and gentlemen," the PA announcer said, "the mayor of Haydenville, the Honorable Bonnie Newman."

Will heard someone calling out his name and turned to see Thomas standing at the curb, wearing his dress uniform.

"Hey, Laurie," Will said. "I'd like you to meet Thomas."

Thomas brought his hand up and doffed the brim of his hat. "T," he said. "That's the nickname Will gave me."

Laurie smiled at him. "It's nice to meet you, T."

"Good parade," Thomas said.

"Yes." Laurie smiled. "Too bad Will's making you work."

"It's fine," Thomas said. "I like my job."

"What does your family have to say?" Laurie asked.

"No complaints." Thomas looked down the sidewalk at the crowd. "Well, I better get back to work. Nice meeting you, Mrs. Magowan."

"Laurie," she said. But Thomas had already waded into the crowd, motioning for people to keep out of the street.

Laurie turned to Will. "He's cute."

"A little young for you, don't you think?"

"That's not what I mean," she said. "I don't know, he reminds me a little of you."

"*Me?*"

"It's hard to describe," she said. "Just his manner, the way he carries himself. It's almost like he's trying to impersonate you. You don't see it?"

He shrugged. "If you say so."

Laurie's hand brushed against the side of his leg, and Will reached down and took hold of it. Her fingers wrapped around his.

A jacked-up truck came around the corner of the square and the crowd began to applaud.

"And now," said the PA announcer, "would you please welcome Haydenville's very own poet laureate, world-famous author Frank Carver . . ."

Will watched as a heavyset woman in a pink tube top jumped up and down, clapping her hands together in the air above her head.

The monster truck rolled toward them on enormous studded tires, its exhaust thick with burning oil. Frank Carver sat in the truck's bed on a folding chair, his white beard piled on his chest. The twins flanked him, throwing candy out into the street. Children darted out from the crowd and scrambled to pick up the pieces.

As the truck rolled past, Frank Carver looked down at Will, his head swiveling, the sun reflecting off the lenses of his eyeglasses like twin flames.

High above the street, the huge neon miner hung from the front of the Dig Inn, as if taking in the scene.

Will turned to Laurie. "Let's get out of here."

She seemed disappointed. "It's not over."

He tugged on her hand. "I've had enough."

FIFTY-TWO

That night, they went to watch the fireworks.

Sawhorses had been set up around the infield of the softball diamond, pyrotechnic equipment arranged on the dirt around home
plate. Will spread out a rough wool blanket on the grass in left field.
They drank white wine and watched the sky darken.

The outfield grew crowded with blankets, the people showing up
now spilling beer as they staggered through the twilight holding plastic cups. Will recognized some of their faces from the Dig Inn.

People began to trample across their blanket. Will sat up, worried that someone was going to step on Laurie. She hugged her knees
to her chest, staring up at their skeletal frames and greasy hair, her
eyes taking in their bad teeth and facial scabs and crudely rendered
tattoos.

Will reached out and put his hand on her shoulder. She turned to
him, the troubled expression on her face feeling like a silent accusa-
tion. He took his hand away, overwhelmed by the enormity of his
failure.

When the sky grew dark enough, there was the sound of an explosion, and a rocket streaked upward into the night. It erupted in a shower of phosphorescent blue sparks, the air so clear that it looked as if he could reach out and touch them.

Will lay back on the scratchy fabric of the blanket, his head close to Laurie's. He could smell the grass and the clean smell of her shampoo. The launcher fired three times, and in the blackness of the sky fireworks bloomed like chrysanthemums.

She took his hand and said, "Sean would have loved this."

Couldn't she go even a day without bringing him up? He had always refused to let himself dwell on Sean's death the way she had; he categorized it under the general heading of *wallowing*, considered it pointless

(i wasn't there——)

and knew that he had to be vigilant, because the thoughts were always there, a song playing inside his head that he refused to sing

(i wasn't there——)

He started to shove the thought from his mind, forcing himself to look back up into the sky, to watch the fireworks exploding in the night, but could no longer see them now, could see only the pair of blue eyes.

Sean sits in the baby jogger in the living room of the house in Van Nuys, his blue eyes filling with tears.

"Hold on, baby," Laurie says. She grabs her house keys off the console table, trying to gather the things she needs to leave the house. Her head is pounding from being up with him for most of the night. She wonders if he's coming down with a cold.

She picks up the cordless phone and dials Will's cell. He's been away from home for two days now working a big case, but he's supposed to be back today. His number once again rolls over to voice mail, and she hangs up, not wanting to leave another message.

Sean begins to cry, his face blotchy with tears. She goes to the dining room table and picks up her bag, but then hesitates. She hates carrying it while trying to push the baby jogger, the strap always slipping down from her shoulder.

She begins grabbing the things she thinks she'll need from the bag. She takes out her wallet, her change purse, the keys to the station wagon. She transfers them to the pocket on the back of the baby jogger and then starts back to her bag for another load.

When she starts to walk away from Sean, his shrieks rise an octave. Her head is splitting; she can't think. There are more things in the bag that she should probably be taking, but the screams are too much for her to bear.

"All right, Sean," she says. "Here we go." She swings open the front door and pushes the stroller out into the overcast morning.

She drives to Griffith Park and parks in a lot near the Greek Theater. She unbuckles Sean from his car seat and sits him in the baby jogger. She pushes him along a wide dirt trail lined with chaparral, the sun beginning to burn through the layer of fog. She hopes that when Will finally gets home he'll call her cell phone, that he'll come and meet them here. Maybe they can all have lunch together at the Trails Café.

The trail zigzags up the hillside toward the observatory, harder work now to push the baby jogger. It's early October, the grasses parched and brown from the long dry season. The trail is dry, dust rising up with each of her footsteps.

Sean starts to fuss, so she pushes the stroller faster to try to distract him. They're all alone now, like being in the middle of the wilderness. Then the trail makes a turn, and she can look down at the white stucco houses of Hollywood far below, basking in the sunlight.

Sean begins to cry in earnest. She keeps pushing the stroller, hoping he'll stop. She wishes she'd taken more of the Motrin before leaving the house, her head caving in.

Sean's wails have become shrieks, so intense that it's as if he's being tortured. Laurie reaches down and strokes his hair, but he only wails louder. She stops pushing and kneels down in front of the stroller. Sean's face is crimson, his mouth gasping for breath between the shrieks. She doesn't know what's wrong with him; he's never acted this way before.

"It's okay," she says. "Everything's fine."

She picks him up and holds him but cannot get him to stop crying. She sets him down on his feet, and he screams even louder. He holds up his hands to her, like he does when he wants her to pick him up. When he takes a step toward her, he seems to limp.

She bends down and sees that his left ankle has become swollen, the skin piled in thick rolls, the leg of an elephant.

"Did you hurt yourself?" she asks him.

She gently presses her thumb against the swelling. When she takes it away there is a white thumbprint, surrounded by a field of red. She can't figure out how he might have injured himself; he's been strapped into the stroller the whole time.

She runs her hands down along his calf, over the ankle, and when she reaches his foot, Sean arches his back and screams out in pain.

Laurie searches his face. "What is it?"

She unbuckles his tiny sandal and works it off the swollen foot. Something falls to the ground. She bends over and looks into the dry grass, sees a yellow jacket turning in slow circles on its back, its mandibles working at the air.

Sean's foot is enormous. She can see white bands where it has been encased by the straps of the sandal. To her alarm, she sees the wildfire of redness working its way upward, his knee now the size of a grapefruit.

"Hold on, Sean."

She goes to the back of the stroller, reaching into the pocket for her cell phone. She's scared by the severity of his reaction to the sting and wants to call 911 to be safe.

She digs through the pocket. In her haste, she tosses things out onto the trail.

But then the pocket is empty, and she knows it's not there, that it's sitting at home in her other bag.

She kneels down next to Sean, seeing that his whole left leg is now red and swollen. She tries to lift up the cuff of his shorts to look at the skin underneath, but it has grown too tight from the swelling.

Mercifully, Sean has stopped crying, but his breath now sounds ragged and laborious, with an odd rattling wheeze that she's never heard him make before.

"Sean?" she says. "*Sean?*" His eyes are swollen shut, and she gently lifts one of the lids with her thumb. The eye is completely white, as if he is staring up at something on the inside of his skull.

Sean's lips are now grotesquely swollen, his breathing like someone has slipped a noose around his neck. If Will were here, he would know exactly what to do. He's been after her to take a CPR class, but she told him it was a waste, since he already knew how to do it.

She can see the bronze domes of the observatory up above her at the peak of the hillside. She grabs the handles of the baby jogger and begins to run up the trail toward it. The trail is steep and sweat runs down her body, soaking her clothes.

She rounds a bend in the trail, and the observatory comes into full view. Its exterior is encased by a skein of metal scaffolding, the observatory closed for a renovation. She can see some people moving around on the deck, though, cameras hanging on straps around their necks.

"*HELP ME*," she screams with the last of her breath. But the distance is too great; they don't seem to hear.

She picks up Sean in her arms and runs toward the observatory. Somebody up there will have a cell phone. One of them might even be a doctor, or at least know CPR.

Sean is heavy in her arms. She begins to run out of breath and has to slow down. The observatory seems to be pulling farther away with every step. It's awkward, trying to run up the hill carrying him.

She weighs her choices, then stops and places him down on the dry trail. She sprints away, feeling light and unencumbered now that she is no longer carrying him, her lips moving to the silent cadence of her fervent prayer.

When she is close to the deck of the observatory, she calls out for help. A man's head appears over the wall of the deck. He is wearing a baseball cap bearing the image of Mickey Mouse.

"Help me," Laurie calls up to him. "My son needs an ambulance. Call nine-one-one."

More heads now appear over the wall. "What happened?" An elderly woman asks.

"He got stung by a bee," Laurie says. "He's having an allergic reaction. Please just call."

"I'm dialing right now," says the man in the Mickey Mouse hat.

Laurie turns and runs back down the hill toward Sean. A solitary and bare tree rises up from the trail behind his small form. When she reaches him, she sees that his face has turned the color of the sky. He does not move. She falls to the earth, taking him up in her arms, clutching the small and inert body against her chest.

"Here I am," she says, consumed by the thought that she has just left him to die all alone. She squeezes him tighter, inhaling the smell of him, the tears on her face shining.

For some reason, Will sees all of this from high above, as though he is floating in the sky. He watches his wife clutching his only son, the two of them tiny and alone, dwarfed by the sweep of the vast hillside.

He is watching as Laurie's face tilts up toward him, her mouth opening in a silent and anguished scream.

Against the black canvas of sky, the fireworks continued to explode, but they now appeared blurred, as if he were viewing them through a kaleidoscope.

"I'm sorry," Will said.

Laurie lay on her back, looking up. "For what?"

His face felt wet. He was glad for the darkness, so that she couldn't see him. "That I wasn't there."

She turned over on the blanket and looked at him. "That you weren't *where?*"

"With you," he said. "When he died."

She reached out and traced her finger along his cheek, drying the tears.

"I'm sorry," he said again. Somehow, he had never said it before.

"It's not your fault, Will. Bad things happen in life. They just do."

"I could have saved him."

Her lower lip began to tremble, her eyes liquid. "I need you to save yourself."

She wrapped her arms around him. He could hear her heart beating inside her, the fireworks booming up in the sky.

"I'm sorry." He couldn't stop saying it now.

"Do you honestly think that everything that goes wrong in the world is your fault?"

He didn't say anything.

"What were you supposed to do?" she said. "Follow him around every minute of his life?"

"No," he said. "Just that one."

"You've got to stop crucifying yourself over the past, Will. It's gone. It only exists in your mind. The thing that's real is what's happening *now.*"

The fireworks grew more frenzied, the launcher booming, sending one rocket after another streaking into the air, the blackness of the sky blotted out by the explosions of light. The crowd cheered.

Will and Laurie stared up into the night, still holding on to each other. The fireworks stopped, and people began to get up from their blankets. The air was thick with the smell of gunpowder.

Will lifted his head from her chest. "Let's head home."

"I always like the finale," she said. "When everything starts going off all at once. But it's sort of sad, don't you think? 'Cause you can tell it's about to end."

He emptied the wineglasses onto the grass. "I feel beat. I'm glad I already set up the foldaway before we came."

She brushed a fallen lock of hair from her eyes and smiled at him. "I don't think that'll be necessary."

"What do you mean?"

She shook her head. "Are you really that stupid?" she asked. "Or do you just enjoy acting like it?"

FIFTY-THREE

The green car had been behind him ever since he left the station.

It was hard to miss, an old and rusting Plymouth Fury, blue smoke trailing from its exhaust pipe. Perched on top of the radio antenna was a giveaway from a fast-food restaurant, a cartoon head the size and shape of a Ping-Pong ball.

His head was pounding from what had turned out to be a miserable day. The crime scene tech from the state had finally made it out to process the crime scene at the pizza restaurant. She'd lifted dozens of latent prints, then told Will it would take two to four weeks before the lab would be able to process them.

Will was almost home now, but instead of turning onto his street, he hung a quick right onto Pine. He glanced up at the rearview and saw that the car was still there. He tried to get a look at the driver, but whoever was behind the wheel wore dark sunglasses and a baseball cap.

He turned left onto Cedar. A woman wearing a blue bathrobe clutched a garden hose, aiming the stream of water at her parched front yard. Will stepped on the gas, going too fast for the residential street.

The green car stayed with him. He had gone in a circle and was now back at Main. Will put on his right turn indicator and checked the rearview. The Fury's right blinker began to pulse.

He waited for a break in the traffic, then floored it, his tires squealing. The station wagon lurched out into the road. Then, instead of turning to the right, he spun the wheel hard to the left.

Behind him, Will heard the sound of horns blaring, but when he looked up at the mirror the car was still following.

He was now heading back toward the square, could see the big round clock hanging from the side of City Hall. He passed the barbershop, with its pole of rotating red, white, and blue stripes, then turned onto Gold Street. He drove slowly, passing the drugstore and bank.

When he reached Court Street he turned right, going along the side of the restaurant where he had taken Laurie to dinner, then turned right again at River. He slowed, watching the rearview, letting the green car draw closer.

An alley ran alongside the bank building. It was narrow, terminating in a dead end, just wide enough for a single car.

Will turned into the alley, drove a few yards, then mashed the brakes and rammed the gearshift lever into park. He drew his gun from the holster, jacked a round into the chamber, and snicked off the safety.

In the side mirror, he watched as the green car turned into the alley. It came to an abrupt stop, the driver realizing there was nowhere to go.

Will pushed open the car door and rolled out of the car. Using the door as a shield, he raised the gun and pointed it at the driver of the car.

"*Police*," he shouted. "Hands where I can see them."

The driver did as instructed, and Will walked toward the car, holding the gun out in front of him. As he drew closer, he could see that the driver was a woman. Her skin was dark, and even with the sunglasses covering her eyes, she looked familiar.

"Why are you following me?" Will said.

"Following *you?*" When she spoke, Will realized it was the librarian, Ernestine.

"Knock it off," Will said. "What the hell are you doing?"

Ernestine smiled at him. "I wanted to talk to you about Frank Carver."

Will held the gun against his thigh, his finger still resting on the trigger. "So you follow me all over town?"

"I didn't want anyone seeing me, going inside the police station."

"Why *not?*"

"I didn't want people getting the wrong idea. To think I'm helping you."

Will shook his head in astonishment. "I can see where that could be damaging to someone's reputation."

A ventilation hood stuck out from the brick wall of the restaurant like a metal mushroom, blowing warm air that smelled of roasting meat.

Ernestine kept her hands on the steering wheel. "Frank told me all about how you've been hounding him," she said. "How you ripped his house apart, arrested those boys—"

"I don't mean any disrespect," Will said, cutting her off. "But I don't understand why you're here."

She looked at him, still wearing the dark sunglasses. It was dim in the alley, the sun blocked off by the roof of the restaurant. "Did you ever stop and consider the possibility you might be wrong about him?"

"Yes."

"So you admit it." She nodded her head, seeming pleased.

"No," Will said. "I stopped and considered the possibility I might be wrong about him."

"And?"

"Then I looked at the facts, and knew I was right."

"You don't know anything," she said. "You come here, to *our* town, you have the gall to accuse a man like Frank—"

"I think it's time for you to go." Will wondered if Frank had put her up to this. "Nice running into you."

She took off her sunglasses and placed them on the dashboard. "Look at you, standing there with your gun and shield. The word that comes to mind is *hubris*."

Will had to fight the urge to laugh out loud at the absurdity of the situation. "Hubris," he repeated.

"From the Greek," she said. "They considered it a crime. You might want to come by the library and read up on Icarus, see how things turned out for him."

Will looked down at the pavement, shards of green glass from a broken malt liquor bottle lying there. He looked her in the eyes and said, "I think Frank Carver has you completely flimflammed. I think you're worried about your next paycheck, because your whole library is bought and paid for by him."

The skin of her knuckles turned white on the steering wheel. "I resent that."

"So resent it," Will said.

He turned his back and started to walk away from the car. He had taken three steps when the car's horn blared, the sound earsplitting in the brick confines of the alley.

"Don't you even want to see what I found?" she said.

He spun around, his chest constricting with anger. "*What?*"

"When you came to the library, you asked me about Frank's past, remember?"

Will wanted to keep walking but found that he couldn't help himself. He started back toward the Fury.

"After you left," she said, "I went on ProQuest at the library. Do you know what that is?"

He felt the last strand of his patience begin to fray. "Just get to the point."

"Most of the things were about his book, and other things I already knew. But I did find something interesting. I think it'll convince you to stop persecuting him."

She leaned over and began to reach inside her briefcase.

Will raised the gun and pointed it at her. "*Slowly.*"

"You are really something else." She shook her head. "Now you think *I'm* some kind of criminal?"

She handed him a manila envelope that was the size of a piece of photocopy paper. Inside was a printout of an old photograph, the colors rendered in faded Kodachrome hues.

Two men stood at a wooden lectern in front of a velvet curtain the color of an egg yolk. One of the men was handing the other a medal that hung from a ribbon striped with the colors of the American flag.

"I found it mixed in with a whole bunch of other documents that were released as part of a Freedom of Information Act request," she said.

Will could see now that the man receiving the medal was a much younger version of Frank Carver. He wore a plum-colored Nehru jacket, his hair and beard jet black. He smiled out at the camera, the photographer's flashbulb reflected in the lenses of his black horn-rimmed eyeglasses.

The other man was short and fat, his head bald.

Below the photograph was a caption that read:

FBN District Supervisor George Hunter White (l) and Frank Carver (r).

"Now you tell me," Ernestine said, smiling at Will as if she had just turned over her hole cards to reveal a straight flush. "Does that look like a criminal to you?"

"Where's the rest of it?"

She shook her head. "I kept searching, but that's all there was. It seems like it's part of a document, but nothing else was there."

Will stared at the photograph. He knew that FBN stood for the Federal Bureau of Narcotics, the predecessor agency to the DEA. But who was George Hunter White? And why the hell was he awarding a government service medal to Frank Carver?

FIFTY-FOUR

The ornate black iron hands of the clock that hung outside City Hall pointed out that it was already nine thirty in the morning.

Will opened the glass door to the building with one hand, using the other to clutch a travel mug filled with coffee.

After his alarm had gone off he had lingered in bed, he and Laurie making love. The two of them ate breakfast on the patio, discussing what would come next. They agreed that Laurie would extend her visit and stay with him through the weekend.

He grabbed the stair rail and vaulted up the terrazzo steps two at a time. He wanted to get to his desk and do a Google search on George Hunter White, see what he could find out.

Before he reached the first landing, footsteps echoed inside the stairwell, people coming down in what sounded like a big hurry. Will moved close to the railing to give way just as Thomas and Mike Lopez came into view. Lopez wore his faded green Forest Service uniform, the Smokey the Bear hat planted on top of his head.

Thomas was carrying the black equipment case that contained

the department's evidence kit. "I've been trying to get you on the radio all morning," he said.

"It's upstairs in my desk," Will said. "What's wrong?"

Thomas started down the stairs. "You better come with us."

"I can't." Will wanted to get upstairs and fire up the computer. "Where're you guys going?"

Lopez unwrapped the cellophane from one of his plastic-tipped cigars. "Remember that missing hiker?"

Will nodded. "The one from the flyers."

"We think we just found him," Lopez said.

"So what do you need me for?"

Lopez placed the cigar in the corner of his mouth. "Because it appears somebody killed him."

They took the Forest Service truck because it was better equipped for off-road driving. Lopez steered the vehicle down a narrow four-wheel trail in the national forest.

"Leader of some church group called it in to dispatch," he said. "They were out on a backpacking trip. Sounds pretty nasty."

Will sat across from him in the passenger's seat. "Nasty how?"

"Details were real sketchy," Lopez said. "Dispatcher said the caller was pretty hysterical about what he found."

The surface of the trail was pocked with deep potholes from the winter rain. Each time one of the truck's tires hit a bump, the vehicle rattled as if it might fall apart.

Thomas leaned forward from the backseat. "You would think they could get you a better truck."

Lopez kept his eyes fixed on the trail. "This administration hasn't exactly made forests a big priority," he said. "Unless you count trying to chop them down."

As they drove deeper inside the forest, the trail narrowed even more, thorns from huckleberry bushes scraping against the side of the truck, the sound like fingernails on a blackboard.

Will shifted in his seat, irritated that he was being dragged all the way out here on the basis of such limited information. "Other than being hysterical, what else did this guy say?"

Lopez chewed on the plastic tip of his unlit cigar. "Something about a hole in the ground, and a lot of blood."

The trail came to a fork, and Lopez steered the truck to the left. They passed into a box canyon that had been burned in a forest fire, the tall trees blackened and naked. Up ahead, the trail ended at an outcropping of granite boulders.

Lopez brought the truck to a stop and switched off the ignition. "Got to hoof it the rest of the way," he said.

FIFTY-FIVE

They made their way through the fire-scarred forest, Lopez leading the way, none of them saying anything.

The trail began to descend, and Will saw a sudden movement on the ground up ahead. The flutter of primeval wings, two turkey vultures perched at the rim of a hole in the earth.

"Shit," Lopez said.

He clapped his hands together and ran at the birds. The vultures swiveled their featherless heads, regarding the forest ranger with dark eyes. When Lopez was almost upon them, they beat their powerful wings against the air and lifted from the earth, landing on the naked branch of a charred tree.

Will approached the edge of the pit. It was perhaps five feet in diameter, the opening partially covered by tree branches and leaves. On one side of the opening, the cover of foliage was missing.

Will leaned out over the pit and peered down into the darkness.

"Careful," Lopez said.

Will could see something moving around in the darkness at the bottom of the hole, maybe seven feet down. There was a rustling sound, Will pulling himself backward from the opening just as another vulture burst upward from the pit, something dripping and red clutched in its sharp beak.

The bird flew up into the dead tree and began to fight with the other vultures over the carrion.

Will looked at Thomas and made a beckoning gesture with his hand. "Flashlight," he said.

Thomas unholstered a Maglite from his belt and handed it over. Will switched it on, adjusting the lens to throw a narrow beam. He shined the light down into the pit, bracing himself to jump back if there were any more vultures down there.

The beam was weak, and he waited for his eyes to adjust to the darkness. "You need new batteries," he said to Thomas.

He could hear the droning of insects down in the pit, smelled something that was like meat spoiling inside a restaurant dumpster. He moved the flashlight, the anemic yellow light passing over wooden poles that pointed straight up at him.

Will's eyes began to adjust, and he could see now that it was a subterranean abattoir, torn flesh stuck to the sharpened tips of the poles and a pool of blood down at the bottom. The dead eyes of an eviscerated man stared up at him from the darkness.

"What is it?" Thomas asked.

"Punji pit," Will said. He stepped back from the edge. "Vietcong used them in Vietnam. You dig the hole and put the stakes in. Then you camouflage it with branches and wait for some poor bastard to come along."

Lopez's face had taken on the olive coloring of his uniform. Without saying anything, he turned and began to walk toward the truck.

"Where're you going?" Will asked.

"Call the EMTs," Lopez said.

"Don't," Will said.

Lopez turned around to face him. "Why *not?*"

"He's dead. An ambulance isn't going to help him."

Lopez shook his head. "But I need to call it in."

"Not now," Will said. "We don't want them to know we were here."

Lopez looked confused. "Who?"

"Whoever dug this." Will pointed at the pit. "It's a trap. They're trying to keep people away from something."

"Like what?"

"If I was a betting man?" Will picked up a fallen tree branch to re-cover the space in the opening. "I'd say it's our clan lab."

FIFTY-SIX

"How many rangers can you get out here?" Will asked.

Lopez chewed on the plastic tip of his cigar. "When?"

"*Now*," Will said. "We need to organize a search for the lab before they find the body."

"There's only one other guy on today," Lopez said. "Everybody worked the Fourth, the government's trying to cut down on OT."

"We need him out here."

"He's over at the Whiskey Creek substation. That's a good hour and a half from here."

Will scanned the woods surrounding the punji pit. Trying to search the area with just the three of them would be difficult, the chances of missing what they were looking for high. But what choice did he have?

"Let's just do this," Will said. He knelt and drew a circle on the ground with a stick. Then he divided the circle into thirds, so that it looked like a peace symbol.

Will pointed at the center of the circle. "This is the pit. We're going to be searching within a half-mile radius of it. Figure that from here, it's a fifteen-minute walk to the perimeter."

He used the stick to point at the wedges, assigning one area to each of them.

"What exactly are we looking for?" Lopez asked.

"Any sign of a drug lab." Will stood up and tossed away the stick. "A structure of some kind. Look out for discarded chemical containers, plastic tubing, anything that shouldn't be out here."

Will made his way through the burned landscape, the tree trunks as dark as lumps of charcoal.

It made him think of the ending of the movie *Bambi*. He'd rented the videotape to watch with Sean, but his son had been too young for it and had fallen asleep on Will's stomach.

Will reached down and unholstered his gun. He pulled back the slide to chamber a round, flicked the safety on, then slipped it back inside the leather holster. He stepped over the trunk of a fallen oak. The forest floor was littered with detritus from the dead trees, a thick layer of decomposing bark and disintegrating branches.

He'd told Thomas and Lopez that they should walk straight out to the perimeter of their segments, then turn to the right, take ten steps, then walk back to the pit. Given the forested terrain and the abstractly defined segment each of them was searching, he knew that the opportunity for missing something was great. The lab could be out there in any direction.

From the little he knew about search and rescue, Will guessed that it would take close to a hundred searchers to conduct a proper grid search of the area.

He wondered if there was a nearby army base or National Guard facility, somewhere where he could get more manpower. But that would take hours—if not days—to coordinate. They didn't have that much time before the body was discovered.

After a few minutes he came to the edge of the burned area, the forest once again becoming dense and green. It was almost as if the fire had made this part of the woods even more hardy, his view blocked in every direction by massive trunks and leaves and hanging pine boughs.

He looked at his watch and saw that he had been walking for almost fifteen minutes. He went a little farther, then turned to his right and started to silently count off his steps.

He had reached seven when he heard the gunshot.

FIFTY-SEVEN

Will ran through the woods, heading in the direction the shot had come from.

The forest had gone silent, the only sounds coming from his labored breathing. He hurdled a fallen tree, gun in hand, safety on in case he fell.

The trail made a sharp turn, and he saw that someone was standing on the trail up ahead of him. He raised his gun before recognizing that it was Thomas.

Will whispered to him. "You okay?"

Thomas nodded his head. "I found something." He seemed perfectly calm, as if he were out for a hike.

Will stared at him. "*You* fired that shot?"

"I wanted to get your attention."

"Something wrong with your radio?" Will asked, still trying to keep his voice down.

Thomas looked confused. "You told me you didn't have one."

Will let out his breath, remembering that the handheld was back in his desk drawer. He looked around the woods; they had now lost any element of surprise.

He heard footsteps and wheeled around to see Lopez coming up the trail, his face flushed from exertion.

"You guys okay?" Lopez asked them.

"I found a house," Thomas said.

Will looked at Thomas. "What did you just say?"

They crouched at the edge of a small clearing, looking at the building.

Thomas was right. It *was* a house, a small wooden bungalow. Like something you'd expect to see in the San Fernando Valley, not way out here, deep in the national forest. It wore a fresh coat of green paint that was the color of canned peas. Its gabled roof was covered with solar panels. An American flag hung from a pole mounted beside the front door.

"Did you know this was out here?" Will asked Lopez.

Lopez looked at the house and shook his head. "It's not on the maps."

Behind the windows, shades were pulled down so that it was impossible to see anything inside. Off to the left was a small dirt parking area, but no cars were there.

Will rose to his feet. "I'm going to knock," he said.

"You really think that's a good idea?" Thomas asked.

Will looked across the dirt clearing that surrounded the house like a moat. Behind the drawn shades of the house, someone could be watching them, perhaps aiming a gun at his chest.

"I don't know," Will said. "But it's the best one I've got."

Will reached his gun from the holster and snicked off the safety. He looked down at Thomas and Lopez. "You two stay here and cover me."

"I don't have a gun," Lopez said.

"Then act like you do." Will thought that whoever might be inside the house would be less likely to try something if there were three of them out here.

In any event, that was what he was hoping.

FIFTY-EIGHT

He walked through the bright heat of the dirt yard, feeling like a sitting duck. The distance seemed to stretch out in front of him, the green house too far away. Sweat ran down his back.

Eventually he came to a concrete front stoop that was for the most part taken up by a doormat, a pattern of twisted vines surrounding large cursive letters that spelled out the word WELCOME.

He didn't see a doorbell, so he rapped on the wooden surface of the door with his knuckles. Then he took a step backward to increase the amount of time he'd have to react, placed the palm of his hand on the butt of his gun, and waited.

He leaned out to his right and tried to look into the picture window beside the door, but couldn't see anything inside because of the drawn shade. There were no gaps for him to peek through. The shade was opaque and lined with some kind of blackout material.

He ran his fingertips over the checkering on the grips of the gun and waited some more. When no one came to the door, he knocked again, this time pounding so hard that it rattled in its frame.

His senses felt heightened, as if he had just drunk an entire Thermos of coffee. Sweat ran down his forehead, stinging his eyes, the sunlight too bright. He wanted to slip on his sunglasses, but was worried that they would prevent him from being able to see inside the house when the door opened.

He moved his head so that his ear was close to the surface of the door and listened. He could hear nothing except for a rhythmic ticking sound.

Will stood there, waiting in the hot sun until he had finally managed to convince himself that there was no one inside.

The three of them split up and searched the outside of the green house.

Will worked his way around the perimeter until he found a back door. He turned the knob, but the door wouldn't open. Above the knob was an expensive dead bolt.

He continued a slow circle of the house, checking the windows, but they were all covered with the blackout shades.

In front of the house, Will found an industrial garbage can made from gray plastic. He lifted off the lid. It was empty inside the can, but an odor wafted up from inside, sickening and sweet at the same time, reminiscent of nail polish.

The dirt parking area was zigzagged with tire tracks. Will knelt to inspect the tread patterns, could see that at least three different vehicles had been there.

All the tread patterns were knobby and deep, made by off-road tires. He matched up a pair of tracks that were obviously from the same brand of tire. The distance separating them told him that they were made by a large vehicle, some kind of truck or large SUV.

He spotted an oil stain on the earth and dipped his finger into it. The oil was still warm, as though it had only recently dripped from an engine block.

He heard footsteps coming toward him across the dirt and looked up to see Thomas.

"I think I found something," he said.

Thomas led Will around to the side of the house, passing a pile of split cordwood stacked against the clapboards. They stopped in front of a white lattice enclosure.

Inside the enclosure was the house's propane tank, a painted metal cylinder resting on its side. The tank was large, the size of a compact car.

Thomas pointed to something at the base of the tank. "Check it out," he said.

Will knelt down, looking at a pressure gauge that displayed the amount of gas inside the tank. Beneath it was a valve with a knurled metal handle.

Will leaned closer to the valve, being careful not to let his skin touch it, making sure that what he was seeing wasn't a trick of the light.

The valve was corroded, as if eaten away by a chemical, and had turned a telltale shade of blue.

FIFTY-NINE

"You're positive?" Kirk Nolan's voice floated from the speaker-phone on Will's desk. "You're *sure* this tank was filled with anhydrous ammonia?"

"I didn't send it to the lab," Will said, watching Thomas across the desk. "But the color and corrosion on the nozzle is textbook."

"Any idea how much is in the tank?" the DEA agent asked.

"I checked the gauge," Will said. "Assuming it's accurate, a hundred and twenty gallons."

"Jesus. I've never heard of that much at one lab."

"That's why we called you," Will said. "What do you want us to do?"

"Just hang tight," Nolan said. "I'll scramble a team out of Sac, chopper in to join them on route to your location."

Will and Thomas stood on the corner outside City Hall, staring at the shimmering heat of Main Street.

Will glanced at the big clock hanging from the side of the building, wondering what was taking Nolan so long. The DEA agent had called from his cell phone over two hours ago to tell him that they were passing through Redding, meaning they should have been here by now.

Will knew they didn't have much time left before whoever was at the lab figured out that they had been there.

He was beginning to wonder if he should have just listened to Thomas. After they'd discovered the tank, Thomas had wanted to break down the door to the house and go inside. Will told him that because of the toxic chemicals inside a meth lab, it was too dangerous to enter without protective suits and full respirators, neither of which the department had.

Will squinted down the black ribbon of pavement and watched a large vehicle coming toward them. As it grew closer, he saw that it was only a rusted Dodge van, an inverted aluminum rowboat strapped to its roof.

Will turned to Thomas. "You bring the warrant?"

Thomas tapped the breast pocket of his uniform with his fingertips. "Right here," he said.

It had been spat out by the fax machine half an hour ago, a "no-knock" arranged by Nolan, signed by a federal judge.

Will heard a sound that was like the drone of swarming insects, and when he looked back down the road he saw the sun reflecting off gleaming paint. A procession of four black GMC Yukons rolled down Main Street, the hulking vehicles spaced at precise intervals, their off-road tires loud against the pavement.

The lead vehicle pulled to the curb in front of Will, the tinted window on the passenger side lowering to reveal a middle-aged man wearing a yellow polo shirt and aviator sunglasses.

"Hop in," Kirk Nolan said.

Will used his chin to indicate Thomas. "Kirk, I'd like you to meet Thomas Costello. You talked to him on the phone."

"Nice to meet you." Nolan gave Thomas a quick glance, then turned back to Will. "We've only got room for one."

The tinted windows prevented Will from being able to see inside the back of the SUV, reflecting his own image as well as a lonely cloud floating up in the sky.

"He's been in this with me from the beginning," Will said. "He's the one who found the lab."

"I'll be sure to put that in my report," Nolan said. "Now let's go."

Will stepped closer to the truck. Kirk Nolan had less hair than the last time Will had seen him, an advanced case of male pattern baldness. A leaping tiger was stitched on the chest of his polo shirt.

"Let's not start off on the wrong foot here, Kirk."

Nolan looked up at him. "I really don't give a flying fuck which foot we start on, so long as we *start*."

Will watched a crow hop across the street on sticklike legs, its body as large as a cat's. "Here's the deal," he said. "He goes along, or we don't show you where the lab is."

Nolan regarded Will from behind the green lenses of his sunglasses. The exhaust of the idling trucks continued to throb, the air growing thick with the smell of burning gasoline.

The DEA agent extended his thumb and pointed it toward the rear door. "You two can ride in back."

SIXTY

The black SUVs stood parked side by side in a clearing a safe distance away from the green house.

The tailgates were raised, and a dozen DEA agents milled about, pulling equipment from the cargo bays. A female agent wearing a baseball cap handed Will and Thomas each a heavy duffle bag that contained personal protective equipment.

Will stepped into the gray Tychem suit, zipped the front, and closed the Velcro storm flap. He pulled on two sets of gloves, first a nitrile surgical glove, then a heavy barrier glove that was the industrial green color of hospital walls.

The female DEA agent sealed the seams at his wrists and ankles with bright yellow tape.

Will hoisted the bulky air cylinder of his self-contained breathing apparatus and slipped the straps of the harness over his shoulders. He pulled the face mask down over his head and adjusted the fit, the tall trees now seeming farther away when viewed through the thick layer of Plexiglas.

He looked over at Thomas, the younger man's eyes wide behind his own face mask. The DEA agents had finished putting on their gear, like a group of alien invaders who had touched down here in the forest.

Kirk Nolan sat at a makeshift command center that had been constructed from a folding plastic table and some canvas-backed chairs. He got up and walked to the front of the group, still dressed in his street clothes. Will knew that this meant he would not be venturing inside the lab.

"Here's the sit-rep, folks," Nolan said. He waited until the DEA agents fell silent. "We're looking at a suspected methamphetamine lab. Our forensic chemist has just confirmed that we have a large-capacity tank of anhydrous ammonia on site, so we can assume the lab is using the Birch, a.k.a. Nazi, method."

Will pulled off his face mask and air tank and set them on the ground, then signaled to Thomas that he should do the same. He had the feeling that Nolan's briefing might go on for a while.

"Therefore," Nolan said, "aside from the caustic hazards of the ani, we can expect the presence of lithium oxide. Do not allow any source of moisture, and that includes your own sweat, to come in contact with any lithium, or we'll all be blown clear to Nevada."

Nolan looked at Will and Thomas. "For those of you who are new to this, listen up. Under no circumstances are you to remove your breathing apparatus while inside the structure. Anhydrous ammonia will dissolve your lungs on contact. I can guarantee this will ruin your day. Are we clear?"

"Yes, sir," the DEA agents answered in unison.

Nolan stared at Will. "Are we *clear*?"

Will felt the group of DEA agents turn to watch him.

He held Nolan's eyes. "Crystal," he said.

Nolan blinked and then shifted his eyes back to the DEA agents. "Be alert for the usual booby traps. Do not switch anything inside the structure on or off. Step carefully and watch out for trip wires. Do not open the refrigerator door."

Thomas had a confused look on his face. Will leaned over and whispered into his ear, "When you open the door, the light comes on. If there are any solvents inside, they'll explode."

Thomas nodded his head. "Got it."

Nolan was staring at Thomas. "Is there something you'd care to share with the rest of us?"

Thomas's face flushed with color.

Will looked at Nolan. "I was just answering a question," he said.

"I'd appreciate any questions being directed to me."

Will felt himself sweating inside the suit. No matter how much time you'd put in working a case, when the Feds showed up, you always felt as if you were on the outside looking in. When he was younger, it had eaten him up. Now, he didn't give a shit who got credit for shutting down the lab, so long as it got shut down.

Nolan kept his eyes on Will, as if trying to read his thoughts. "Moving *on*, we believe the building to be unoccupied, but until that is confirmed we will assume otherwise. We go in with a five-man entry team."

Nolan looked over at a group of agents that had dark blue ballistic vests strapped on over their protective suits. "Due to the likely presence of volatiles, we will not be using flash-bangs. No one else is to enter the structure until it has been cleared and secured by the entry team. Keep the radios clear, no nonessential chatter. I will have command of this operation, and all orders will be relayed by me, and *only* by me. Any questions?"

When no one said anything, Nolan turned to the entry team and said, "Let's go."

The agents picked up their equipment and ran in a crouch across the clearing.

An agent lugging a black metal Ram-It went up the steps and stood in front of the door. A pair of agents holding riot shields took positions on either side of the steps, directly in front of two other men who wore sling-mounted Heckler & Koch MP-5 submachine guns.

The agent standing at the door turned back to check that the others were ready. Then he swung the battering ram backward, away from the door. It reached the top of its arc, then began to swing forward like a pendulum.

It struck the door just below the knob. The door sprang inward, the agent holding the ram stepping aside as the others entered the house in a snake formation, swallowed up one at a time by the darkness of its interior.

SIXTY-ONE

Twenty minutes passed before one of the DEA agents emerged back out onto the concrete stoop, his features unreadable behind his face mask. He looked toward where the rest of the agents were waiting and raised the thumb of his gloved hand.

"All right," Nolan said. "We're clear."

Will shouldered his air tank, fitted the face mask, and pulled the hood of his suit up over his head. He opened the valve to his air supply, checking the thick black hose to make sure there were no kinks.

Then he joined Thomas and the rest of the agents as the group moved toward the house.

It was dark inside the living room, the windows of the house still covered by the blackout shades. Will stood there and waited for his eyes to adjust, feeling isolated from the rest of the world inside the protective suit.

The features of the room appeared in chiaroscuro, flashlight beams raking the walls. The furniture was carefully arranged, like a living room set on display in a department store. Lace doilies were draped over the arms of the sofa and easy chair. The seat cushions looked as if they had never been sat on.

A built-in bookcase occupied an entire wall of the room, the books all hardcovers. The remaining walls were covered with a collection of taxidermied birds. A peregrine falcon peered down, its scaled talons wrapped around a plastic tree branch, glass eyes glowing with light from the flashlight beams.

Will heard the sound of ticking again, the same noise he had heard through the door this morning. He moved his flashlight, searching for the source of the sound.

He spotted it in the dark corner of the room, a tall wooden cuckoo clock, its wooden case filigreed, like something out of the Black Forest.

Will moved into the kitchen. His peripheral vision was cut off by the face mask, and he turned in a slow circle on the linoleum floor, taking in Formica counters that were bare except for a small jar of honey and a ceramic cookie jar shaped like a dog.

Will peeked quickly inside the tiny bathroom, but there was nothing to see aside from the pedestal sink, tiled shower, and toilet.

The bedroom was the only other room in the small house. He walked down the hall that led to it, the hissing sound of the respirator loud in his ears. The lab had to be back here; it was the only other place where it could be.

The bedroom was crowded with DEA agents. Will stepped inside, careful not to bump anyone's air hose. He saw a double bed neatly covered with a green chenille bedspread. Above it on the wall was a framed needlework sampler, the image of a horse-drawn carriage above words stitched in colorful wool letters:

TRAVEL EAST
TRAVEL WEST
AFTER ALL
HOME'S BEST

The DEA agents had the closet door open. Clothes encased in plastic dry-cleaning bags hung on a wooden rod. Will moved closer, seeing that it was all women's clothing, paisley-patterned dresses and polyester pantsuits, the styles all dated, as if they had come from a mid-seventies time capsule.

Will turned and rechecked the room, but there was nothing else to see. His hands sweated inside the two layers of rubber gloves.

Kirk Nolan's voice startled him, the sound loud over the earpiece of the two-way radio. "This is Command. What've you got?"

Will felt for the switch on his mike and spoke before the DEA agents had a chance to respond. "Still searching," he said.

"What do you mean?"

Will hit the TRANSMIT switch again and said, "I need this channel clear."

A group of the DEA agents were now standing around him in a tight semicircle. Because of his face mask, Will talked to them over the two-way. "Tear up the carpeting," he said. "Look for a trapdoor."

The agents stood there without responding, the air hoses that dangled from their face masks making them look like a swarm of anteaters. Will started to worry that they wouldn't accept an order from him. But then one of the agents nodded to him and motioned for the others to go ahead.

Will went back out into the living room so that they would have room to work. The fireplace mantel was empty except for a plastic snow globe. Will bent to look at it, careful not to touch it. Inside he could see the buildings of a small western town, the flakes of ersatz snow piled incongruously on the desert landscape. Debossed plastic letters spelled out the name of the town, ALAMOGORDO, N.M.

He stepped to the bookcase and slid out a dog-eared copy of *Othello*. He opened it and saw that someone had marked it up, all of the parts crossed out except for that of Iago.

The group of DEA agents came out of the bedroom. The one

who seemed to be in charge spoke to him over the radio. "We pulled the carpet," he said. "There's nothing there."

Inside his spacesuit, Will felt his sweat-drenched body go cold. "Move this furniture, check underneath."

The DEA agent didn't look happy about it, but he went over to the couch and used an inspection mirror to check underneath it for booby traps. The agents pushed the couch against the wall, but there was nothing there other than a small mound of rat droppings.

Then the small room all at once filled with a clangorous sound. Will whirled around, the beam of his flashlight illuminating the cuckoo clock, a small and painted bird thrusting forward on its hidden mechanism of gears and springs.

The DEA agents traded looks, some of them shaking their heads from side to side. Then they began to move aside the remaining pieces of furniture.

When they'd finished, Will heard the voice of the DEA agent in his earpiece. "There's nothing here."

Will could hear the hissing of the oxygen tank but couldn't seem to get enough air. He turned to face the agents, trying to think of where he might tell them to search next, but couldn't think of anything else.

SIXTY-TWO

The sunlight outside the house was blinding.

Will staggered down the concrete stoop and across the dirt of the clearing. The ground lurched from side to side, as if he were walking across the deck of a storm-tossed ship.

A portable decontamination shower had been set up upwind from the house. He went over to it, and a DEA agent hosed him down. He stepped out of the shower and dropped his suit and SCBA equipment on a blue plastic tarp that had been put there for that purpose.

He spotted Nolan talking to two of the DEA agents who had been inside the house. Will walked toward them. When he drew close, their conversation stopped.

Will started to speak, the words painful inside his parched throat. "I think——"

Nolan held up the palm of his hand in the *stop* gesture of a traffic officer. "Save your breath. I've already heard it from my men."

"I don't know——"

"You don't know?" Nolan said. "You just blew seventy-five K of the government's money on this little exercise, that's the best you can do? You don't *know*?"

Will felt his pulse throbbing along the side of his neck. "You saw the tank of ani. When I found it, I called you in. Isn't that what you wanted?"

"You should have checked it out," Nolan said. "You should have been *sure*."

"It's funny how I didn't hear you saying that a little while ago. It seemed like you were happy to jump in and take charge."

Nolan shook his head. "Not anymore. You think I'm taking the hit for this debacle, you're out of your mind."

Nolan's nipples stood out against the piqué material of his polo shirt. Behind him, Will could see the DEA agents packing up pieces of equipment and loading it into the trucks.

"Nobody has to take a hit for anything," Will said. "The lab, it's got to be here."

"We just searched the entire house." Nolan pointed up at the canopy of the trees. "So tell me, where is it you think it's hiding, inside a bird's nest?"

"I don't know yet. We've just got to keep looking."

"*You* keep looking." Nolan said. "Best of luck."

Kirk Nolan turned his back and walked away, the two DEA agents falling into step in his wake.

SIXTY-THREE

"You're not talking," Laurie said.

They sat outside at the picnic table, lingering over their empty dinner plates. The sound of crickets came from the shadows of the bushes.

Will took a sip from his glass of sauvignon blanc. "Sorry," he said.

She was wearing a white V-neck T-shirt and a pair of shorts, the night air still warm, even though it was past ten. Buddy sat on the brick surface of the patio, his head in her lap.

"Do you ever cut yourself a break?" she asked.

He didn't answer, but she kept staring at him, an expectant look on her face. "I'm sorry," he said. "I thought it was a rhetorical question."

"It wasn't," she said. "You need to stop torturing yourself over this thing. You look exhausted."

"I've got to figure out what the hell's going on."

He couldn't stop thinking that Frank Carver was somehow behind this, that the whole setup at the house had been Frank toying with him. But what did it mean? Was the house some kind of elaborate decoy?

Was the real lab out there, hidden away in some completely different location?

"In meditation class, they teach us that the obstacles in life aren't our enemies," Laurie said. "They're really our friends, because they teach us where we're stuck."

A gentle wind came up, carrying the smell of charcoal fires and pine trees. "I already know where I'm stuck," he said. "I just don't know how to get unstuck."

"You need to just accept it, the *not* knowing."

He couldn't keep from smiling. There seemed to be no shortage of things he didn't know. "That may cut it in yoga class, but I'm not sure how well it works in criminology."

"It works in *life*." Laurie stared at him, her eyes studying his face. "You need to stop struggling, Will. It only makes things worse. Try to practice letting go."

"How am I supposed to let go?" He shook his head. "It's got to be there. Or maybe it was there, and they moved everything. I don't know."

"You hear that?" She smiled at him. "You've just accepted that you don't know. Now stop thinking about it."

He laughed. "I don't think that's gonna happen."

"Try putting your attention on something else."

"Yeah?" he said. "Like what?"

She reached up and brushed her golden hair back from her face. The orange tip of the candle flame danced in the blackness of her pupils.

"*What?*" he asked.

She lifted one of her eyebrows, so that it looked like a tilde placed over her eye. "Do you really need me to spell it out?"

SIXTY-FOUR

He came awake with a start. Through the sheer curtains of the window he could see the outline of the waxing moon, its horns pointing up into the black sky.

Will was certain that he now had the answer, although he was unsure of how or when it had come to him.

He swung his bare feet to the wooden floor, picking his weight up slowly from the mattress in an effort to keep the springs from making noise. Laurie slept on her side of the bed, facing toward him, the white sheet pulled down across her naked hip. The moonlight wrapped around the curve of a breast, her belly rising and falling.

One of her eyes came open, not focusing. "Don't leave," she said, half asleep.

"I need to make a call."

She lifted her head from the pillow and looked at the glowing red numbers of the alarm clock on his night table. "It's four in the morning."

"I know," he said. "Go back to sleep."

She reached down and pulled the sheet up to her neck, turning away from him, the mattress holding an impression of her form in the place she had just vacated.

He went down to the kitchen, not bothering to switch on the lights, the silver moonlight enough for him to find the numbers on the wall-mounted telephone. He asked the directory assistance operator for the number of the Gold Rush Inn, which was the only motel in the area. The night clerk at the motel confirmed that Kirk Nolan was registered there, and Will asked her to ring his room.

Nolan's voice was slurred, as if he'd been drinking. "Do you know what fucking time it is?" he asked.

"I know where the lab is."

Nolan let his breath out in a sigh. "I'm listening."

"When I was at Frank Carver's house, he had a copy of the *Aeneid*."

"The *what?*"

"The *Aeneid*," Will said. "You know, the book. By Virgil."

"You call me up in the middle of the night to tell me what's on this guy's reading list?"

"It's his prized possession." Will tried to keep his voice down, not wanting to wake Laurie. "When I remembered that, it's how I figured out where the lab is."

"You're losing me."

"The *Aeneid*, it has the story of the fall of Troy—"

"Are you using again or something?" Nolan asked. "Because you're making about as much sense as a junkie."

"The Trojan horse," Will said. "Something was *wrong* about that house. But the thing is, it's only a decoy, like the Trojan horse. The lab, it's somehow hidden inside."

"We already searched inside," Nolan said. "Remember?"

"It's *hidden*. We've got to go back out there."

"Don't you think you've already blown enough of the taxpayers' money?"

"Just listen to me," Will said. "We've got to go back. *Now.*"

Nolan didn't reply. Will stood there in the moonlit kitchen, looking at the snapshot of Buddy hanging on the door of the refrigerator. Somewhere far away he could hear the rumble of a lumber truck.

"All right," Nolan said. "It's not like I'm gonna be getting any more sleep tonight, anyway. We'll check it out. But then I'm getting the fuck out of Dodge."

SIXTY-FIVE

They stood in front of the green house, the predawn sky the color of lead.

Nolan sipped coffee from a steaming foam cup. The rest of the DEA agents still sat inside their trucks. "Let's get this over with," Nolan said.

"What about the suits?" Will asked.

Nolan took another sip before answering. "You only need protective equipment if you're going inside a lab," Nolan said. "Since there's no lab, I don't see why we need to bother."

"I know it's here," Will said. "The whole setup—"

Nolan held his palms up in a gesture of surrender. "Spare me. I'm only out here because I want to see you make an ass out of yourself. I mean, more than you have already."

Will forced himself to stay cool, remembering why he was here. "Let's just do this."

Nolan leaned back against the sculpted black fender of one of the SUVs. "Go ahead. We'll be right here if you need us."

*   *   *

By the time Will walked back out of the house, the sun had come up.

"Had enough?" Nolan asked. He was surrounded by a small cadre of DEA agents.

"I need a tape measure," Will said.

"You can measure your *shvantz* on your own time."

The agents cracked up at Nolan's joke. Will stood there in the warm morning air, waiting for them to stop.

Waiting to tell them what he had found.

"The reason I need a tape measure," he said, "is because it looks like the inside dimensions of the living room are a lot less than the outside."

"Ever hear of insulation?" Nolan was trying for humor, but this time the other agents didn't laugh.

"It's too big a difference," Will said. "I paced it off, but I want to make sure."

It was quiet now as what he had said began to sink in.

Nolan turned to one of his agents. "Get it," he said.

Thomas pulled up in the department's truck as they were measuring the exterior of the house. He looked at the two DEA agents stretching the yellow ribbon of the tape measure from the front door to a corner.

"What's going on?" he asked Will.

"Hang on a minute," Will said.

The DEA agent near the door checked the tape measure. "Twenty-one and a quarter," he said.

Nolan stood next to him on the stoop. "You're sure?"

The agent pulled out a pocket notebook and consulted one of the pages. "Positive," he said. "The inside wall measures five and a half feet shorter than the outside."

Will clicked on his flashlight, the watchful eyes of the dead birds staring down at him. Everyone, Nolan included, had changed into protective gear, and it was crowded inside the small living room of the house.

Will went to the far wall of the room, the one covered by the built-in bookcase. He began taking out the books, feeling as if Frank Carver was mocking him as he read the titles:

Great Expectations
Look Homeward, Angel
To Have and Have Not

He abandoned any pretense of caution or neatness, pulling the books out in handfuls and flinging them out into the room, the covers spreading open like wings.

When the bookcase was empty, one of the DEA agents stepped up and raised the heavy head of a sledgehammer into the air. He swung the hammer downward, one of the shelves exploding. He repeated this over and over until he had knocked a jagged three-foot opening in the wall behind the bookcase.

Will stepped forward and shoved his flashlight inside the hole. Sheetrock dust danced in the beam, making it difficult to see anything.

As the dust began to settle, Will could make out the shape of something in the space on the other side of the wall. He aimed the flashlight downward, so that it was pointing toward the floor.

The yellow light gleaned off something metallic. Will stuck his head farther inside the hole, careful not to snag the air hose of his respirator, not sure of what he was looking at.

He could see a steel step. He moved the flashlight beam until he saw another, the massive spiral staircase disappearing from view and down into the darkness below.

SIXTY-SIX

There was no safe way to fall with a thirty-pound air tank strapped to your back.

Will held on to the handrail as he descended the metal staircase, using his toe to feel for each stair tread. He looked down at the DEA agents milling around in their protective suits. The subterranean room was large, the walls craggy where they had been carved from the earth.

It was as if he had stepped inside a manufacturing facility at Merck or Schering-Plough.

Flashlight beams crawled over objects in the room: long laboratory tables with commercial-grade equipment lined up on their dark gray tops, large coffin freezers, black fifty-five-gallon drums, and steel shelving stocked with containers of Freon and hydrogen chloride gas.

Will went down the rest of the stairs, finding it difficult to get enough air inside his face mask.

One of the tables was covered with large glass flasks that were shaped like globes, filled with liquid that was the color of blood. They were known as twenty-twos, and they were expensive and difficult to come by. Will counted ten of the flasks; he'd never heard of a clan lab that had this many of them.

Someone came up beside him, anonymous within the protective suit. He saw that it was Thomas, his eyes wide behind the Plexiglas mask. They looked at each other for a moment, no way to speak unless they did it over the two-way.

Thomas raised a gloved hand up and held it in the air in front of him. Will looked at him, unsure of what he was doing. Then he understood and brought his own hand up, slapping it against Thomas's. Thomas smiled, his face youthful and alive behind the faceplate.

There was a flash of light. Will turned to see one of the agents taking a photograph of something against the wall. A long metal table was stacked with vacuum-sealed bags of white crystals. Each of the bags was the size of a small loaf of bread; there were probably close to thirty of them on the table.

Will went to take a closer look. He ran the beam of his flashlight over one of the bags, looking at the crystals that were like pieces of rock salt, glowing with a bluish inner light.

SIXTY-SEVEN

A camera flash fired.

Kirk Nolan posed himself in front of the command table outside in the clearing. He had slipped on a navy blue windbreaker over his polo shirt, block lettering on the chest spelling out DEA. The table was now piled high with the neatly stacked bundles of crystal methamphetamine.

He put a purposeful look on his face as the flash went off again, photographs for the DEA press release.

Will leaned against the trunk of a cedar and watched, drinking from a warm bottle of spring water. He had taken off his protective suit; his street clothing was damp with sweat. The sun was about to set, hanging just above the ridgeline now, the pine trees casting elongated shadows across the dirt floor of the clearing.

The photographer snapped off a few more shots, then arranged the other agents around Nolan for a group photo. Nolan put his arms around two of the other agents and looked at the camera.

He noticed Will standing there. "Want to get in this one?" he asked.

Will shook his head. "I need to talk to you."

"Hang on." Nolan turned back to the photographer and smiled as the flash fired. Then he patted one of the agents on the back and walked over to where Will was standing. "What's wrong now?"

"We're wasting time," Will said. "We've got to move on Frank Carver. If he figures out we're here, he'll leg-bail."

"We're not moving on Carver," Nolan said.

Will looked at him. "What are you talking about? Why not?"

"Lack of evidence, for one thing." Nolan unsnapped the front of the windbreaker. "Look, Will, you know the drill. We've got the dope, we shut down the lab. Another victory in the war on drugs."

"You haven't *arrested* anyone," Will said. "He'll just start up another lab, and you know it."

A female DEA agent walked by them carrying an equipment case. The other agents were busy packing up their gear and loading it into the backs of the trucks.

Nolan waited for the woman to move out of earshot, then turned to face Will. "Can't you be smart?" he said. "Just for once in your life?"

Will searched Nolan's face. "What are you saying?"

"That you've done good work here, Will. Play your cards right, you could have a real job. Get yourself out of this shit hole."

Will saw the trees begin to sway, the breeze cold through the damp fabric of his clothes. "And what happens to Frank Carver?"

"That's what I'm trying to say here," Nolan said. "Frank Carver is a nonstarter."

Will stepped forward, Kirk Nolan's face zooming closer to his own. "What the fuck aren't you telling me?"

A bulky DEA agent appeared next to Nolan. "Everything all right here, sir?"

"Chief Magowan was just saying his good-byes," Nolan said.

The agent nodded. "Everything's pretty much packed up. We're about ready to go."

Will stared at Nolan. "We're not done."

Nolan spoke to the agent. "Go wait in the truck. I'll be there in a second."

The DEA agent took a step toward the trucks, then turned back to Will. "You've got a good man in there," he said. "A real hard worker."

"Thomas?" Will was confused. He looked around the clearing but didn't see him.

The agent pointed his thumb toward the green house. "He's still inside."

Will pulled the radio from his belt and pressed the TRANSMIT button. "Thomas, it's Will. Do you copy?"

He lifted his thumb from the button, listening to the sound of static. He was about to transmit again when he heard Thomas's voice. "I'm here, Will."

In the background, Will could hear the hissing of Thomas's respirator. "Where are you?"

"Down in the lab," Thomas said.

"What for?" Will said. "Everybody else's already out."

"I know." Thomas paused. "Are you by yourself?"

"What are you talking about?"

"Can anybody else hear me?"

Will turned down the volume knob on the radio and walked a few steps away from Nolan and the other agent, turning his back to them. "No," Will said. "Now tell me what's going on."

"I found something," Thomas said.

"What?"

"It's a computer, Will. A laptop."

Even over the radio, Will could hear the pride in the boy's voice.

"Nobody else saw it," Thomas said. "Just me. It was duct-taped underneath a table."

Will was alert now, his fatigue falling away. "Don't turn it on, Thomas. I repeat, do *not* turn it on."

Thomas's voice sounded confused. "Why not?"

Will spun toward where Nolan and the other agent were standing. "GET *DOWN*," he shouted.

Will watched the two men drop to the ground in the moment before the air seemed to be sucked from the atmosphere, his eardrums drawn inward as if he were on board an airplane plunging from the sky.

The clearing filled with a sudden flash of orange light as fragments of shattered glass and chunks of wood and tendrils of fire shot past him. Will found himself being hurled through the air, like being tumbled inside a powerful ocean wave.

Then he slammed into the rough trunk of a pine, the wind knocked from his lungs, searing pain radiating outward from the base of his spine.

SIXTY-EIGHT

The green house was gone now, the flaming rectangle of the front door frame the only thing left standing.

Will used a branch of the pine tree to pull himself to his feet, the pain from his back jolting him so hard that his vision dimmed. He stumbled through the clearing, weaving his way through an obstacle course of burning pieces of furniture and collapsed sections of the roof.

Flames licked upward from the hole in the earth where the house had once stood. Will approached the edge and looked down into an abyss filled with dark smoke and mounds of burning rubble, exploded chemical tanks and steel tables now twisted into abstract forms.

A DEA agent ran up behind him, moving in a low crouch. "You can't be here." He pointed at the shifting clouds of noxious smoke. "It's not safe."

Will scanned the rubble at the bottom of the pit. "I've got a man down there," he said.

The DEA agent reached out and pulled at Will's elbow. "At least put on a suit."

Will pushed him away. "Get off me."

The agent stumbled backward, shook his head at Will, then ran off in the direction of the trucks.

Will leaned out over the pit. The smoke made his throat burn and had an odd smell that reminded him of rotting citrus. Down at the bottom, one of the taxidermied birds lay on its side in flames, like a fireplace log.

"*THOMAS*." There was no response from the pit other than the crackling of flames and an ominous creaking sound.

Will waved his palm in front of his face, trying to fan the smoke away. He saw something sticking up from beneath a pile of broken concrete.

A man's dress shoe, the polished black surface coated with a layer of gray dust.

"*THOMAS* . . ." he called again.

He turned to see if the DEA agents were coming to help. Off in the distance, they stood in a tight circle around one of the black SUVs.

Will looked back into the burning pit. He bent his knees like a man poised at the end of a diving board, then leapt down into the abyss.

SIXTY-NINE

Will worked his way through the rubble, disoriented by the thick smoke.

When he found the shoe, he fell to his knees and began tossing aside the heavy chunks of concrete foundation that surrounded it. He managed to uncover Thomas's ankle, encased in a black dress sock, but the rest of the leg disappeared down beneath the pile of rubble.

Will craned his neck to look up at the rim. "I NEED HELP DOWN HERE," he called.

Then he turned back to Thomas, working as fast as he could to uncover him. The acrid smoke made his eyes water and the air painful to breathe. He was able to free the leg all the way up to the top of the thigh, the rest of Thomas's body hidden underneath the top of a lab table.

Will grunted as he lifted one end of the heavy tabletop, pushing it off to the side. He looked back down and saw with growing horror that nothing was there, that there was only a dismembered leg that was no longer attached to anything.

Will fell back on his rear end, choking on something caught in his throat. He sat there, surrounded by the drifting smoke, until he noticed something sticking out from beneath a wooden foundation beam.

A hand, the flesh dark with char, the fingers moving as if beckoning him forward.

Will ran over and shoved aside the beam. Thomas's blue eyes stared up at him, his face coated with ash.

"Will," Thomas said.

Will couldn't believe that he was still alive. He glanced up at the rim high above and called out, "MEDIC . . ."

Will knelt beside Thomas, examining the bloody stump that was white with shattered fragments of his hip socket.

"I can't feel my legs," Thomas said.

"You're going to be all right," Will said. He tore off his shirt, folding it into a square. He placed the fabric against the stump and pushed on it as hard as he dared.

Thomas's body arched backward against the ground, his mouth opening to form the shape of an O.

"Just hold on, Thomas."

"T," he said.

There wasn't enough of Thomas's leg left for Will to apply a tourniquet. The folded shirt was already heavy with Thomas's warm blood, every beat of the boy's heart causing more of it to seep out between Will's fingers.

"I didn't tell them, Will," Thomas said.

Will looked down at his face. "Tell them what?"

"About the laptop," Thomas said. "Just you."

Will looked up at the rim. *What the fuck was taking them so long?*

Thomas was staring up at him, his face pale and sheened with beads of perspiration. "I'm sorry I told the mayor."

Will looked at him. "Try not to talk," Will said. "Save your energy."

Thomas closed his eyes.

Will touched the boy's shoulder. "Don't do that," he said. "You've got to keep your eyes open, T."

Thomas's eyelids fluttered, coming open in stages, as if he were lifting a great weight.

Will pressed harder against the stump, the shirt drenched and warm. The pulsing was faint now, as if coming from far away. He looked down at Thomas's face, wanting to make sure that he was keeping his eyes open, but it was hard for him to see, everything going blurry.

"It's okay, Will," Thomas said.

Will blinked his eyes. "I'm sorry, T."

"Why?" Thomas asked.

Then it was as if a bubble had burst somewhere deep inside the boy, his open mouth filling with a grainy black substance that looked like coffee grounds.

Will reached down and turned Thomas's head to the side. There was no resistance, the dark and viscous fluid running down Thomas's pale cheek and pooling on the earth.

Will ran through all of the things he was supposed to do next, his mind racing as he thought about clearing the airway, checking for a pulse, beginning cardiopulmonary resuscitation.

But as he held Thomas's cooling face at the bottom of the burning pit, he knew that there was no use, knew that he had once again failed.

SEVENTY

He turned into the motel parking lot and parked beneath the porte cochere.

An overweight man wearing a leather bolo tie stood behind the front desk inside the air-conditioned office.

Will badged him. "Which room is Kirk Nolan in?"

The clerk punched some keys on a computer. "That group's already checked out."

"When?"

The man shrugged. "You just missed them."

Will went back outside and scanned the parking lot. Down at the far end of the building he spotted the red glow of taillights, the procession of black SUVs rolling toward the exit of the parking lot.

He sprinted down the walkway. When he reached the lead vehicle, he rapped his knuckles against the passenger window.

The tinted glass glided down. Kirk Nolan stared out at him, his expression blank. "Yes?"

Will was out of breath from running. "Why the fuck are you protecting a piece of garbage like Frank Carver?"

Nolan frowned and turned to the driver. "Excuse me a second."

He climbed down from the truck and closed the door behind him. "You don't know what you're talking about."

"Then why don't you tell me?" Will said. "Why was his record expunged?"

"How should I know?" Nolan said.

Will stepped toward him, so close that he could see the individual pores on the man's nose. "Who's George Hunter White?"

Nolan's eyes blinked. "Never heard of him."

"He was a high-ranking agent in the FBN," Will said.

Nolan looked down at his wristwatch. "Look, I'm sorry about your man, but we've got to hit the road."

Nolan began to turn toward the truck. Will grabbed him by the collar, then reached down and drew his gun, pointing the barrel at Nolan's face.

Will heard the doors of the other trucks opening, a chorus of safeties being clicked off. He glanced over his shoulder and saw the muzzles pointing at him.

He looked back at Nolan. "Tell your men to stand down, or I swear I'll put a bullet in your brain."

Nolan studied Will's face, as if trying to take the measure of his seriousness. Will held the gun steady, staring back into the other man's eyes.

Nolan signaled to the agents. "It's all right," he said. "Get back in the truck."

Will waited until he heard the last door slam shut. Then he lowered the gun to his side.

Nolan attempted to straighten the collar of his polo shirt. "You've lost it, Will. You know that?"

"I'm just getting warmed up."

"Why don't you stop being so fucking naive? You think this is the Boy Scouts?"

Will raised his elbow and slammed the point of it into Nolan's face. "You're trying my patience."

Nolan raised his hand and wiped the blood from his lips. "Believe me, you don't want to know. It'll just piss you off."

Will glared at him. "I'm already pissed off."

Nolan raised his hands in a gesture of supplication. "All right. But it's not like I know everything."

"Try starting with what you *do* know."

Nolan took a breath. "You remember something called MK-ULTRA?"

Will nodded his head. It had been a Cold War–era CIA project to research the potential of LSD and other psychoactive drugs for their use in espionage. "Go on," he said.

"The head of MK-ULTRA was a CIA chemist named Sid Gottlieb. By the mid-fifties, he decided that they needed to start testing the materials in real-life situations on nonvolunteer subjects."

"You mean slipping acid to unwilling people," Will said.

Nolan nodded. "If you want to put it that way," he said. "Gottlieb needed someone to run the project. He decided George White was the perfect man for the job."

"I didn't think he was CIA."

Nolan shook his head. "He wasn't, but they didn't care. White had drug experience from the FBN, and he had worked for OSS during World War II. So Gottlieb asked the FBN to loan him out, as a consultant on a subproject called Midnight Climax."

Nolan's face was bathed in the red neon light of the motel sign. "White set up safe houses in some apartments in Frisco, outfitted them with movie cameras and two-way mirrors. They used prostitutes to lure men up to the apartments, then gave them cocktails spiked with acid."

"What does any of this have to do with Frank Carver?" Will asked.

"Carver worked for White, mostly as a procurer."

"Of LSD?"

Nolan shook his head. "The government already had boatloads of that," he said. "Frank lined up the whores."

Will tapped the gun against his thigh. "Is Frank still working for the government?"

Nolan shook his head again.

"Then why are you protecting him?"

Nolan looked away. "They're all afraid of him."

"*Why?*"

"Isn't it obvious?"

"I don't think anything you told me would come as much of a shock to the American public."

"It's not just that," Nolan said. "After George White retired in 'sixty-six, Frank went on to another project. Something really heavy."

"What do you mean, *heavy?*"

Nolan shrugged. "I already told you, I don't know everything."

"*Bullshit.*" Will raised the gun, jamming the barrel into the soft flesh below Nolan's jaw. "Tell me what it was."

Will heard the truck doors opening, but he was beyond caring now. He put his thumb on the hammer spur and pulled it back until it clicked in place. But when he looked into the other man's eyes he saw the resignation and embarrassment there.

He doesn't know.

Will lowered the gun. An electronic mosquito trap made a crackling sound, something caught inside it so that the noise went on and on.

Nolan rubbed his fingers over the red spot on his throat. "You're going to burn for this."

Will watched Kirk Nolan slip back inside the SUV. The truck engines turned over, the big tires making a crunching sound as they began to roll.

Someone had hosed down the parking lot, the puddles reflecting

the letters of the motel's neon sign. Will stood alone on the slick pavement, watching as the caravan of trucks receded toward the horizon
until they were nothing but red pinpoints of light that faded away into
the blackness.

SEVENTY-ONE

On the other side of the kitchen window the light was still on, casting a yellow rectangle of light out onto the dark grass. Will rummaged through the cargo area of the station wagon until he found a jacket to wear over his bloody T-shirt. He didn't want Laurie to see it and get upset.

She sat at the small circular table in the kitchen. The wooden surface of the table was empty except for his vial of Vicodin. When he came into the room she picked it up in her hand and shook it like a maraca.

"Look what I found," she said.

Will slumped against the door frame. "I was in pain—"

She shook her head. "*Don't.*"

He looked at her, trying to think of something to say. He was so exhausted that it was as though his brain had shut down.

"You promised me, Will."

"I know." He looked down at his hands. They looked like a palm reading chart, Thomas's blood dried red in the creases.

She stared at him. "That's it?"

"I'm sorry," he said. "Can we please just talk about this in the morning?"

She looked down at the tabletop. "You know, I feel like such an idiot. Because for a while there, I actually thought this could work. Can you believe that?"

"I still believe it," he said. He looked past her into the dark living room, the shadowed emptiness of the house.

"You know what it's like?" she said. "It's like we're on a wheel, just going around and around. And the only thing I know is, I can't do it anymore."

He took a step into the room and could see now what was on the other chair. Her blue duffle bag, like someone else sitting there at the table. "What's that for?" he asked.

"I'm going back to L.A.," she said. "I was just waiting for you to get home so I could say good-bye."

"Please," he said, taking another step. "I need you."

"For *what*? To have someone to ignore while you run around getting high?"

"I just need a little more time, to finish this."

She shook her head. "I'm not going to stay here and watch you destroy yourself. I wish you could see yourself, what this is doing to you."

"What choice do I have?"

"You need to get away from here, Will. This is no good for you. You can stay with me if you want. Go see Dr. Stock, get yourself some help."

"I can't just leave," he said. "Not now."

She put the vial down on the table and looked up at him. "You know, I think I finally figured something out."

"What's that?"

She tapped her fingernail against the side of the plastic bottle. "You're not really addicted to these."

He looked at her.

"These pills, the heroin, whatever—they're only a chaser. What really gets you off, what you're really high on, is *idealism*."

"I didn't realize that was a bad thing."

"It is when it blinds you to reality." She picked up the duffle bag and went to the kitchen door. "I think you see yourself as some kind of saint."

He opened his mouth to speak, but she held up a finger and pressed it to her lips, shaking her head. "No, it's OK. That's your choice. But the thing is, I never asked for it. All I wanted was a husband, not something I could wear on a medal around my fucking neck."

She stood there in front of the door, staring at him, waiting for him to say something.

"I don't know what it is you want from me," he said. "To just give up? To quit? Is that what you want?"

She reached out her arm and put her hand on the doorknob.

He kept talking, trying to make her understand. "Because if I just leave. If I just walk away, then *what*? I mean, then what am I?"

Her eyes became bright and filled with tears.

He took a step toward her, but she turned away from him and wiped at her eyes with the back of her hand.

When she looked at him again, it didn't look like she was crying anymore. "If you ever figure it out, you know where you can find me."

Then she turned and went out through the door.

SEVENTY-TWO

The funeral was held on Sunday, in a cemetery set on an oak-studded hillside overlooking the town.

The open sky was cloudless, the strong morning sun beating down on the mourners. Will counted eight, himself included, all of them standing around a rectangular hole that had been dug into the red soil.

This was the first funeral he had been to since Sean had died. It wasn't as if he hadn't had any opportunities, it was just that he hadn't been able to bring himself to go.

The minister read from a black leather book embossed with a large golden cross. His lips moved as he recited the eulogy, Will not really hearing any of the words. He looked around and recognized a waitress from the Café. Lila was there, the backup dispatcher covering for her. A frail-looking woman sat on a folding chair at the head of the grave, her face hidden behind a black veil.

The town had paid for the burial, since Thomas had been killed in the line of duty. His coffin was plain, one step up from a pine box. An American flag was spread out over the top of it like a tablecloth.

When the minister finished, he asked if anyone would like to speak. The mourners looked down at the ground and shifted their feet. Will realized that he should say something, but he had nothing prepared. He started to organize his thoughts, recalling images of Thomas, trying to arrange them in a way that would convey what he was feeling.

But when he looked up, he saw that he had missed his chance. The minister shut the Bible and took the flag off the coffin. He folded it into a neat square, handing it to the woman wearing the veil.

A cemetery worker flipped a switch on the metal framework that surrounded the grave and the casket began to descend down into the hole. People started to leave. Will went up to the rim of the grave and bent to pick up some of the red-hued dirt.

The ground was baked hard by the sun and webbed with cracks, and he had to use his fingernails to scrape some of the dirt loose. He leaned out over the grave and opened his hand, watching the dirt drop down into the hole. It seemed to fall for a long time, finally landing on the polished top of the coffin, Thomas all alone down there.

He heard the noise of a diesel engine starting up and turned to see a cemetery worker seated on a backhoe, waiting for Will to move out of the way so that he could fill up the hole.

Will wiped his hand against the front of his pants. The woman in the veil was still seated in her chair at the head of the grave, the folded flag on her lap. Will looked around the cemetery and saw that the others had already left; she seemed to be all alone.

He walked up beside her. "Mrs. Costello?"

The veil tilted up at him, but he couldn't see her face. "I'm Will Magowan. I worked with your son."

The woman's head nodded. "You were his boss."

"That's right," Will said. "I'm sorry. He was a good kid."

She held out a small plastic package toward him. "Would you like a tissue?"

"I'm OK," Will said.

She reached up and lifted away her veil. For some reason, he had expected her to be older. She looked to be the same age that he was.

"It's something you never picture yourself doing," she said.

"What's that?"

"Attending your child's funeral."

He felt himself sweating. He only owned one suit, and it was woolen, too heavy for the summer heat.

"Is there anyone here to help you?" Will asked her.

She shook her head. "Thomas used to live with me."

"What about his father?"

"He went out for a pack of cigarettes."

Will looked around the small cemetery, confused.

The corners of her mouth turned up. "Nineteen years ago."

He forced himself to smile at her joke.

White lines of salt had dried on her cheeks. "Do you think this is what he would have wanted?" she asked.

"I don't understand."

"They called me up, asked whether he wanted to be cremated or buried. I didn't know what to say. It wasn't something we'd ever talked about."

"I'm sorry," Will said. "That this happened."

She had Thomas's blue eyes. "You say it like it's your fault."

Will looked away. Crows filled the sky, wheeling and cawing like madmen, so many of the birds that for a moment they blotted out the sun.

"Was he in much pain?" she asked. "At the end?"

He didn't quite know how to answer. "He didn't act like it."

"Who are these people? That could do something like this to my son?"

"I'm sorry," he said. "I can't tell you that."

She studied his face. "But you know who they are?"

Will nodded.

"What will you do to them?"

Will felt uncomfortable, the way she kept staring at him. "That's for the courts to decide," he said.

She picked up the folded flag from her lap and held it up to him. "He would have wanted you to have this."

Will didn't take it. "I can't," he said.

She pressed it against his stomach. "He looked up to you a great deal. He told me how you always tried to look out for him."

When it was clear that he had no choice, he took the flag. "I should have tried a little harder."

SEVENTY-THREE

The red light on the answering machine pulsed on and off.

Will pressed the button, hoping that it might be Laurie. Instead he heard the voice of a "Mr. Johnson" calling from American Express, dunning him for his unpaid May statement, which sat on the counter along with the rest of the bills he could not afford to pay.

Will opened the back door for Buddy and sat down on the couch, his holster still clipped to his waistband, the hammer of the gun digging into his side.

In the silence of the house, the buzzing in his damaged ear was loud.

The translucent plastic box filled with photographs sat on the seat of a dining room chair. Will stared at it. He already knew that he would finally open it, but he didn't move, like holding off on scratching an insect bite.

When he pulled the plastic lid off the box he was hit by the smell, a Proustian sense memory of the house the three of them had once shared.

Inside the box were envelopes printed with the name of the fast photo place on Cahuenga he had once used. He reached inside and pulled out one of the packets. The pictures were from a vacation they had all taken to San Francisco, maybe fourteen months after Sean was born. Will had been the photographer, so it was mostly scenes of Laurie holding Sean in her arms. The two of them smiling at the camera in front of Coit Tower, on the running board of a cable car, looking out at the sea lions at Pier 39.

The big mistake, he thought, is that you think they'll always be around.

Buddy jumped up beside him on the couch. Will moved the box over so the dog could lay his head in his lap.

He opened another packet. This one was only half full, and he flipped through the photographs, trying to figure out where the rest of them had gone. Then he realized they were from the roll of film that had been in the camera at the time Sean had died.

He looked at the last photograph he had taken of his son. Sean extended a tiny hand toward the camera, as if to wave, looking directly into the lens. Will was transported back in time to the moment when he looked through the viewfinder, their eyes coming together in the instant that the shutter clicked.

Will carried the photograph into the kitchen. He went to the door of the refrigerator and slid the picture of Buddy over to the side. Then he centered the photo of Sean on the door, using a small magnet to hold it in place.

The American flag that had covered Thomas's coffin was draped over the back of one of the kitchen chairs. Will leaned against the refrigerator, trying to think about what he might do next. He felt as if he had been traveling for a long time down a narrow road, only to find that it had suddenly ended at the edge of a cliff.

The shadows grew long inside the room. He stood there until it had become completely dark, turning the possibilities over inside his mind, not knowing if he would be able to live with any of them.

SEVENTY-FOUR

The next morning, Frank Carver was arrested and booked into custody at the Haydenville Police Department.

It had gone easier than Will had expected, Frank putting up no resistance other than mocking him from the backseat of the truck, telling him how his lawyer would have him back home in time for lunch.

Will placed Frank inside the interview room, then left him there to marinate for awhile.

He went into the records room, slid open the drawer of one of the tall steel filing cabinets, and ran his fingers along the file jackets until he found what he was looking for. He opened the folder and removed Glen Sexton's Confidential Source Agreement.

Lila sat at the reception desk, her headset pulled down so it rested around her neck. She was eating a piece of buttered toast from out of a square of tinfoil.

Will held out Glen Sexton's Confidential Source Agreement to her. "Could you please scan this and send it to my computer?"

Will went into his office and closed the door. On the seat of his chair was a pink message slip with the words WHILE YOU WERE AWAY printed at the top. He picked it up and saw the mayor had called. A checkmark inside a small box indicated that it was URGENT. He crumpled the paper into a ball and tossed it into his garbage can.

He opened his desk drawer and took out a file folder that was thick with papers. The label on the tab read CARVER, FRANCIS XAVIER.

He placed the file on his desk blotter and sat down in front of his computer. He opened up the document that Lila had scanned for him and went through it line by line.

Each time he came to Glen Sexton's name he deleted it. When he finished, he double-checked, making sure that Sexton's name no longer appeared anywhere on the agreement. Then he saved the document twice, renaming the file each time so that he now had two sets of the edited Confidential Source Agreement.

He opened one of the documents and began to go through it again. He moved the cursor to one of the blank spaces where he had deleted Sexton's name. He watched it blinking at him on the screen, like a traffic sign.

Then he placed his fingers on the keys and began to type.

SEVENTY-FIVE

Frank Carver raised his large head and watched Will enter the interview room. He sat at the table wearing a faded green T-shirt that promoted the Concert for Bangladesh.

"This should be entertaining," he said.

Will placed the file folder in the middle of the table, turning it so that Frank could see his name on the label. "It's over, Frank. We found your lab."

Frank's laugh was the rasp of an elderly smoker. "*My* lab?"

Will wasn't surprised to hear Frank deny it. "Never thought we'd find it, did you?"

"To be real honest, I never thought about it at all," Frank said. "Let me ask you something. Why would a world-famous writer be running a meth lab?"

"I've seen your royalty statements. Your family would have starved a long time ago."

A thick and greenish vein pulsed against the side of Frank's forehead. "Fuck you," he said.

"Your command of the language, I really can't understand why you aren't selling more books."

Frank glared at Will, the anger rising off him like a physical presence inside the room.

Will felt the hair stand up on his forearms. "Tell me about the work you did for the FBN."

Behind the lenses of his black eyeglasses, Frank's eyes snapped into focus. "Where'd you hear *that*?"

"From someone at DEA."

"And you believed him?" Frank said. "That's sort of like the Cretan Paradox."

"I'm afraid I don't know what that is."

"Epimenides, the philosopher. He famously said, 'All Cretans are liars'. But he himself was a Cretan. Get it?"

"You're saying you can't trust anyone at DEA."

Frank lifted his bearded chin in Will's direction. "Give the man a prize."

"Now tell me something I don't know," Will said.

Frank smiled. "How does it feel, knowing your whole life's built on a foundation of lies?"

"I didn't realize it was."

"I mean, you seem like a reasonably intelligent man. Have you ever stopped—even for a moment—to ponder the hypocrisy of what you're doing?"

"In what sense?"

"Open up your fucking eyes, man. There was no drug culture in this country until the government created one. There never would have been a supply of LSD if the CIA hadn't contracted with Eli Lilly to manufacture it for them. Ginsberg, Kesey, Leary, all the pied pipers of the psychedelic movement, they all got turned on for the first time inside government research labs."

Frank's pink-rimmed eyes stared at Will, not blinking. "The

Castalia Foundation, the Society for the Study of Human Ecology, they were all funded by the CIA. And here's a little piece of trivia Tom Wolfe never bothered to write about: When the Merry Pranksters climbed on board that magic bus for their psychedelic tour across America, who do you think supplied the acid?"

"If it wasn't you, I don't really care," Will said. "What was it *you* did after George Hunter White retired?"

"Now, that's the kind of information our government friends would refer to as need-to-know."

"Tell me," Will said.

Frank leaned back in his chair, smiling. "You know what they say about the sixties—if you can remember what happened, you probably weren't there."

Will pushed his chair back from the table and stood up. "You might want to take that smirk off your face," he said. "Before I'm through, you're going to have a lot more to worry about than drug charges."

"Oh yeah?" Frank asked. "Like *what*?"

Will reached out and tapped the file on the tabletop. "The way I see it, you're responsible, either directly or indirectly, for at least three homicides: Glen Sexton, Tony Canepa, and Thomas Costello."

Frank cocked his head. "Who the fuck is Thomas Costello?"

Will swallowed hard, his hands balling into fists. The air in the room felt humid and smelled like a locker room. He stood over Frank, the other man grinning up at him without a trace of fear. It took every ounce of Will's self-control to keep from striking him.

Just stick to the plan.

Frank shook his head. "Let me ask you a question," he said. "Do you have any evidence? I mean, even just a tiny *shred*?"

"I've got something better."

"If you're holding out for some kind of confession here, let me assure you that you're sadly mistaken."

"What if I told you I had an informant?" Will said.

Frank laughed. "First off, let me state for the record that I'm innocent. *Completely.* But speaking hypothetically for a moment, no one I know would ever be stupid enough to turn rat."

"Maybe they think there's safety in numbers."

"The fuck's that supposed to mean?"

"That I don't just have one informant inside your organization, Frank. I've got two."

The smile remained frozen on Frank's face. But something almost imperceptible shifted inside the other man's eyes, like a cloud drifting past the moon.

Will walked over to the door and placed his hand on the lever. "I need to take a break."

SEVENTY-SIX

Will went into his office, the morning sun bright through the windows. He twisted the plastic wand on the venetian blinds to angle them closed.

He sat down behind the desk, slid open the desk drawer, and searched through it until he found a pair of nail trimmers. He dragged the black metal garbage can along the floor, positioning it between his legs. Then he used the nail trimmers, watching the tiny crescents tumble down inside the pail.

He had just finished the nails on his left hand when Lila knocked on the frame of the open door.

"What are you doing?" She stayed at the threshold, watching him.

"Grooming," he said. "What's up?"

"I just looked through the two-way. You left the prisoner all alone."

"So?" He transferred the clippers to his left hand and placed his thumbnail into the metal jaws.

"You forgot your file in there." Her hand fumbled with a button on the front of her blouse. "He's going through it."

Will pressed the lever and watched his nail fall down into the blackness of the can. "I guess I've been a little absentminded lately."

She stood there, looking at him. "Aren't you going to get it?"

He nodded. "Soon as I'm finished."

"Are you all right, Will?"

He looked up at her. "I think I'll be OK," he said.

Frank Carver's attorney was a tan and middle-aged man wearing a maroon golf shirt and a gold Rolex with diamonds encircling the bezel.

When Will stepped into the reception area, the lawyer rose from his chair and immediately began threatening him with a laundry list of legal countermeasures that included harassment, false imprisonment, and some other things that a judge would only laugh at.

Will waited for him to finish. "Does Frank pay you by the word?"

The lawyer seemed confused by the question. "No."

"Then how about shutting up?"

Will led the lawyer down the corridor and let him into the interview room. The file folder lay on the tabletop, some of the papers sticking out of it. Will picked up the folder and left the lawyer alone in the room with Frank Carver, locking the door behind him.

Less than a half hour later, Stuart Isgro called, ordering Will to release Frank Carver from custody. The district attorney seemed taken aback when Will didn't put up any resistance.

Will watched from his office window as Frank Carver and his attorney went down the front steps of the building and out onto the bright squares of the sidewalk. They got into a black Mercedes that was parked at the curb and drove away down Main Street.

When he heard the sounds of Lila leaving for lunch, Will got up from his chair.

He took Frank Carver's file with him to the deserted reception desk. He took the two sets of Confidential Source Agreements that he had created from the folder and fed them into the paper shredder.

The gears of the motor whirred, the documents slowly being drawn into the mouth of the machine, pieces of confetti dropping down into the bin. Will watched the pages disappear. The names of the two men that he had typed into the documents seemed to jump out at him, both of them sharing the same last name.

SEVENTY-SEVEN

Through the binoculars he could see that the large glass windows of Frank Carver's house were coated with grime, the wooden frames stranded with cobwebs.

Will lay flat on his stomach on the forest floor, propped up on his elbows a hundred yards or so from the house. The ground was covered with a carpet of fallen pine needles, pieces of twigs poking into his stomach and rib cage.

It was two days now since he'd stopped with the pills, and he felt it most in his bones, a dull ache that was worse lying here on the cool ground.

He glanced at his watch and saw that it was coming up on seven, the house already deep in shadow. Behind it, the fire tower rose from the woods, the windows of the building set on top reflecting the orange of the setting sun.

He'd been out here for close to five hours now. Watching the house, not sure what he was expecting to see.

He wasn't all that happy with his plan, but it was the best he could come up with. It was the old "Turd in the Punch bowl" tactic:

By inserting the twins' names into the agreement and letting Frank see it, he hoped to shake things up, to push Frank into doing something stupid.

And to be there waiting for him when he did.

The blue light of a television flickered on the far side of the glass, the twins seated on the couch watching the screen. Will turned the knob on the binoculars, the television screen snapping into focus. An MTV show called *Cribs*, some rapper Will didn't recognize showing off a garage filled with Hummers and pimped-out Escalades.

The woods grew darker, mosquitoes swarming his face, the sound of buzzing loud in his ears. He forced himself not to swat at them, knowing the activity would only attract more.

An aluminum screen door at the back of the house swung open, and Frank Carver stepped out into the dusk, holding a longneck Budweiser. He went to a black kettle grill, lifted the cover, and filled it from a bag of charcoal briquettes. He squirted a stream of lighter fluid inside the grill and tossed a lit match inside, his face glowing red from the flames that licked upward.

Frank went back inside the house until the coals were ready, then reemerged carrying a platter of raw hamburger patties. He used his bare hands to toss the meat onto the grill, smoke rising up and drifting over into the trees. Will was surprised to find his mouth filled with saliva; he hadn't had much of an appetite since he cut off the Vicodin.

Frank used a long spatula to turn the hamburgers. Then he suddenly looked up, his head swiveling around, staring into the woods where Will lay.

Will pulled the binoculars away from his face and lowered his head. He held his breath, the buzzing mosquitoes swarming over his cheek.

Frank continued to stare into the woods, his body shrouded in smoke, his eyes obscured by the lenses of his eyeglasses. The screen door opened, and one of the twins stuck his head outside. He said something to his father, who began lifting the meat from the grill.

Will allowed himself to breathe again, looking through the binoculars in time to watch Frank walk back inside, the screen door
slamming shut behind him.

The woods grew dark, and yellow lights winked on inside the
house. Will continued to watch through the binoculars, the sounds
of night creatures moving behind him in the forest.

His eyelids began to feel heavy, and he bit into his tongue to keep
himself from falling asleep. He didn't know how much longer he'd be
able to stay out here. With Thomas gone, there was no one to relieve
him, no way to work the surveillance in shifts.

A little after ten, the lights shut off inside the house. An hour
crawled by, the night air beginning to cool on his skin. Will trained
the binoculars on the large and blank windows, but nothing moved
inside.

He gave it another fifteen minutes and then rose to his feet, his
back stiff, the pine needles stuck to his clothing. He began the long
hike through the dark woods, back to where he'd left the truck.

The thunder was loud, shaking the glass of the darkened windows.
Will turned over in the bed and looked at the glowing red digits on
the alarm clock: 3:47. He'd been asleep for less than three hours.

He could hear Buddy whimpering, and when he looked over the
side of the bed, the dog was sitting there, bright in the moonlight, his
eyes wide with anxiety. He pawed at the side of the mattress, wanting to climb up into the bed.

Will shook his head; the dog knew that this was not permitted.
Buddy continued to stare up at him, silently negotiating, as if trying
to assure Will that it would only be for this one time.

The thunder boomed again, and the dog jumped, his claws scrab-
bling against the wooden floor.

"You win again," Will said. He slid over to Laurie's side of the
bed, patting the empty space on the mattress. The dog climbed up
and turned around in a small circle on top of the sheets, as if he

didn't quite know what to do now that he had gained entrance to this forbidden territory.

Will patted the mattress again. The dog finally lay down on his side, head on top of the pillow. He watched Will with one eye, his front legs stretching out toward him, the leathery pads on the bottoms of his feet almost touching Will's face.

Will stroked his hand along the fur on the dog's side, watching as Buddy's eyelid fell shut.

When the rain came, Will heard a single drop hit the metal roof, like a gunshot. Then it began to fall faster and harder, building into a deluge, the water drumming against the roof and running loud inside the gutters and downspouts.

SEVENTY-EIGHT

The bodies were discovered the next morning.

Mike Lopez came by the department a few minutes past noon to pick Will up. Lopez wore his ranger's hat, the peak of the felt crown brushing against the headliner of the Forest Service truck. The cabin smelled of stale cigar smoke.

"One of my men found them." Lopez chewed on the plastic tip of his unlit cigar. "Saw some smoke, thought it might be an illegal camp-fire."

They drove past the rusting Rotary Club sign at the edge of the town. A young girl sat by the side of the road at a folding card table that held a plastic pitcher of lemonade and a stack of Dixie cups.

The palms of Will's hands were coated with sweat; he laid them down on the fabric of his jeans.

Lopez turned onto a Forest Service road, driving into the farthest reaches of the woods, until Will no longer had any sense of where he was. The road started to climb the flank of a mountain, the growth of trees becoming so dense that Lopez removed his sunglasses so that he could see.

The truck's radio was tuned to a sports station, but the signal began to fade until it was only static. Will reached out and turned it off, the two of them sitting there in the cabin of the truck, the only sound that of the off-road tires on the uneven ground.

Lopez stole a glance over at Will. "I'm sorry about Thomas."

Will kept looking forward, out through the dusty windshield. Droplets of water clung to the underside of tree branches, like tears.

"So am I," he said.

They came to a clearing ringed by tall pines. Lopez pulled on the parking brake and turned off the engine.

A fog hung in the air, the warmth of the sun evaporating the fallen rain. Puddles of water lay scattered on the ground. On top of a large flat rock there was a pyre of split wood. The logs were only partially burned, extinguished by last night's rainstorm. Otherwise, there would have been nothing left for them to find.

The air smelled of wood smoke and scorched skin, buzzing with insects that he could not see.

Will felt himself moving closer to the wooden pyre, as if he were on a conveyor belt. Two blackened forms lay on top of it, a burnt offering.

The corpses were dressed in clothing that had mostly been burned away by the flames, the visible flesh blistered and turned the color of charcoal. Their hands and feet were bound with lengths of baling wire. Both of their throats had been sliced open by a sharp instrument.

Will recognized one of the faces as that of Ike Carver. His eyelids were singed shut, the skin of his face runneled like dripping candle wax. His mouth was opened in a rictus of pain, the enamel on the teeth melted away.

The face on the other corpse was nothing but a scorched and bubbled caul. But the size and shape of the body was almost identical to Ike's, and it was evident to Will that he was looking at the corpse of Ike's twin brother, Trevor.

Will's stomach shifted inside him. He felt nauseated and weak and wondered in passing if he would ever be able to feel good again.

Mike Lopez stood a short distance away, watching him. "You okay?"

Will swallowed. "Why does everybody keep asking me that?"

Will thought about whether to use the radio in Lopez's truck to call the state lab and request a crime scene tech. He decided that it would take too long, that he would attempt to process the scene himself. It wasn't all that hard to know what to look for when you already knew who did it.

He had brought the department's evidence kit, and he now went to get it from the cargo bay of the Forest Service truck.

He looked over at Lopez. "Can you stay here with me?"

Lopez looked at his wristwatch. "What for?"

"I want a witness while I do this," Will said. "In case it goes to trial."

Lopez nodded. "What do you need me to do?"

"Just watch."

Will pulled on a pair of surgical gloves and started with the perimeter, walking in a circle, slowly working his way inward toward the flat rock. He spotted something in the damp earth and crouched to take a closer look.

An oblong shape was pressed into the ground. He examined it and saw that it was the heel of a man's boot, adjacent to the imprint of a Vibram-type sole.

Will took an L-shaped measurement scale from the evidence kit and placed it on the ground alongside the boot print, then used the digital camera to snap some photographs. It would have been nice to take an impression, but the kit did not contain the necessary materials.

He approached the pyre and took some pictures of the two charred bodies, the shutter clicking inside the camera. His throat burned with stomach acid; he wished he had brought along a bottle of water.

He started with Ike, beginning at his feet and working his way upward, gagging on the smell.

The right leg of Ike's blackened jeans was ripped at the calf, the flesh beneath torn away. Will looked closer, puzzled to see that there was no sign of bleeding. He raised the camera to take a picture, but when he looked through the viewfinder he noticed the pattern of bite marks and realized that an animal had been gnawing at the corpse.

Ike Carver had been wearing an inexpensive watch on his left wrist. The heat from the fire had melted the plastic casing, the face stretched out, the numbers distorted.

Ike's hands were clenched into fists. Will took hold of Ike's left wrist, as if he were grabbing a handful of dry leaves. He pried open Ike's rigor-locked fingers and used a magnifying lens from the evidence kit to look underneath the fingernails, but didn't see anything.

He opened Ike's right hand. When he examined the fingernails with the lens, he spotted something right away. He switched the camera to the macro setting and took a close-up of the tip of the fingernail.

He put the camera down and took a pair of forceps and a plastic evidence bag from the kit. Working carefully, he plucked the pieces of hair from beneath the nail, dropping them inside the evidence bag.

Will held the bag up toward the cobalt sky, examining the hair samples. They were coarse and curled slightly at the ends and were the white color of Frank Carver's beard.

SEVENTY-NINE

In the dimness of the forest, Frank Carver's house glowed with the incandescent light coming from behind the large sheets of glass.

Will checked the clock on the dashboard of the department's truck, surprised to see that it was only a few minutes before five, the dense trees blotting out the afternoon sunlight.

He switched off the ignition, listening to the ticking of the engine.

He drew his gun and racked the slide to feed a round into the chamber. He checked that the safety was on and slid the gun back inside the holster.

He opened the glove compartment and took out an extra clip for the gun and loaded it from a box of Hydra-Shoks. He shoved the clip into the front pocket of his jeans, then climbed down from the truck.

Will stood on the doormat at the front door of Frank Carver's house and pressed the illuminated button for the doorbell. He listened to the sound of the chimes bounce around inside the house, but heard no sign of movement. He pressed the bell again and waited, breathing slowly through his nose in an attempt to calm his heartbeat.

When no one came to the door, he peeked through one of the panes of glass.

The living room was a disaster area, one of the avocado-colored sofas upended, the glass top of the coffee table shattered. Books that had been knocked from the bookcases lay open on the floor.

Will decided that what he was looking at constituted probable cause, that it was reasonable evidence that some kind of struggle had occurred. He pressed the thumb lever on the door handle, and the front door swung open. He drew his gun before stepping into the living room.

"POLICE," he shouted. "Anybody home?" His words echoed up in the room's cathedral ceiling, but there was no response.

Will took a step and felt a piece of glass crunch beneath the sole of his boot. He looked down and saw a picture frame smashed on the floor, a photograph of a young Frank Carver holding his infant twins, one in the crook of each tattooed arm.

"*POLICE*," he called out again. "Anyone here?"

He stood frozen in place, listening, holding his breath so that it wouldn't interfere with his hearing.

He could hear a faint sound. It sounded like the clapping of hands, and it seemed to be coming from the kitchen.

A rectangular cutout in the wall led into the kitchen. Will pressed his back against the Sheetrock, off to the side of the opening. "This is the police," he called. "Is someone in there?"

No one answered. Leading with the gun, he went into the kitchen.

Will swept the room, looking over the front gun sight. Knotty pine cabinets and a harvest gold side-by-side. Butcher-block counters. A mop bucket sat out in the middle of the vinyl-covered floor, a blue sponge floating in soapy liquid.

He smelled the cloying fragrance of Pine-Sol, but also something else, like rotting meat. He walked over to the counter and saw a large mound of ground beef sitting in a yellow foam butcher's tray. The plastic wrapping had been torn open, the meat starting to turn brown, crawling with black flies.

Next to the sink, a boning knife lay on top of a green dish towel. The blade was clean but patterned with droplets of water.

He heard the sound again. Definitely people clapping, what sounded like a large crowd. He turned and saw a door in the far corner of the room. It was slightly ajar, the sound coming from the other side of it.

Will stood beside the door and listened, his heart loud in his ears. He could hear a lot of people now, clapping and cheering.

"GIVE ME AN 'F' . . ."

Will jumped. It was a man's voice, shouting, as if he were leading a cheer at a high school pep rally.

An enormous chorus of voices answered in unison, so loud that the door vibrated. *"FFFFFFF . . ."*

Will sneaked a quick peek through the gap in the doorway, saw stairs leading down into darkness. A basement.

"GIVE ME A 'U' . . . ," the man shouted.

Will stuck the gun around the door frame, then followed it with his head.

"UUUUUUUU . . ." The sound of the crowd's chant was earsplitting inside the confines of the stairwell. Down at the bottom of the stairs was a strange orange and red light, moving across the carpeted floor like dancing flames.

"GIVE ME A 'C' . . ."

In the darkness, Will pressed his back against the railing and felt with his boot for the tread of the first step. The air reeked of marijuana smoke. He kept the gun pointed down toward the orange light, his hand shaking.

"GIVE ME A 'K' . . ."

Both sides of the stairwell were enclosed with plywood paneling, restricting his vision. All he could see was the orange and red light moving across the floor down at the bottom.

"WHAT'S THAT SPELL??? WHAT'S THAT SPELL??? WHAT'S THAT SPELL???"

He listened to the crowd chanting the answer, suddenly placing what he was listening to, remembered listening to it when he was a teenager.

The sound track album *Woodstock*.

He listened to the sound of the crowd, so lifelike it seemed to be down there in the basement with the strange lights. He heard a single strummed chord from an acoustic guitar, and then a man began to sing. Will thought it was the band Country Joe and the Fish, but he couldn't remember the name of the song.

He had now reached the bottom step. He could see that the basement floor was covered with shag carpeting, the strange lights moving across the surface.

"And it's one, two, three, what are we fighting for?" The singing was so loud that it was difficult for Will to think.

He took the last step, convinced he was stepping into some kind of trap. His foot sank into the deep pile of the carpeting. He could see a tall stack of stereo equipment, the dials and gauges glowing with green light. Other than that, the room's only source of illumination was a lava lamp, orange and red globules swimming around inside.

Will's view of the room was still partially blocked by the wall of the stairwell, but he saw a pair of legs propped up on an oak coffee table, the feet shod in heavy black engineer boots.

Will took another step into the basement, screaming out the word, "POLICE."

His voice was swallowed up by the music, making him question whether anything had even come from his mouth.

"And it's five, six, seven, open up the pearly gates . . ." The sound came from two massive speakers on the far side of the room.

Frank Carver sat on a futon couch, his eyes closed. A joint burned in a metal ashtray set on the coffee table, blue smoke curling upward from the tip. He wore a faded T-shirt that read STEPPENWOLF.

Will pointed the gun at the other man's chest. "FRANK CARVER," he shouted.

Frank didn't seem to hear. His eyes remained closed, his right hand hidden from view behind a cushion.

Will looked at the stereo and saw a record spinning on the platter of the turntable. He went toward it, trying to keep one eye on Frank. The smoke filling the room made his eyes tear.

He lifted the plastic dustcover of the turntable and reached out for the tonearm. His hand shook as he tried to grab the headshell, an amplified scratching sound coming through the big speakers as the needle skittered away across the spinning vinyl.

The music stopped.

Frank Carver's eyes snapped open, like those of a lizard that had been dozing on a sun-warmed rock. "What the *fuck?*" he said.

Frank's hand was still hidden behind the cushion. The orange and red patterns of the lava lamp moved across his face. Then his arm began to move.

Will centered the gun sight on Frank's chest. "*FREEZE.*"

Frank grinned and shook his head. "It's a bottle of *Bud.*"

Will held the gun on him. "Slowly."

Frank took his hand out from behind the cushion. It *was* a bottle of beer. He brought it to his lips and drank from it. "You need to chill."

"How do you turn on the lights?" Will asked him.

Behind the lenses of his eyeglasses, Frank's eyes were glassy and bloodshot. He raised both of his hands and clapped them together. A floor lamp in the corner switched on.

Frank held out his open palms as if he had just performed a magic trick. "As seen on TV."

Will could now see the room, hazy with smoke. The paneled walls were covered with framed memorabilia, like a museum dedicated to the psychedelic era. Hanging behind Frank's head was a poster promoting an appearance by the Grateful Dead at the Avalon Ballroom.

The colorful artwork featured a skeleton, the skull adorned with roses the color of blood.

Frank picked up the joint from the ashtray and took a hit. "Feel like telling me what you're doing in my crib?"

Will held the gun on him. "You're under arrest for the murders of your sons."

Frank blew out twin streams of smoke through his nostrils. "Why would I murder my own sons?"

Will stared at him. "You could have at least tried to act surprised when I told you they were dead."

Frank looked at him from the couch. "That doesn't prove shit."

Will reached into his shirt pocket and took out the evidence bag. "Yeah, but I think this does."

He held the bag out toward Frank. The color of the hair seemed to be a perfect match with his beard. "I found this under Ike's finger-nail. Too bad for you it rained."

Frank looked at the evidence bag. "Into each life some rain must fall."

A long gouge ran down his left cheek, fresh blood crusted at the edges.

"What happened to your face?" Will asked.

Frank reached up and touched the scratch. "Goddamned cats," he said.

Will took a laminated Miranda card from the pocket of his jeans and began to read from it. "You have the right to remain silent. Any-thing you say can—"

Frank began to talk over him. " 'And he made a trumpet of his arse . . .' "

Will looked up. "What did you say?"

"Do we really have to go through this fucking *charade*?" Frank asked. "Again? You dragging me down to the police station, just so Isgro can cut me loose?"

"I'm not taking you to the police station," Will said. "The sheriff's department has a chopper on its way here. You're going to the county lockup."

Frank looked at him and shook his head. He seemed unfazed, as if he were talking to a neighbor who had dropped in for a cup of coffee. "You just don't get it, do you? You could take me to *Leavenworth*, it wouldn't make a lick of difference."

Will felt claustrophobic. It was as if he were getting a contact high from the air inside the room, making it hard to think straight. "What makes you so sure?"

Frank lifted his head, the green lights of the stereo reflecting on the lenses of his eyeglasses. "Because I'm the man who knew too much."

EIGHTY

"There are a lot of people in high places who wouldn't want me pissing outside the tent," Frank said.

Will stood there, looking down at him. "They already let you go to prison once."

Frank took a hit off the joint. "I made it explicitly clear I wouldn't be willing to do that again."

"What is it that you did? What could be so bad that they'd protect you like this?"

"I could tell you," Frank said. "But then I'd have to kill you."

Will drove his fist into Frank's face. It was his left, the hand that wasn't holding on to the gun, but it still managed to break open Frank's lip.

Blood ran down into Frank's white beard. "Now I might have to kill you anyway."

Will whipped the barrel of the gun across Frank's cheek. His glasses flew off his face and landed beside him on the futon.

"Tell me," Will said.

Frank smiled up at him from the couch. The blood had turned

the beard surrounding his mouth a bright crimson, like the makeup on the face of a clown.

Will brought the gun up to strike Frank again, but Frank raised his hands. "Save your energy." He picked his glasses up and fitted them back on his face. "I suppose I can tell you. From what I've seen, nobody listens to you anyway."

Frank took another joint from his pocket and lit it with a plastic lighter. "Back in the midsixties, the government put together a joint task force," Frank said. "FBI, CIA, National Security Agency, to prepare for defense against American youth unrest."

Frank exhaled, blue smoke rising up and wreathing his head. "McNamara and the generals were freaked, because the whole hippie movement was getting out of control. 'Sixty-seven was the march on the Pentagon, the following summer there were riots at the Chicago Democratic Convention. They thought the peace movement was growing too powerful, that it posed a legitimate threat to the war."

Frank stopped talking, looking at Will to see if he was following along. A framed black-and-white photograph hung on the wall behind him, a Buddhist monk setting himself aflame on a Saigon street, his body encased in a cocoon of fire.

"I'm listening," Will said.

"They put together lists of U.S. citizens deemed threats to national security. They decided to start with the cultural leaders of what they were calling the New Left, musicians, celebrities, people they saw as role models. They wanted to get rid of them or discredit them."

"How?"

"They started slipping them drugs."

"Why?" Will said. "Couldn't they get them on their own?"

Frank shook his head. "Not like this. They spiked their beer with sixteen hundred mikes of pure LSD-25. Or gave them bags of China white and told them it was coke. Trying to get them to freak out in public, or OD."

"I don't believe you," Will said.

Frank smiled. "What, you thought it was a coincidence, all those musicians suddenly start choking to death on their own puke?"

Will's head throbbed from the smoke. "So that's what you did? You slipped drugs to somebody?"

Frank shook his head. "They used me for something a little bigger."

"Like?"

"The Army Chemical Corps had started testing a new hallucinogen called BZ."

"Brown acid," Will said.

Frank pointed a finger at Will and nodded. "That's what they called it on the street. This stuff was ten thousand times more powerful than LSD, you'd stay high for days. Problem was, it caused a lot of bad trips, made people crazy violent."

"I thought this story was supposed to be about you."

"It is," Frank said. He took another hit off the joint, ashes falling down into his beard. "By the fall of 'sixty-nine, the government was in full-blown panic mode. Things were spinning out of control. Half a million freaks had just turned out for Woodstock, massive peace rallies were being held all across the country."

The gun was growing heavy in Will's hand. "Thanks for the history lesson. But what does any of this have to do with Frank Carver?"

Frank smiled. He was enjoying this, as if he'd been dying for the chance to tell someone. "The powers were desperate to find some way to put the genie back inside the bottle. By that time, I was second in command at the Oakland chapter of the Angels. We got hired to provide security for a Stones concert at the Altamont Speedway, remember?"

"Altamont, the death of the sixties," Will said. "The crowd went crazy, an African American man was stabbed to death by the Hell's Angels."

Frank shook his head. "*Four* people died that day. The spade just got all the attention."

Will felt his patience give way, as if it were a physical thing that had broken. "What's your fucking *point?*"

Frank's lips and teeth were smeared with red. "The point is this," he said. "My agency handler gave me fifteen thousand hits of BZ to give away at Altamont."

Frank sat back on the futon couch, the orange and red light playing over his face. "The rest, as they like to say, is history."

EIGHTY-ONE

The basement was silent except for the sound of the air-conditioning compressor as it labored to cool the house.

Will tried to think of what he should do next, how he might alter his plan. He understood now why Frank was being protected, why they wouldn't want him making an appearance on *Larry King*.

It was hard to think. His head felt like someone had stuffed it with cotton, no sense of time here in this subterranean room with no clock or windows.

He gestured with the gun at Frank Carver. "Get up."

Frank looked up from the futon couch. "What for?"

"Get on your feet."

Frank shook his head as if he were dealing with a slow child. "You're still going to arrest me?"

"No," Will said.

"Then what are we doing?"

"Let's take a walk," Will said.

* * *

The yard was lost in shadow, but the air was still warm.

Will kept the gun centered between Frank's shoulder blades, following him over the uneven ground that was littered with dead pine needles.

The fire tower rose up ahead of them. It stood on tall wooden stilts, a staircase zigzagging upward inside of them. The observation room perched at the top, high up above the darkness of the trees, the sun flaring off its glass walls like the beacon of a lighthouse.

"Where are we going?" Frank asked.

Will pointed at the tower. "Up there."

A hot breeze blew through the boughs of the pines, shadows moving across Frank's back. "Why?"

"I'm going to assist you."

"With *what*?"

"Suicide," Will said.

They climbed the wooden staircase of the fire tower, moving upward toward the burning sun.

Will kept his left hand on the railing, his other hand pointing the gun at Frank Carver's back. He took no pleasure in this task, an executioner dutifully climbing the gallows. He only wanted it to be over.

Frank spoke as he climbed. "What are you doing this for?" he said. "I mean, what makes you so sure you're wearing the white hat?"

"I need for you to keep moving."

"Ever heard of John Mulholland?" Frank asked.

Will could hear the sound of the sheriff's department helicopter, coming from somewhere off to the east. He now regretted calling for it, but at the time he had no way of knowing the way things were going to play out.

"He was a famous magician," Frank said. "The agency hired him to teach us sleight of hand. So we could slip acid into people's drinks. You can look it up on the Internet."

They had risen above the tops of the trees, Will squinting his eyes against the bright sunlight. He kept a safe distance away from Frank, wary that he was going to try something. He wished he could put him in cuffs, but didn't want to leave any marks on Frank's wrists that would raise questions at a postmortem.

"All that Orange Sunshine the Manson family gobbled before they killed Sharon Tate?" Frank said. "It came from a group called the Brotherhood of Eternal Love. They were a front for the CIA. You can look it up."

They continued to climb into the blistering sun. Will wanted Frank to be quiet. His head was still throbbing from all the second-hand smoke he had inhaled.

Frank continued to speak. "When Timothy Leary was testing psychedelics at Harvard, the head of the department was ex-CIA. One of their test subjects was a young man named Ted Kaczynski, later known as the Unabomber."

"What's your *point*?" Will said.

Frank's head swiveled around. "What makes you so sure you're working for the good guys?"

"I'm not working for anybody," Will said.

They reached the top of the staircase. The glass-walled lookout cabin was encircled by a narrow balcony that was like a widow's walk. The balcony was enclosed by a waist-high railing, the wood painted white. Beyond it, the view was dizzying.

Will looked down on the tops of the trees and the twisting jade ribbon of river, the faraway shingled rooftops of the town. The sound of the approaching helicopter was louder now. He needed to get this over with before anyone inside the chopper had a view of what he was about to do.

"Move down to the end," Will said.

Frank looked a question at him but moved forward, his heavy boots clomping on the wooden decking.

Will moved along the wall of windows, clouds and sky reflected in the panes of glass. He could see Frank's office on the other side, a chair and desk, the shape of a typewriter hidden beneath a green vinyl cover. All of it covered by mounds of dust like dirty snowdrifts.

Will turned back just as Frank made his move. The other man's right hand snaked down, spatulate fingers disappearing inside the back pocket of his jeans.

Will drove his forearm against Frank's broad chest, shoving him back against the wooden railing. He jammed the barrel of the gun up underneath Frank's jaw, the gun sight disappearing into his beard.

"Don't fucking move," Will said.

Frank didn't try to struggle. "Relax. I just want to show you something."

Will's gut screamed that it was some kind of trick, or at least a stall tactic. The sound of the helicopter's rotor was closer now, coming from the far side of the ridge. Not much time left.

Frank's breath smelled like moldering leaves. "Trust me," he said. "You really need to see this."

Will took a step back, centering the gun on Frank's chest. "Take your hand out," he said. "Slowly."

Will watched Frank's hand emerge from the pocket, something that looked like a piece of paper between his fingers.

"What is that?"

Frank held it up for him to see.

It was a Polaroid photograph, the colors lurid, imparting a surrealistic quality to the image.

Laurie sat at the foot of a bed covered with a green chenille spread. Silver duct tape wrapped around her head, covering her mouth. She looked directly into the lens of the camera, frozen in the white light of the flash, her eyes glassy and wide with fear.

"I tried to get her to smile," Frank said. "But she wouldn't do it."

Behind Laurie's head, a television sat on top of a dresser. It was switched on, the image on the screen from a news show, a banner showing the date, JULY 8, 2006.

Four days ago.

Far below, Will watched the ground begin to spin, as if he were on a carnival ride. He suddenly felt acrophobic, desperate to get back down to the earth.

Will stared at the photograph. "What is that?" He tried to make his voice sound even, but he could hear it break. "What *is* that?"

Frank Carver's gaze was as blank and pitiless as the sun. " 'Though lovers be lost, love shall—' "

Will grabbed the front of Frank's shirt and drove him backward. His boots came off the deck, his body cantilevered out over the railing, the ground far below.

"Where is she?"

"Somewhere you'll never find her," Frank said.

"I'll kill you, you sick fuck."

"You still don't get it, do you?" Frank was smiling now. "You kill me, you'll never find your wife."

Will continued to grasp the bunched material of Frank's shirt, the weight of his body heavy, a chore to hold him there against the force of gravity. "What've you done to her?"

"Let me break this down for you," Frank said. "Your wife is hidden in a place where no one will ever be able to find her. She has no food, no water. You will allow me to go free while you wait here. When I'm someplace safe, I will call you and tell you where to find her."

Birds reeled above them in the sky, their shadows moving across Frank's face. "If I am arrested or otherwise inconvenienced, I will not tell you where she is hidden. She will die, and it will all be on you."

"How do I know she's not dead already?" Will had to raise his voice over the roar of the approaching helicopter. In a few seconds it would clear the ridgetop and come into view.

"Trust me, she's fine." Frank smiled. "Just spending a little time in isolation."

Will stared into Frank's eyes. The phrase had triggered something inside his mind. He tried to remember who he'd heard say it recently.

When the memory clicked into place, he allowed his fingers to come open, letting go of Frank Carver's shirt.

EIGHTY-TWO

From behind the lenses of his black-framed eyeglasses, Frank's eyes widened with surprise.

The smile faded from his lips as he dropped backward over the railing, his eyes still locked on Will's.

For a long moment he seemed to hover there in the air, like some enormous bird of prey.

Then the forces of gravity took over, and the ground seemed to rush up to embrace him. His mouth opened as if to speak, but whatever he was attempting to say was cut off by the impact of his body slamming into the earth.

One of his boots flew off and came to rest upright at his side, the ground turning red.

Will leaned out over the railing. He was surprised by how small Frank's body looked now, lying there on the ground, a shattered urn. He lay on his back, one arm thrown above his head as if he were swimming the backstroke.

Will stared down, waiting to feel something. A gust of wind swayed the treetops, the warm breeze seeming to pass right through him, as if he were no longer solid. He closed his eyes and saw the charred bodies of the twins on their smoldering pyre. He wondered what the rest of his life would be like, trying to carry these images around with him.

Then the sound of the helicopter became a deafening roar, and when he glanced up it cleared the tall and pointed trees of the ridge.

The helicopter set down in the dirt clearing behind Frank Carver's house, the rotor churning up waves of dust and brown pine needles.

Will held up his hand to shield his eyes and watched a man drop from the cockpit of the chopper. He wore a khaki-colored jumpsuit, a star-shaped sheriff's department badge pinned to the left side of his chest.

Will ran toward him, crouched low to stay clear of the still beating rotor. He held his opened badge holder out in front of him.

He had to shout over the noise of the helicopter. "You have a map?"

"What kind?" the deputy said.

"Topo, if you've got one."

The deputy leaned back inside the helicopter and said something to the pilot. When he turned back around, he was holding a rolled-up tube of paper.

Will took it and slipped off the rubber band. He unfurled the topographic map, looking at the green of the printed woods, the blue of the lakes and rivers.

"Where are we?" Will asked.

The deputy came around to look over his shoulder, then put a fingertip down on the surface of the map.

Will scanned outward from the indicated spot, running his eyes over the brown contour lines, crowded together in the steep areas, spread apart in the flats. He had to keep a firm grip on the edges of the map because it kept trying to roll itself back up again.

Almost due west of where they were now standing, Will spotted what he was looking for. A symbol, one pickaxe crossed over another, forming an **X**.

Will checked the scale markings printed at the bottom of the page, estimating that it was less than a mile away over mostly flat terrain.

The deputy cleared his throat. "Where's your prisoner?"

Will looked up at him. "Dead." He had shouted the word, speaking too loud, now that the helicopter's rotor had finally spun down.

"What happened?"

"Suicide." Will rolled the map back into a tube, then slipped the rubber band back in place. "Can I take this?"

The deputy seemed confused. "Where are you going?"

Will's thoughts were racing, conscious of precious time being wasted. "I have to find my wife."

The officer shook his head. "I need you to stay here."

Will didn't have time to explain, aware of the sun sinking lower in the western sky. He pointed toward the base of the tower. "The body's over there."

When the officer turned to look, Will ran off.

EIGHTY-THREE

He could hear the shouting as he ran, but it soon began to fade away behind him, and he knew that he was not being pursued.

In the dirt yard, Will stopped to grab his backpack from the passenger seat of the truck. He shouldered it on, then plunged into the dense woods.

He ran through the lengthening shadows, nothing now but the sound of his ragged breath and twigs snapping under his feet. He was in a box canyon, no trails here in this part of the forest. He threaded his way around the trunks of cedars and madrones and pines, branches tearing at his clothes and face.

The dense foliage blocked out the sky. He could no longer see the position of the sun and became unsure if he was heading in the right direction. He wished that he had asked the deputy for a compass.

The horrible image from the Polaroid appeared in his mind, Laurie sitting there on that bed, the look in her eyes. The date on the television screen had been from Saturday morning, meaning that Frank had snatched Laurie right after she had walked out on him.

He should have called her, made sure she'd made it home safely.

But he hadn't wanted to seem needy, wanted to give her time to calm down. The enormity of his selfishness revealed itself to him with breathtaking clarity. It was all his fault; he should never have invited her up here, should have acknowledged the danger.

He needed to find the water. That was his landmark. On the map, the mine had appeared just on the far side of a creek.

It felt as if he had been running for an eternity. He had nothing left, but he forced himself to run faster, his heart bursting in his chest, each breath filling his lungs with fire. He welcomed the pain as a kind of self-flagellation, a way to drown out the accusatory thoughts.

He saw the sunlight reflecting off something up ahead of him, shimmering over the rough bark of the trees. He came to a creek bed, nothing but a thin trickle of muddy water flowing through some rocks.

He took the map from the backpack and unfurled it, finding the blue vein of the creek. Could this really be it? On the map it looked the size of a small river. He couldn't seem to catch his breath, his brain starving for oxygen. He decided that this had to be the creek, that its waters had been dried up by the summer heat.

On the map, the crossed pickaxes appeared just millimeters away from it, just off to the west, on the other side of the creek.

Standing there, beside the dry creek bed, he now had a clear view of the sun. He checked his watch. It was just past six; he figured the sun should be almost due west in the July sky.

He ran toward it.

EIGHTY-FOUR

After a few minutes a wooded hillside rose up in front of him. Will sprinted to the top of it and found himself standing in a small clearing enclosed by tall evergreens.

He scanned the clearing, not sure what he was looking for. He'd never seen a mine in real life before. He'd been hoping for something obvious, maybe a big timber-framed opening in the side of a mountain, like a ride he'd once gone on at Disneyland.

But there was nothing here, aside from a few rocks and a small and scrubby oak. He must have misread the map, or somehow gone wrong in his orienteering. He looked off into the distance, nothing but green for as far as the eye could see. The mine could be anywhere.

He cupped his hands to his mouth and shouted out Laurie's name, but there was no answer. He paced around the small clearing, trying to figure out where he might have gone wrong.

Will turned, ready to leave the clearing and begin retracing his steps, but then he felt something underfoot.

He backed up, walked over the patch of ground again. The earth was softer here, almost spongy. He used the toe of his boot to push aside some of the dirt and pine needles.

He saw a piece of wood, weathered and dark. He dropped to his knees and used his hands to clear away the dirt. Underneath there were wide boards that had been fashioned into a trapdoor.

On one side of it he found a handle, a circle of black cast iron. He took hold of it and pulled upward, but the door didn't move. He pushed more of the dirt out of the way until he had uncovered all of the door. At the top was a steel hasp closed with a brass padlock, both much newer than the rest of the door.

He climbed to his feet and went off to find a rock. He selected one that came to a point.

He knelt down beside the padlock and raised the rock into the air above his head. He smashed the point of the rock down on the shackle of the lock. Then he did it again, over and over until the rock became slick and red with his blood.

He checked the shackle of the lock. There were only a few small nicks in the metal. He pulled on the lock, but it was solid.

He drew his gun from the leather holster. He hesitated before thumbing off the safety. If the bullet went down into the mine shaft, it would ricochet forever, hitting Laurie. He decided to risk it, holding the body of the gun parallel to the ground. He squeezed the trigger once, a blast of fire coming from the muzzle.

Birds lifted from out of the treetops, darkening the sky.

Will took hold of the black ring and pulled. The door was heavy and swung upward on rusted hinges. Cold air wafted up from the darkness, carrying the smell of rotting things.

The opening in the ground was framed with redwood timbers. Will lay down on the ground and stuck his head into the opening.

He could see nothing, his pupils still constricted from the bright sunshine. He heard the repetitive sound of water dripping, like a leaking faucet.

"LAURIE?" He shouted. "It's Will, are you down there?"

There was no answer, just his own voice echoing back at him.

His eyes began to adjust to the darkness. A tunnel had been scooped from the earth, just tall enough for a man to stand up, the rock walls mottled with white patches of efflorescence. The shadows of the trees moved across the stone, shadow deepening shadow. He could see perhaps six feet down into the tunnel before it disappeared into blackness.

He grabbed the backpack from the ground and rummaged inside for the flashlight, but couldn't find it. He upended the pack, dumping the contents out onto the ground.

It wasn't there. In his haste to flee from Frank Carver's house, he must have left it in the glove compartment of the truck.

He climbed to his feet and stepped into the opening of the mine shaft. The ground sloped away underneath his feet, like walking down a steep ramp, drawing him down into the earth.

EIGHTY-FIVE

With every step, the sunlight and air retreated behind him. The temperature dropped as if he were entering a walk-in freezer, the cold air penetrating his sweat-soaked shirt.

His body blocked out most of the light coming through the opening, only a few particles managing to sneak through. He forced his eyes to open wider, willing them to adjust to the darkness.

The ceiling dropped down, forcing him to lower his head and crouch as he moved, his spine spasming with pain. Just ahead, he saw that the tunnel turned sharply to the left.

He turned the corner, the darkness utter and complete now, like sitting in a movie theater in the moments before the film is projected onto the screen. Colorful shapes swam across his field of vision.

Will extended his arms out in front of him, using his hands to feel along the cold and hard stone. His feet splashed as they moved, as if there were a small stream running along the ground.

He could smell something, the sulfurous odor of rotting eggs. His eyes began to burn. He blinked his eyelids, but it didn't help.

Then he froze. In the darkness he heard something move.

"LAURIE?"

The sound came toward him, like the flutter of wings. He strained to see in the blackness.

Something slammed into his face.

Will staggered backward against the wall of the tunnel, leathery wings beating against his cheeks and lips. He swatted at the bat with his hands, felt it drop down on his foot. He kicked at it in blind panic, then heard the beating of its wings as it flew away.

He continued to shuffle forward, the tunnel growing narrower as he went, the stone walls scraping against his shoulders. He grew worried that he wouldn't be able to turn around, would somehow have to back his way out.

He called out her name, over and over now as if it were a mantra, but there was no answer from the darkness.

She's not here.

Inside the narrow tunnel, there was nowhere for him to escape the accusing Greek chorus of his thoughts, convinced now that he had guessed wrong. He had seized on a single word, "isolation," had gambled Laurie's whole life on it in his lust to kill.

The blackness of the mine shaft poured into his heart, his thoughts tearing him to pieces.

In the purity of his despair he could see the truth, his victory over Frank Carver no more meaningful than that of Pyrrhus, his losses too devastating. If he had only been willing to let Frank live, he would have been able to find her. The librarian had pegged him correctly after all, had been right to accuse him of hubris.

The smell of rotten eggs was stronger now. His head pounded and he thought he might need to vomit. He grabbed the stone wall for balance, wondering if there might be some kind of gas down here. He'd read about miners who had been killed that way; it was the reason they had used canaries.

Will knew he needed to turn back, to get back to the surface while he still could. What would be served by him dying down here?

But he continued to shuffle forward, moving deeper into the blackness. He had managed a few steps when his toe slammed into something down on the ground.

Will pitched forward into the blackness, the side of his head banging against a protruding rock.

He fell to the damp ground. Ice water ran around his cheek and up into his nostrils. He tried to lift his head, but it was far too heavy.

He spoke Laurie's name one more time, only a whisper, using the last of his energy.

Then he passed out.

EIGHTY-SIX

He opened his eyes, but it made no difference.

In the absolute darkness of the mine, there was only the slightest shift from one shade of black to another. He had lost all sense of direction, had no idea which way led back to the entrance. The rotten egg smell was nauseating.

He lifted his arm and looked at the phosphorescent green face of his watch, surprised to see that only ten minutes had gone by since he had entered the shaft.

He couldn't recall ever feeling so tired. He wanted nothing more than to shut his eyes and go to sleep.

But then he remembered Laurie, and with a grunting effort he managed to push himself up onto his hands and knees. He crawled along in the darkness, feeling the ground with his hands, trying to find what it was that he had tripped over.

His arm bumped into something, and he reached over and touched it, its texture rough as sackcloth.

It felt like a large bag. He ran his hands over it, the shapes inside familiar to him. Even in the darkness, he knew what it was. He began to sweat in spite of the cold.

He shook the sack. "Laurie?"

There was no sound or movement. He found a small opening at the top of the sack, just large enough for him to insert his hand. He felt the fine strands of her hair, ran his hands over her face, as if he were a blind person trying to feel what someone looked like. He held his open palm beneath her nose, but couldn't feel her breathing.

Will used both hands to try to rip the sack open, but the material was too strong. He considered using his pocketknife, but thought it was too dangerous in the dark.

He scooped the bag up in his arms, straining to stand upright. His head slammed into the rock ceiling, pinpoints of white blooming in front of him. Will staggered ahead, hunched over at the waist, struggling to hold her weight close to his chest. She did not move inside the bag, like a sack of stones, the heaviest thing he had ever carried.

He felt as if he were being torn apart. He tried to cling to some shred of hope that she was still alive but was afraid to invest too much in it.

He moved forward, faltering, his progress coming in inches. He would have given anything to be able to stand upright, to stop the bolts of electricity that shot down the backs of his legs.

How much farther? He grew worried that he was going in the wrong direction, heading deeper inside the mine, lost in the labyrinth of darkness.

He couldn't smell the rotten egg odor anymore. He wondered if it was still there, if he had just gotten used to it. He was convinced that it was some kind of toxic gas: He was having trouble keeping his balance, his head splitting.

He wanted to sit down and rest, just for a minute, the urge overpowering. But he was afraid that if he did, he would never get up again. He kept going; not for himself, only for her. He didn't want to leave her down here in this dark place.

The ground now began to pitch upward more steeply, and he thought that he could detect light, just a gray apparition at first, then filling the tunnel so that he could see nothing but white, like walking into the sun.

EIGHTY-SEVEN

Will laid the sack down on the carpet of pine needles.

He unsnapped the blade of his pocketknife and cut open the burlap, working as carefully as a surgeon.

When he saw her face, a strangled sound escaped from his throat. Her eyes were closed, her skin the color of the open sky.

Her wrists and ankles were bound with silver duct tape. He used the sharp blade to free them, then pulled away the piece of tape that covered her mouth. He worried about hurting her, but there was no reaction when he tore the tape from her skin.

He knelt beside Laurie's chest on the floor of the clearing. He tilted her head back to open her airway, then placed his ear close to her nose and mouth and listened. He could hear nothing, not even the slightest hint of her breathing.

Will filled his lungs with the pine-scented air and fitted his lips over hers. He was shocked by how cold they were, like meat that had just been taken from a freezer. He tried to extract a measure of hope from this, because if she was hypothermic it would slow down her metabolism, increasing the window of time she could survive without oxygen.

He pinched her nostrils shut between his fingertips and blew into her mouth, moving his eyes to watch her chest rise. He gave her another rescue breath, then placed two fingers on her carotid artery and felt for a pulse.

He squeezed his eyes shut with concentration, but after ten seconds of feeling nothing he knew that her heart was not beating.

He placed the heel of his left hand between her breasts and laid his right hand on top of it. He pushed down hard, watching her chest depress a couple of inches. Then he relaxed and let it rise again. He did this quickly thirty times before giving her two more of the rescue breaths.

Will forced himself to focus on his technique, trying not to think. In his first-responder training the instructor had told the class that only 10 percent of people who undergo CPR will survive. But he'd also drilled it into them that *doing something in an emergency situation is better than doing nothing.*

He pumped her chest hard and fast. He worried again that he was hurting her, then realized that it probably didn't matter.

There were so many things he didn't know. How long had it been since her heart had stopped? He thought about medications, airways, heart monitors, all the things he did not have. She needed to be in an emergency room, not lying here in the middle of the forest.

He moved his lips back to hers. He blew the air inside her, forcing her to breathe, trying to do this one simple thing for her.

She showed no sign of life, and he moved back to her chest, his grief coming in waves.

He knew that he had failed her, just as he had with Sean and with Thomas. His arms began to cramp, his head buzzing with dizziness, but he refused to let himself stop. If he stopped, if he gave up now, he would be admitting that she was lost.

He blew into her mouth, his head crowded with thoughts, wondering if there was some physical limit to the amount of suffering the human heart could endure. Time lost all meaning; he had been here for a lifetime.

The sun dropped lower in the sky, slits of orange light piercing the tall pines, their trunks casting long shadows across the floor of the clearing.

He tried to summon his memories from the life they had shared but was devastated to find that he could not even do this. He could only come up with small things, fleeting moments and images, her hair spread across the top of a white pillowcase, the two of them standing side by side as they bathed Sean in the kitchen sink, the tentative and halting sound of her voice as she attempted to sing along to a song playing on the car radio. These were the things he remembered.

He sat back on his heels and wiped his sleeve across his brow, his head spinning from lack of oxygen.

There was no point in going on.

EIGHTY-EIGHT

Her eyes were open, staring sightlessly up at the sky. He thought he remembered them being closed before. They must have somehow come open while he was trying to resuscitate her.

Will reached out his hand to close the lids, his body shaking now, as if he had a fever. When his fingers drew near her eyes, he could have sworn that he saw her blink.

He was sure that it was only a trick of the light, the shadow of a swaying pine bough moving across her features, but he brought his face close to hers, gazing down into her eyes, his lips moving in a silent prayer. A teardrop fell from the tip of his nose, cutting a track across the dirt smeared on her cheek.

Her eyelid fluttered closed, then came open again, his image snapping into sudden focus in the darkness of her pupil.

"Will?" Her voice was a soft rasp.

He reached out and put his hand on her shoulder. He could feel the warmth through the soft fabric of her shirt. "Here I am," he said.

EIGHTY-NINE

He helped her to turn over onto her right side. "How do you feel?"

"Thirsty."

He went through the pile of objects that had been dumped out of the backpack. He twisted the cap from a bottle of spring water and placed the opening against her lips.

"Take it slow." He watched her drink from the bottle of water. "Can you stay here while I go and get help?"

She stopped drinking and shook her head. "Don't leave me."

"You need a doctor," he said. "I can try and carry you out."

"Let me rest for a minute," she said. "I think I can walk."

He lay down beside her, on top of the fragrant pine needles. He took hold of her wrist, the pulse steady now. He put his arm around her, taking in the rhythmic rise and fall of her breath.

Her arm moved as she hugged him back, her strength surprising. "You found me."

Will felt the warmth of the breeze, heard the whispering pines and the distant sound of the river.

"What happened?" she asked.

"He's dead."

He tilted the bottle so she could drink some more of the water. He looked at her, their eyes inches apart. "Did he . . ."

She shook her head. "He just kept talking, like he couldn't stop."

"What was he saying?"

"He wasn't making much sense. He told me that there was something I was supposed to tell you, if I ever saw you again."

"What was it?"

Her forehead became furrowed, as if she were struggling to remember. "He said to tell you that you should be glad your son was dead. That it saved you a lot of pain." She searched his face. "What did he mean?"

Will looked off, toward the sound of the river. He started to think about it, then stopped himself. He didn't want to let Frank crawl back inside his head. "Forget it. He was crazy."

He sat up and dug through the pile on the ground until he found a PowerBar. He tore open the wrapper and handed it to her. "See if you can eat this."

Will looked across the clearing at the entrance to the mine, the wooden door lying open on the ground. It bothered him, somehow offending his sense of orderliness. He thought he should close it, that it would be unsafe to just leave it open.

He rose to his feet and moved across the clearing, feeling almost weightless, no sense of delineation between where his body ended and the air began. He took hold of the iron handle and lifted the heavy door, the rusted hinges grating. He became lightheaded from the effort and the lingering effects of oxygen deprivation.

Cold air drifted up from the depths of the tunnel. He hesitated, holding on to the weight of the door, staring down into the dark earth.

He remembered watching Sean being lowered down into that blackness, his coffin disappearing, remembered thinking *it's too small.* Not even crying at the time, too busy silently bargaining with God.

Begging for the chance to trade places with his son, to please just let him be the one down there.

"Will?"

He stopped and looked at her. Laurie was up on her feet, standing in a yellow column of sunlight that danced with grains of pollen. The color had returned to her skin, the sylvan light causing the years to fall away. In the flattering glow, she appeared to him now like the first time he had seen her, emerging from beneath the surf at Zuma, childlike and filled with life, kelp swirling around her face in the foam-flecked water.

A soft breeze floated through the treetops, pine needles drifting down through the warm air. Laurie smiled at him, reaching out her hand, as if waiting for him to take hold of it and lead her from the forest.

Will turned away from her and looked once more down into the darkness.

Then he shut the door.

Frank Carver quotes or paraphrases Dylan Thomas ("And Death Shall Have No Dominion"), Dante Alighieri (Canto XXI of "Inferno" from *The Divine Comedy*, as translated by Henry F. Cary), Leo Tolstoy (*Anna Karenina*), and James Joyce (*Ulysses*), without bothering to give proper credit to the sources.

The title for Frank's novel, *The Silent Men*, was appropriated from Oscar Wilde's "The Ballad of Reading Gaol."

In Will's last encounter with Frank Carver, the description of Frank's gaze is indebted to William Butler Yeats's "The Second Coming."

ACKNOWLEDGMENTS

The author would like to thank the following individuals and organizations (in alphabetical order, and with apologies in advance to everyone who's been forgotten):

John M. Anderson at Coblentz, Patch, Duffy & Bass LLP

Chris Barnett

Billie M.

Officer Bruce Borihanh of the Los Angeles Police Department

Linda Carreon at Dilbeck/GMAC Realtors, Sherman Oaks, California

Michael Connelly

Andre Dubus III

The Hon. Kenneth R. Freeman of the Los Angeles Superior Court

Tracey Gant

Acknowledgments

Susan Goldsborough

Liza Heath

Michael Homler, Andrew Martin, Kelley Ragland, Bob Berkel, Tara Cibelli, Hector DeJean, David Rotstein, and everyone else at Minotaur Books

Judith Israel

Heward Jue, photographer

Don Jung at Jung Novikoff Bellanca & Company

Dr. Steven B. Karch, MD, FFFLM

Rick Kurnit and Maura Wogan at Frankfurt Kurnit Klein & Selz, PC

Bob Licht, Steve Hayward, the real Mitch Powers, and the rest of the crew at Sea Trek Ocean Kayaking Center, Sausalito, California

Barry Mandelbaum and Gary Poplaski at Mandelbaum, Salsburg, Gold, Lazris & Discenza, P.C.

Elaine Markson, Gary Johnson, and Julia Kenny at the Elaine Markson Literary Agency

Country Joe McDonald at countryjoe.com

Jim Patterson

Lieutenant Adam Perez of San Quentin State Prison

Elaine Petrocelli, Sheryl Cotleur, Reese Lakota, Kathryn Petrocelli, and Karen West at Book Passage, Corte Madera, California

Amy Schiffman at Intellectual Property Group

Sheldon Siegel

Most of all, I'd like to thank my wife for all her support, love, and everything else that allows me to get the writing done.